Bad Housekeeping

Also by Maia Chance

Fairy Tale Fatal Mysteries

Beauty, Beast, and Belladonna

Cinderella Six Feet Under

Snow White Red-Handed

Discreet Retrieval Agency Mysteries

Teetotaled

Come Hell or Highball

Bad Housekeeping

AN AGNES AND EFFIE MYSTERY

Maia Chance

CROOKED
LANE

NEW YORK

This is a work of fiction. All of the names, characters, organizations, places, and events portrayed in this novel either are products of the author's imagination or are used fictitiously. Any resemblance to real or actual events, locales, or persons, living or dead, is entirely coincidental.

Published in the United States by Crooked Lane Books, an imprint of The Quick Brown Fox & Company LLC.

Crooked Lane Books and its logo are trademarks of The Quick Brown Fox & Company LLC.

Library of Congress Catalog-in-Publication data available upon request.

ISBN (hardcover): 978-1-68331-167-6
ISBN (ePub): 978-1-68331-168-3
ISBN (Kindle): 978-1-68331-169-0
ISBN (ePDF): 978-1-68331-170-6

Cover design by Louis Malcangi
Cover illustration by Teresa Fasolino
Book design by Jennifer Canzone

Printed in the United States.

www.crookedlanebooks.com

Crooked Lane Books
34 West 27th St., 10th Floor
New York, NY 10001

First edition: June 2017

10 9 8 7 6 5 4 3 2 1

Chapter 1

My name is Agnes Blythe, and sure, I may have neglected to do any exercise since I completed my high school PE requirement, but I'm in the prime of life. I'm twenty-eight years old. I have a college degree. I am in perfect health if you don't count cellulite as a medical affliction (I don't). I can take care of myself. Okay, maybe not in like a bar brawl in Honduras, but every day I pull on the big girl pants.

Which is why after moving back to my hometown, the idea of starting over basically from scratch was alarming. To say the least.

Let's set the scene. My hometown of Naneda (population 13,721) in the Finger Lakes region of upstate New York is a picture-perfect college town. Trees arch over big lawns and lovely homes. Think prize-winning roses, picket fences, porch swings, and lifetime subscriptions to *This Old House* magazine for every mailbox, and you're on the right track. Main Street is like a television sitcom set thanks to the Naneda Historical Society and its draconian ordinances. In leaf-peeping season, the entire region blazes with Technicolor nostalgia, inspiring even the grimmest city slickers to buy pounds of maple fudge and drool over the real estate listings in the Naneda Realty window.

Honestly, Naneda is *too* perfect. Creepily perfect. It's just asking for trouble.

That's what I was thinking as I hurried along Main Street the day before I found the dead body. That, and something along the lines of, *Coming back here was a massive mistake. This town is going to smother me like a nursing home pillow.*

I was breathless and a little sweaty by the time I reached the Cup n' Clatter Diner on Main Street, where I was late for lunch with Dad and my long-lost great-aunt Effie. I paused outside, trying to slow my breathing, making sure all traces of murderous rage and/or panic were hidden behind my thick glasses. I hadn't bothered with my contacts that day because I'd been cleaning the new apartment—*our* new apartment—when Roger broke the news that he's through with me. Cheating weenie. I smoothed my yellow T-shirt over my jeans, tucked my shoulder-length, straight brown hair behind my ears, and pushed open the door.

Inside, fry oil hazed the air, and the lunch crowd babbled. I heard Great-Aunt Effie before I saw her.

"*Darling*," she shrilled from one of the booths in the back. "You're an absolute *riot!*"

And off we go.

I threaded my way through crowded tables heaped with burgers and fries, tuna melts, biscuits and gravy, and chicken-fried steaks. I was ready to plow through any and all of it because I'm a Blythe, and when we're upset, we don't cry if we can eat.

"Agnes," Dad boomed. "Here's Agnes, Aunt Effie." He patted the red vinyl seat next to him. "Take a load off. Did you walk all the way here?"

"It was only four blocks, Dad."

"Say, why do you look so down?" he asked.

Dad is the mayor of Naneda and has been for longer than I've been alive. He always wears a suit, and his gray hair is trimmed each Friday at Eddie's Barber Shop. Everybody loves Mayor Gary Blythe. He's like Perry Mason crossed with a teddy bear.

"Down?" I said. I took off the stupid minibackpack I'd grabbed because I couldn't find my purse when fleeing Roger and the apartment. I slid into the booth. "Not me."

"Just look at you, Agnes," Great-Aunt Effie—short for Euphemia—said.

I sent her a cool stare across the table. "Ditto."

"Pretty as ever."

I held my tongue.

If Barbie were allowed to achieve the age of seventy-something, she'd look like Great-Aunt Effie. And, well, *wow*. Kinda scary. Effie's sleek, platinum-silver bob fell at a chic angle. A dazzling sunflower print saturated her silk blouse, but it was saved from seeming clown-like by wafting the distinct smell of money. Effie had been a fashion model a gazillion years ago, and she still had the good bones underneath only slightly wrinkled and undoubtedly nip-and-tucked, Botoxed, fillered, lasered, and Retin-A slathered skin. After the modeling gigs wound down, Aunt Effie had subsequently worked as a serial trophy wife and alimony recipient. Nice work if you can get it.

"What brings you to town, Aunt Effie?" I asked. I picked up my greasy laminated menu and pretended to study it, even though I already knew what I'd be ordering: cheeseburger, extra cheese, extra mayo, hold the green stuff. Oh, and extra fries. Why? Because Roger is a cheating weenie who had just ruined my life, that's why.

"I am here to stay," Effie said.

"Are you kidding?"

"No."

"Remember how we were scrambling to find Great-Uncle Herman's will last month?" Dad asked me.

I nodded. Great-Uncle Herman, a fragile fossil stored on the shelf at Honeybee Hollow Retirement Home, had finally passed away in his sleep last month. Effie was Dad's aunt on his mother's side, and Herman was Effie's cousin. This actually made Herman my third cousin twice removed (I think), but I'd always called him great-uncle.

"Cousin Herman willed me the Stagecoach Inn," Effie said. She took a tiny sip of ice water.

"Oh, so you're here to sell it," I said. I turned back to my menu.

"No, I mean to restore it and open it up again in all its former glory."

I snorted. "Okay, first of all, that place may have been glorious in, what, 1856?"

"It has potential," Effie said. "Glorious potential."

"And second of all, isn't it a condemned building?"

"We were just talking about that," Dad said. "It *is* condemned. It has been deemed unfit for human habitation."

"I am *going* to restore it," Effie said. "I don't care if it kills me. I'll fix whatever is wrong with it, have it reinspected, and get a new certificate of occupancy issued. It'll be a snap."

Dad and I exchanged sidelong looks: *This is weird.* Because the thing is, Effie just doesn't fit into Naneda. Granted, I don't either—at least, not anymore. I feel like Jane Goodall every time I go to the post office. But Effie *really* doesn't fit in. It's like sticking a designer cocktail dress on the clearance rack at Walmart.

"Why do you want to restore the inn?" I asked, mainly to make Effie stop inspecting my face. She had shrewd eyes, a sharp bottle-glass blue. I'd never noticed that about her before, but of course, the last time I saw her, I was thirteen years old.

"Why?" Effie said. "Because I adore that show about the Vermont inn—what was it called?"

"*Newhart?*" I said. "You adore *Newhart?*"

"Yes. Hilarious."

I didn't buy it; Effie looked like she only watched black-and-white art-house films.

The waitress arrived, took our orders, and left.

"Did you know the Stagecoach Inn is supposed to be haunted?" I asked Effie.

"Agnes," Dad said, "I'm sure she doesn't want to hear about that."

"No, it's fine," Effie said. "Do tell. Ghosts? Goblins?"

I shrugged. "Lights and weird noises and things."

"Teenagers," Dad said firmly.

"I don't believe in ghosts," I said, "but I thought you should know." The waitress dipped over the table long enough to deposit my Diet Coke. I took a long sip. *Ah.* Maybe everything was going to be okay. Just as soon as I toilet-papered Roger's office.

"Of course you don't believe in ghosts," Effie said, "because you have a college degree—archaeology, was it? King Tut and so forth?"

"No. Anthropology. The study of human culture."

"Oh! That's what *I* study too, darling."

I rolled my eyes.

Dad shifted in his seat. The vinyl made a farty noise beneath his substantial frame. "Agnes, I was hoping you and Aunt Effie could put that business behind you. It's been ten years now."

"Sixteen years," I snapped, and stuck the straw in my mouth. "I was only a kid."

"I *have* apologized about all that," Effie said, "and anyway, you took it *entirely* the wrong way, Agnes."

"Don't think so," I said.

Here's the thing. When I was thirteen years old, Effie took me on a trip to New York City—Central Park! Art museums! Broadway shows! Oh, and a trip to a modeling agency where she pitched me as *a husky teen model*. I had never been particularly confident about my looks. *This* was the final nail in the coffin. Effie—gorgeous, willowy Effie—just couldn't see how much being labeled *husky* had hurt. Even if it was more or less accurate. There are some things you just don't say, right?

I felt that bug-crawly sensation of someone watching and slid my eyes to the side. Sure enough, the Realty Sisters—that's what everyone in Naneda called Bitsy and Lily Horton of Naneda Realty—were staring at Effie.

"I already had a bit of a run-in with those two," Effie said softly. "They asked me if I would like to sell the inn. I'd forgotten how quickly word travels in this town. When I said no, the one in the terribly snug pantsuit looked like she wanted to bite me. I suppose they would just sell the property to a condo developer. The piece of land it sits on is gorgeous, and the deed says it's one and a half acres. In-town lakeshore property like that just isn't available anymore."

"It is nice," I said, "and I'm sure if it wasn't a total pit, you'd be booked solid with tourists all year round." The inn had been sagging there, gray and empty, for years. It was the sort of place kids dared each other to sneak into on Halloween.

Effie gave me another penetrating look. "Agnes, have you been crying?"

I hadn't, actually, but my eyes *had* felt hot and squinchy when Roger had dropped his nuclear bomb. "Allergies," I said.

"I didn't know you had allergies," Dad said.

"I do. It's, um, pollen."

"In September?" he said.

Effie tipped her head. "No. You look a bit—not *weepy*—more like, well, like you'd enjoy throttling someone."

I could start with *her.*

"Everything all right with Roger?" Dad asked.

"What?" I slurped Diet Coke. Where the freak was my cheeseburger?

"He seemed a little jumpy at Sunday dinner," Dad said. Roger and I hadn't missed a Sunday dinner at Dad's house since we'd moved to Naneda a month ago, after Roger had landed a job at the university.

"Look, she's shredding her paper napkin," Effie said to Dad.

I threw the napkin down.

"Agnes?" Dad said.

"Fine!" I yipped. I took a couple deep breaths. My upper lip perspired. "Roger and I, well—he said he wants to break up—there's this . . . this *person*, Shelby—"

"Oh, dear God," Effie said. "You're engaged to be married, aren't you?"

"We are—*were*—engaged."

"Where's the ring?" Effie asked.

"There is no ring," I said.

"What?" Effie looked disgusted. "He's a young professor, your father tells me. I know the type—I'll bet he's a pompous, pontificating ass."

"He's not a *type*," I said. But you know what? Roger kind of was. Or at least he *aspired* to be a type, which was probably

7

worse. He had a tweed jacket with suede elbow patches, for goodness sake.

"What is she?" Effie said. "Makeup counter girl? Cocktail waitress? *Undergraduate student*?"

I swallowed hard. "Pilates instructor."

"Hideous!" Effie shrieked.

Half the diner swiveled to gape at Effie. She ignored them all, and for the first time in my life, I warmed a little to the taxidermied old swan. Not, of course, that I forgave her for the husky teen model episode.

"There, there," Dad said awkwardly, patting my hand. My mom died when I was little, but Dad never got very good at dealing with the waterworks.

"So Roger dumped you for a fitness bimbo," Effie said. "He's moving in with her, I suppose?"

"I think he'll come around," I said. "We've been together since we were twenty! What will he talk about with a Pilates instructor?"

"Oh, he doesn't want to *talk* with her, darling."

My eyes felt hot and squinchy again. I removed my glasses, even though without them, I felt like a mole in a Velma Dinkley wig.

"Aunt Effie, she's um . . ." Dad said.

I blotted my eyes with the shredded napkin. Luckily, I never wear makeup, so it wasn't the sludgy mess it could've been. "He kicked me out. He's keeping the Prius—it's in his name. And he said that things had been shuffled around at the university so *he's* going to be my graduate advisor." Roger had also accused me of being "not very adventurous," but somehow I couldn't admit that aloud.

"Putrid," Effie said. "Simply putrid. Couldn't you simply ask for a new advisor?"

"I guess so." It suddenly hit me. "I'll have to defer my enrollment. I can't face him at school every day."

"But you've been planning on going to graduate school for years, honey," Dad said. "That was your plan with Roger, right? You helped get him through school, and then he'd help you." Dad looked at Effie. "Agnes basically put Roger through grad school, working as a barista and a hotel clerk in Boston so that they didn't have to take out too many loans."

"He's slime," Effie said.

"Stay in school, honey," Dad said to me.

"No. I'm taking the semester off." I had only just decided on this, but it made me feel less panicky, so I was going with it. I'd figure out the rest later. Suddenly, I wasn't even sure if I wanted a graduate degree in anthropology. What do you do with *that*?

"At least you have your library job," Dad said.

"That ended yesterday," I said. "It was only a temp job." I had spent the last month entering book bar codes into the library's new computer catalog. "I was supposed to be starting school next week."

"Oh." Dad looked worried. It wasn't a financial thing, I knew; Dad comes from a fairly well-to-do family, and I know he'd always be capable and willing to help me out. I'm his only child. No, the worry I saw in his eyes had something to do with fears for my sanity. I get bored. "You can come stay with me," Dad said, patting my arm.

"Only for a few weeks. I've got to get out of this town."

"*I* know!" Effie crowed. "You can come work for *me*. At the inn."

Dad and I both stared at her.

"No thanks," I said.

* * *

By the time I'd wolfed down my lunch, I had realized that, number one, I needed to go to the Naneda Public Library and beg to keep my temp job a little longer, at least until I figured out how I was going to get the heck out of Naneda. No way could I work as a barista again; I was all frothed out.

I said good-bye to Dad and Aunt Effie—mumbling to Dad that he should expect me at his house later—and left the Cup n' Clatter. I passed the Flour Girl Bakery and my best friend Lauren's vintage clothing shop, Retro Rags. I considered going in to talk to her. She'd definitely be able to cheer me up with her wry wit, perennially upbeat attitude, and hilarious talent for impressions. But I saw she was busy with customers, so I kept going. I'd call her later.

"Watch out, lady!" someone shouted as I stepped onto the crosswalk. A motorcycle screeched to a stop, its rear tire skidding sideways. Numbed by greasy carbs and by being dumped, I hadn't noticed it coming.

I stepped backward onto the curb. "I was on a *crosswalk*. Are you blind in that helmet?"

The guy's legs were splayed—muscular, long legs in faded jeans—to keep his balance, and he wore a white short-sleeved undershirt. He flipped up his helmet's visor. "Wait," he said. "*Agnes?*"

I hitched up the straps of my minibackpack. "Yeah. Who are you?"

He lifted his helmet off. His longish honey-brown hair stood up and didn't lie back down.

"Oh." My pulse quickened. "Otis."

"I didn't know you were in town, Agnes. You look great."

He didn't even sound sarcastic. Weird. "What's up, Otis?"

"*What's up?* I haven't seen you for, what? Ten years?"

"I've been in town almost every Christmas."

"That explains it. I go down to see my mom in Philly at Christmas." Otis's coffee-bean-brown eyes shone.

Great. Otis was just as good-looking as he'd been in high school. Scratch that. He was *more* good-looking, because when guys start getting little wrinkles at the corners of their eyes, it's a good thing. No one drops hints about SPF thirty to guys. He still had the same firm chin; the slightly crooked prominent nose; the quick, broad white grin; the thick dark eyebrows. Otis and I were "buddies" for about a year in senior AP English even though, well, I'll put it this way: we both had letterman's jackets, but Otis's said *swim team*, and mine said *debate squad*. He still had the swim team body. I suppose I still have a debate squad body.

Oh, and those quotes around "buddies"? Those are because in high school, I was secretly, madly in love with Otis. He was officially the first guy to have broken my heart. I was over it, though. Of course I was.

I set off on the crosswalk, finally mustering a smile for Otis. "Nice to see you again."

"Glad you're back in town," he said. I heard his motorcycle engine turn over, and he blatted away.

This is the problem with hometowns. You can't escape your high school self.

11

Chapter 2

The Naneda Public Library is an old brick building set back from the sidewalk on a lush lawn overarched by maple trees. It's a five-minute walk from Main Street, so by the time I mounted the steps, my bangs were stuck to my forehead, and I was out of breath.

There had been maybe a *miniscule* grain of truth in Roger's parting shots regarding me and exercise. Hypocrite.

A poster on the library door said, "Local Celebrity Author Gracelyn Roy, Best-Selling Author of *Country Kitsch-ins*, book signing tomorrow, 7 PM," accompanied by a photo of a lady with dimples and curly red hair.

I went into the cool, hushed library foyer. Historical documents and photos about Naneda filled display cases. More Gracelyn Roy posters bedecked the walls. Rooms through archways housed the library stacks and public reading rooms, and the office was behind a glossy oak door. Chris the Slug would be in the office. Chris was the one I needed to talk to about getting my job back for a little longer.

I shoved the door. It hit something solid. I heard shrieks and a *thunk*, and then something shattered.

Crud.

The door had two-way hinges, so instead of pushing the door again, I carefully pulled it. On the other side, a woman knelt, picking orange-and-white shards off the floor. Beside her lay a cardboard box. Another woman stood over her with another box.

"Oh my gosh!" I said. "I'm so sorry!"

"Did you shove the door, young lady?" the standing woman snapped. With her ash-blonde hair helmet, WASPy good looks, and silk paisley scarf, she could've been Martha Stewart's stunt double. "Just *look* at the mess you've made."

"It was an accident," I said. I knelt and gathered up a couple shards.

"Oh, thank you," the kneeling woman twittered. She was plump, and she wore a rumpled floral dress with a lace collar. Her short cottony hair was drugstore blonde.

"*Thank you*, Dorrie?" the Martha stunt double snapped. "You're *thanking* her for destroying one of our town's irreplaceable relics?"

"Oh, well, Kathleen, I only . . ." A flush mottled Dorrie's cheeks.

"*This* was an irreplaceable relic?" I held up one of the orange-and-white shards. "It looks like a mixing bowl my grandma used to have."

"Pyrex," Kathleen said. "It belonged to one of Naneda's most famous ladies, the cookbook author Mary Whittaker, and it is my sworn responsibility to protect these relics at any cost."

This was getting dippy. I picked up the last shard, handed it to Dorrie, and stood.

"Agnes?" a man said.

13

"Hey, Chris," I said. "I was just coming to see you."

Chris the Slug, head librarian, trundled toward us in a shirt that looked like a tablecloth. "Agnes, are you bothering Mrs. Todd?"

"I—"

"This young lady destroyed one of Mary Whittaker's Pyrex bowls," Kathleen said. "I think she did it on purpose."

"Agnes!" Chris hissed. "Seriously?"

"On *purpose*?" I said.

"Anyone else would have pulled that door," Kathleen said, "yet you heard us coming and shoved with all the might in your doughy little body."

I narrowed my eyes. I am not a confrontational person *at all*, but something in me just snapped. "Watch it, lady. I've had a pretty rotten day so far, and I'm not really feeling like I have a lot to lose."

"It looks like you've got about *twenty pounds* to lose," Kathleen said.

Chris said, "Treat Mrs. Todd with some respect, Agnes. She's the chairman of the historical society."

"Chair*woman*," Kathleen said.

Okay. This was starting to make sense. Kathleen Todd was the rich widow who had donated the boxes of old magazines that Chris was too chicken to get rid of. The mildewed 1960s issues of *Good Housekeeping* and *Better Homes and Gardens* were in bad shape, and the library already had copies of those issues, anyway. But since Chris clearly kowtowed to Kathleen, they were sitting in a utility closet in the nonfiction stacks. I didn't think I'd met Kathleen before, although Naneda was small enough that she looked familiar.

"Apologize, and I won't press charges," Kathleen said to me.

"Press *charges*? You're insane!"

"How dare you!"

"I'll just go take this box to the temporary storeroom," Dorrie whispered.

"No." Kathleen stopped Dorrie with a hand. "I want as many witnesses as possible."

"Witnesses to what?" I said. "Witnesses to me wringing your neck?"

"Oh!" Kathleen cried.

"*Kidding*," I said through gritted teeth.

"Please, Mrs. Todd." Chris twisted his pudgy hands. He turned to me. "Agnes, are you here for your final paycheck? Because I put it in the mail this morning."

"Um, no. Well . . ." I swallowed. Kathleen and Dorrie weren't going to budge. Fantastic. "I was wondering if I could have my job back. At least for a few more weeks."

"I hired a permanent employee. Someone with a library science degree."

"Do you want me to beg?" I asked.

"I'm sorry, Agnes, but the job is no longer available. Now, Mrs. Todd, let's get all this sorted out. Here. I'll take the box with the broken pieces and—yes, Mrs. Tucker, why don't you take Mrs. Todd's boxes and—right. Good."

My glasses began the slow slide down my nose. I watched the three of them maneuver through the doorway with the boxes.

On the way out, Kathleen swiped at the Gracelyn Roy book-signing poster taped to the door. She shredded it right down the middle of Gracelyn's curly red head and tossed it to the floor.

Chris scooped up the torn poster. "Uh, Mrs. Todd—?"

"Gracelyn Roy will ruin this town," Kathleen snapped.

"Oh, Agnes, I almost forgot," Chris said over his shoulder. "You'll still be helping out at the book signing tomorrow, right? You wouldn't want to give the Blythe family a bad name, would you?" He made a juicy wink, but I knew he wasn't joking. He is, after all, the slug. Once, for example, Chris suspended a six-year-old's library card for a year after the little boy returned a book with chocolate smeared on the title page. He's ruthless.

"I'll be there," I said. I pictured myself booting Chris's creased khaki butt as he waddled after Kathleen and Dorrie. The door swung shut.

*　　*　　*

I spent the rest of the day in Dad's den watching an Alfred Hitchcock marathon, eating muffins, and e-mailing my friends who lived in cool places like San Francisco and Brooklyn, asking if they needed a roommate. Even if Roger was going to come to his senses, I had to be proactive, right? And I kept telling myself Roger *would* come to his senses, even though he had not called. But I hadn't brought my cell phone charger in my backpack when I'd stormed out of our apartment before lunch—I hadn't brought much of *anything*—and now my phone was out of juice. Of course, Roger had a low-genius IQ (that's what his mom told me once), so surely he knew he could call me at Dad's.

Dad's phone didn't ring. I began to have a hard time remembering exactly why I had ever liked Roger in the first place, which made me feel guilty.

After gorging on a Betty Crocker–style dinner prepared by Dad's housekeeper, Cordelia—roast chicken, scalloped potatoes, creamed spinach, and Jell-O with marshmallows suspended inside—I went upstairs to my childhood pink-princess bedroom. Cordelia kept it spick-and-span, along with the rest of Dad's large white colonial house.

I stayed up late reading one of my old Nancy Drew books. It was almost one o'clock when I checked my e-mail for the last time on Dad's study computer. Nothing in my in-box but spam. Nothing from Roger. Nothing from my friends in San Francisco and Brooklyn.

As I lay in a miserable ball in my canopied bed, I had this sensation that everything holding me up—the mattress, the floor, the house, the ground—was giving way like cake in a rainstorm.

* * *

The next morning, I decided that the way to cope was (a) to *refuse* to think about Roger and his abs bimbo, (b) to eat more muffins, and (c) to distract myself by asking Great-Aunt Effie if I could help out at the Stagecoach Inn for a few weeks. Sure, I had turned her offer down, but I was running low on options, and she *was* family. Hey, maybe it would even be fun watching her dig through cobwebs and mouse poop.

At breakfast, Dad told me he had no idea where Great-Aunt Effie was staying but that she might be found at the inn since she'd said something about getting started right away with lifting its condemned status. "She'll sure be glad for a hand," Dad said. "I'm worried about her, you know." He tapped his temple.

"What?" I said. "Dementia?"

"No, it's just that she's always been . . . skittish, I guess is the word. Erratic. She's had five husbands, for Pete's sake."

Cordelia the housekeeper was at the kitchen counter, dumping fresh grounds into the coffeemaker. She had a short brown perm and wore a ruffly apron over crisp slacks and a blouse. She kept herself trim with artificial sweetener in her coffee and by not eating the food she cooked. "Agnes, don't forget to keep the security system armed," she said. "The code to disarm it is 8-7-8-7."

Cordelia insisted on a security system for Dad's house as well as for her private apartment above the garage. In my analysis, this was just her being territorial, since Naneda is the kind of town where people leave their doors unlocked.

* * *

After four of Cordelia's famous strawberry muffins and two cups of coffee, I dug my old ten-speed bicycle from the garage and wobbled off in the direction of the Stagecoach Inn. It was a quarter till eight o'clock.

Ten minutes later, I turned off Main Street, near where it fed out to Route 20, and onto the inn's overgrown driveway. Potholes booby-trapped the asphalt. Rusty beer cans, a toilet seat lid, and a crumpled lawn chair lurked in the ditch. An orange-striped cat sprinted across my path and disappeared into a hedge. The driveway opened out onto a big weedy lawn graced with large trees. Naneda Lake sparkled in the morning sun. Across the lake, vineyards striped sloping fields. The first hints of autumn gold tinged the rolling forestland beyond.

And there was the inn. Three stories of circa-1850 peeling paint, dangling shutters, and missing windowpanes. An enclosed porch stretched along the lakefront side. Chimneys hosted cawing crows. The entry porch had once-white pillars and grand double doors. A red sign on one of the doors said,

Condemned
as
Dangerous and Unsafe
Danger—Keep Out

So basically, a horror movie set.

I hopped off my bike and leaned it on its kickstand in the drive.

Great-Aunt Effie emerged on the porch just as I was mounting the steps. She wore huge sunglasses, white slacks, a black blouse, and electric-pink pumps. "Oh, it's you, Agnes," she said. "I *thought* I heard crunching on the drive." She took a calm puff of her cigarette and inspected my blue T-shirt, which read *Naneda High Band Camp*. I'd found it, along with a pair of too-small jeans from high school, in my closet at Dad's.

"I used to play the clarinet," I said.

"I see. And the . . . shoes?"

I glanced down at my orange sneakers. "They're comfortable."

"But at what *cost*, darling?"

"I'm not here for a makeover, okay?" I leaned my butt on the porch railing. I heard a crack and felt it give, so I straightened and folded my arms. "I just came to see if you were okay. And, um, I was hoping I might take you up on your offer after all. To help you here at the inn, I mean." I told her my terms: it was a temporary arrangement, no blowing cigarette smoke in my face, and no discussion *whatsoever* of Roger.

Effie agreed. "This is because you didn't get your library job back," she said.

"Well, yeah."

"And because you are somewhat straitened, financially speaking."

"Um. Yes, actually." I had maybe eight hundred dollars in my bank account. Thankfully separate from Roger's.

"And then, of course—since you are a Blythe, and Blythes always have a surplus of neurotic energy that must be channeled, or they become morose and fixate on carbohydrates—you require a diversion until you figure out a way to leave town, at which point you will promptly do so without looking back and go on to lead a fruitful and exciting life elsewhere, in . . . Paris?"

"I was thinking Brooklyn."

"Oh, dear God. Well. I've always adored honesty." Effie dropped her cigarette onto the porch and swiveled her pink shoe to crush it. "It saves *so* much time. Come through the inn— I've got to collect my handbag in the kitchen, and the car is out back. I was just on my way to the hardware store. They open at eight. I've got piles of tool-type thingies to buy, apparently—that's what your cousin Chester said. He rattled off an entire shopping list when he stopped by last night."

"Chester?" *He* was in on this insane project? Chester and I have been fighting over the last slice of Thanksgiving pecan pie since we were toddlers. He's . . . well, you'll see.

"It seems that the inn is condemned only because all the wiring is hopelessly out-of-date and dangerous—this is what the code-compliance officer at City Hall told me yesterday—and it just so happens that Chester worked as an electrician once." Effie led me into a grand, murky entry hall with a long spill of dirty staircase.

"Looks like the Addams Family would find it pretty homey," I said.

"Use your imagination, Agnes."

"That's the problem. I am."

We went past the staircase, through a door, and into a kitchen. The kitchen was spacious, filthy, and outdated, with saggy linoleum floors and dank and musty odors.

Effie said, "I think they remodeled in the fifties—see? The stove and refrigerator are salmon pink. They didn't shut the business down until the seventies, and after that, the inn served as a boarding house until the late eighties."

"Great-Uncle Herman and his wife, right?"

"Yes, and Herman's father and grandfather before that. It's a family tradition."

"Which is why you're hoping to resuscitate it."

"Not *hoping*. I will."

I was too young to remember the inn as a boarding house, but I'd seen old postcards of the place in its heyday from the late nineteenth century up until World War II. The headquarters of the prosperous Chester Stagecoach Company had been built on the site in 1808 by my ancestor Joseph Chester (yes, my cousin's namesake). In 1847, the place burned down, as nineteenth-century buildings so often did. Blame it on the whale-oil lamps. By this time, the railroad had mostly driven stagecoaches out of business anyway, so Joseph Chester built a hotel instead—but the Stagecoach Inn name stuck. With its scenic location, charming hospitality, and wholesome old-fashioned offerings like canoeing, fishing, and swimming, the Stagecoach Inn became a summer holiday destination for generations of families.

Effie had collected a costly looking white leather handbag from the table. "Just through here, darling." She opened a door off the kitchen, which led to a glassed-in back porch.

I went first. I tripped on something and stumbled. I braced my fall on another door that led outside and turned to see what I'd tripped on. It was a foot in a driving moccasin. A foot attached to a leg. Attached to a body.

Chapter 3

My heart squeezed. "Oh my gosh," I whispered. "*Oh my gosh!*"

"Whatever is the matter with . . . oh. Oh, dear me."

Effie and I stared at Kathleen Todd's body, sort of half lying, half hanging by the neck with her scarf—the silk paisley scarf she'd been wearing in the library yesterday—caught in the wringer of an old-fashioned washing machine. Kathleen's face was bloated and livid, but her ash-blonde hair helmet still looked perfect.

"That's some strong hair spray," I said stupidly. A pause. "Um, Aunt Effie? I think she's . . . dead."

Effie drew a shuddery breath. "It would seem so. Strangled herself with her scarf—Ferragamo, but likely a knock-off because I do see a few stray threads—"

"How could she have possibly strangled herself? Look! Her scarf is caught between the rollers of the wringer, and it has been—" I swallowed bile. "It has been—"

"Cranked?" Effie suggested.

"Yes, her scarf has been *cranked up*. Someone *else* cranked it up." I couldn't look away. I wasn't even sure if I was breathing anymore.

The washing machine was comprised of two round steel tubs sitting on sturdy wooden legs, and in between the tubs was a double-roller crank on a wooden frame. I assumed you'd feed your wet clothes through, cranking all the while, to get out the extra moisture. I couldn't help thinking it was exactly like one of those handmade pasta makers . . . uh-oh. I was *so* close to being sick.

"We've got to call the police!" I fumbled in my backpack, but then I remembered my phone was out of power. "Do you have a phone?"

"Of course I have a phone." Effie pushed past me, through the back door and out into a scraggly backyard. She fumbled in her handbag and pulled out a pack of Benson & Hedges and her lighter. Her hands shook so it took a few tries to light up.

"Where's your phone?" I shouted.

She dug into her handbag again and tossed me a sleek white phone.

I dialed 9-1-1. I calmly told the lady on the line that I'd just tripped over the corpse of Kathleen Todd at the Stagecoach Inn. Then I ran behind the ramshackle garage and threw up muffins.

* * *

Almost immediately, sirens wailed up in the distance. Effie went back inside, and I went around to the front porch to wait. I heard Effie clunking around inside, and a little bit later, I heard a car trunk slamming. Then she joined me on the porch.

"What are you doing?" I asked.

"Nothing."

An ambulance blared down the driveway first, followed by two police cars and, for some reason, a huge fire engine. I guess everyone wanted in on the action. The next part was a blur. Walkie-talkies blipping on and off, polyester uniforms rushing around, the flashing lights just about sending me into an epileptic seizure. And the weird thing was, despite hurling muffins, I would've given anything for *more* muffins. Effie stood on the porch the whole time, sunglasses on, chain-smoking.

Then a police officer told Effie and me that we needed to ride with him to the police station for questioning.

* * *

At the police station, Effie and I waited for more than an hour in a room with a water cooler, folding chairs, bedraggled issues of *People*, and a noisy clock. Effie started fidgeting. Nicotine fit, I guessed. I kept my nose buried in *People*. Finally, a squat lady with a bona fide beehive asked Effie to come with her.

I waited for another hour all alone, drinking too-cold water from a Styrofoam cup. I didn't even think Styrofoam existed anymore. I thought about calling Dad for help but decided against it. Sunday was his day to play golf at the course in Lucerne with his buddies. Of course, it was likely that he'd already heard the news about Kathleen and about Effie and me being taken in for questioning. He could be calling my out-of-power cell phone frantically, for all I knew. I could just hear his weary, caring sigh, and it bogged me down with guilt.

Then I was called in for questioning. Two men waited for me in a small, windowless room. I'd seen both of them earlier at the inn. One had a police uniform on, and one wore a baggy brown suit and—I noticed under the folding table—brand-new white sneakers that were maybe size thirteen.

"Ms. Blythe," the baggy-suited man said. He was in his midthirties, small, brown-skinned, and with his thick glasses, he looked like a cartoon goldfish. He reached over the table to shake my hand. "I'm Detective Sam Albright of the Naneda Police, and this here's Sergeant Hooks."

Sergeant Hooks took a huge bite of a maple bar.

Seriously? A donut?

"Have a seat, Ms. Blythe," Albright said.

I sank onto a chair across from them. The waist of my jeans pinched into my midriff, and I winced. Albright looked at me as though my wince was one of guilt.

"It's my jeans," I said. I'd fastened them with a hair tie since I'm several pounds thicker than I was in high school. "They're too tight."

"What?" Albright said. "Never mind. Tell me about finding Kathleen Todd's body. From the beginning."

I felt like puking again. Could the cops already know about my run-in with Kathleen at the library yesterday? No. Impossible.

I explained how I'd met Kathleen for the first time at the library yesterday but omitted how we'd butted heads.

"Uh-huh," Albright said, shoving his glasses up his shiny nose. "The thing is, Kathleen Todd was murdered—"

"*Murdered*?" I shook my head. "Things like that don't happen in Naneda."

"Tell me about it," Albright said. "I took the job up here as a sort of early retirement. After ten-plus years in Gotham, I've seen enough dead bodies."

Gotham? I looked at Albright more closely. Yeah. He *did* bear traces of being a comic book collector.

Albright's eyes bored right back at me through his thick glasses. Two nerds sizing each other up. He said, "Mrs. Todd was murdered—the washing machine had been cranked up after her scarf was caught between the rollers—and I think you may have had something to do with it."

"Me? What do you mean? Like I—like I killed her? I only met her for the first time yesterday, and we weren't even properly introduced. She treated me like something nasty she'd accidentally slipped on." *Crapola*. I shouldn't have said that.

"Which is why you said you were going to wring her neck."

My mouth flopped open. "Who told you that? Did she report me to the police for bumping into that stupid box of Pyrex bowls? She said she was going to but—"

"No," Albright said. "The head librarian, Chris McCavity, told me that you said you'd like to"—he glanced down at his notebook—"wring Mrs. Todd's neck with her paisley scarf."

The Slug. "Well that was fast," I said.

"Word travels fast here in Naneda. Seems like Mr. McCavity thought it was his civic duty to inform me of your threats when he learned Mrs. Todd had been killed. What is more, your former domestic partner, Dr. Roger Hollins—I spoke to him just a few minutes ago—"

"Wow, you're really on the ball."

"—Dr. Hollins described you as a woman who is going through a life change at the moment and that your actions have been, lately—what did he say, Sarge?"

Sarge set down his maple bar and flipped back a few pages in his notebook. "Erratic."

"Erratic?" I said. *Erratic* is how Dad had described Great-Aunt Effie. "Roger said I'm going through a life change? We just broke up *yesterday*, and anyway, he's the one who has taken up with the town floozy."

"And who is that?"

"The Pilates teacher from that studio on Oak Street."

"Shelby Adams?" Albright said. "I take a core-toning class with Shelby every Saturday. She's a delight."

I stole a look at Albright's core. It was about as toned as a deflated beach ball.

He caught me looking. "I'm working on it," he said stiffly.

"Okay, so what's your hypothesis, Detective?" I said. "That Kathleen Todd ticked me off, so I *strangled* her? That's ridiculous."

"Is it, now?" Albright's glasses gleamed softly. "I'm not going to say it was premeditated, exactly. But there was a confrontation last night—"

"She died last night?"

"Around midnight. And there was a confrontation. Maybe Mrs. Todd's scarf accidentally caught on that wringer contraption, and then maybe she wouldn't shut up, so you and your great-aunt *made* her shut up. Mrs. Todd could be pretty provocative, is what I hear."

"Me and my *great-aunt*?" Oh. My. Gosh. Was this a nightmare? I knew it wasn't healthful watching that Alfred Hitchcock marathon.

Albright went on, "Mrs. Todd told your great-aunt that she would never allow the inn to receive a new certificate of occupancy. There were witnesses to an altercation between your great-aunt and Mrs. Todd at the Green Apple Supermarket yesterday evening. Tell me, Miss Blythe, where were you last night at midnight?"

"At my dad's house. Asleep."

"Can that be corroborated?"

"Sure. Call my dad." I swallowed thickly. "Mayor Blythe." It always sounded like I was doing that *Do you even know who I AM?* routine when I said my dad was the mayor.

But Albright didn't so much as elevate an eyebrow. "Mrs. Winters is a person of interest in the case, and so are you, Ms. Blythe. Do not leave town. I will contact you when you are wanted for further questioning. I understand you're no longer living with Dr. Hollins?"

"Yeah." I was sinking in my chair.

"How could he break up with a bright and attractive young lady like you?"

Um, can you say *inappropriate*?

"You'll continue to stay with your father?" Albright asked.

"Yes." I rattled off Dad's address and home phone number, and Sergeant Hooks scribbled them down.

Albright was studying my Naneda High Band Camp T-shirt. "What instrument?"

"Clarinet."

"I play the tuba."

Naturally. I folded my arms since Albright was still studying the boob sector of my T-shirt with that spaced-out look guys get when they're studying boobage.

To my great relief, he let me go.

* * *

I went to the bathroom and then made my way toward the police station exit. As I passed the reception desk, the squat lady with the beehive hairdo watched me furtively from behind her computer.

I stopped in front of her desk. "What?" I said.

Beehive sipped a green smoothie through a straw. "Nothing." She clicked at her computer keyboard, looking busy.

"Yes, I'm Mayor Blythe's daughter," I said, "and yes, I had the misfortune of tripping on a dead body this morning. But I didn't *do* anything."

Beehive kept up with the keyboard clicking, saying in a prim voice, "That's not what *I* heard."

I blinked. "What did you hear?"

"Nothing."

"Something."

"I'm really *very* busy, Ms. Blythe." *Clickety-click-click* went her keyboard. Her crayoned eyebrows arched in permanent surprise.

I could tell she wanted to blab, though. She had that bottled-up look gossips get when they've got something juicy. So I waited. The clock ticked five seconds.

Beehive heaved a sigh and looked up. "Just like your dad, aren't you? So darned persistent. All that happened was, when I went to the farmer's market just now to get my green smoothie at the smoothie stand—did you know you can live only on kale *indefinitely?*"

"I doubt it," I said. "If nothing else, that would take an emotional toll."

Beehive took an aggressive sip of smoothie. "Rosalie at the smoothie stand told me that someone told *her* that you and your great-auntie were there at the old inn all last night, doing golly gosh and gee knows what, listening to weird music with crashing waves and sea gulls, and that they heard you arguing loudly with Kathleen Todd in there."

"Well, that's a lot of baloney," I said.

Beehive shrugged and went back to her typing.

I stomped out of the police station.

Outside, I squinted in the burnished Indian summer sunlight. A horn beeped. A pearl-white Cadillac idled in the parking lot, and I glimpsed two black circles behind the windshield. Great-Aunt Effie's sunglasses.

When I went closer, I saw the Florida license plate. Effie zipped down the window. Smoke billowed out. "Need a lift?" she asked.

"I guess." I wasn't sure where I was going, actually, but I circled around and got in. The seats were buttery-white leather. The dashboard looked like real wood. It felt like a luxury plane, or so I imagined; I've never been on a luxury plane. I've done my share of traveling, but I always buy the budget tickets that stuff you back by the bathrooms. Talk about the study of human culture.

I turned to Effie. "So we're both persons of interest," I said.

"Don't sound so accusing, darling. I had nothing to do with that woman's death."

"They said you had a fight with her at the supermarket."

"They said *you* had a fight with her at the library."

We scowled at each other.

I slouched against the seat. "Did that receptionist in there with the beehive and the green smoothie tell you the rumor about us?"

"No."

I told Effie what Beehive had said. "What is she talking about, weird music with crashing waves and sea gulls?" I asked. "She made it sound like we were holding a witch's Sabbath in there."

"That must have been my sound machine," Effie said.

"Go on."

"I can't sleep without it. It plays white noise and soothing nature sounds."

"You slept at the *inn* last night?" Effie seemed like the type who only stayed at five-star hotels and *only* if they had a spa. "Why?"

"The inn is my new home."

"Well sure, but—is there even running water?"

"I'm not sure. To be safe, I bought out the gallon jugs of spring water at the supermarket and three LED lanterns and an enormous ice chest at the sporting goods store. Oh, and luckily, my sound machine can run on batteries."

I decided not to ask about the potty situation. "So you're *camping* in that dump?" Something was . . . off. Effie was supposed to be loaded, *seriously* loaded, so why wasn't she staying at another hotel or renting a house until the inn was habitable? Dad was right. She was erratic.

"Agnes, at my time of life, you simply do whatever the hell you feel like doing," Effie said. "One day you wake up not caring what other people think."

"Okay, fine. You're living at the inn." Presumably with a battery-operated straightening iron, unless that was a wig. "But you care what the *police* think, right?"

"Well I don't want to go to *jail*. Especially not this week."

"What's so special about this week? You can't possibly care about the county fair coming up."

"The *county fair?* These slacks will no longer fit if I even *look* at a fried Twinkie. No. Didn't the detective tell you? It seems that Kathleen Todd managed to get a date set for the city to raze the inn on September seventeenth."

"Are you *serious*?"

"Mmm. Kathleen's last hurrah. Although the inn was condemned, no plans had been made yet to demolish it. But it seems that after we had words at the supermarket last night, Kathleen got on the phone with someone at City Hall and set the big day."

"Why did she care so much whether the inn was demolished or not?" I asked.

"Perhaps she felt that the inn brings down the quality of the neighborhood. She lived right next door, you know. That big brick lakefront place hidden behind the hedges?"

It was looking like Aunt Effie really *did* have a good motive for murder. Great.

"Wait a minute," I said. "Wait a goldarn *minute*. The rumor! According to Beehive's rumor, your sound machine was playing during this supposed argument we had with Kathleen, right?"

"Right."

"Detective Albright said Kathleen was killed around midnight. Didn't you hear anything?"

"No. I took a sleeping pill, and the room I chose to sleep in is rather distant from the kitchen porch where she died."

"And did you turn off your sound machine before the police came?"

"Yes, when I woke up."

"Don't you get it?" I said. "Whoever started that rumor was at the inn *last night when Kathleen was killed*—they had to be, if they heard your sound machine. Which means . . ." I couldn't say it out loud.

Effie said it for me. "The murderer started the rumor."

"Oh my gosh," I whispered. I shoved open the car door. "I'm going to go tell Detective Albright. Back in a minute."

"Wait!" Effie cried.

I ignored her and trotted back into the police station. Beehive seemed to enjoy telling me that Detective Albright and Sergeant Hooks had gone out.

"I didn't see them leave," I said, looking past her to the station's inner sanctum.

Beehive shrugged. "They took the back way." She unpeeled a pink sticky note and jotted down a number. "Here is Detective Albright's cell number."

I returned to the Cadillac and got in. "They're gone."

"*Oh, thank God,*" Effie said on a smoky exhale.

"What do you mean, 'oh, thank God'? This sound machine thing is a major clue! Pass me your phone—I have Albright's number."

Effie didn't pass me her phone. "There's a bit of a . . . snag."

"Uh-huuuh . . . ?"

"It's, well—" Effie shifted in her seat. "The snag is that if the police learn that I was sleeping at the inn last night, they will arrest me for trespassing."

"What? Trespassing on your own property?"

"That's what can happen with condemned buildings, apparently. If they've been deemed unfit for habitation, it's *illegal* to inhabit them. Detective Not-bright told me as much. So you can't tell the police about the sound machine because that would necessarily entail explaining that I was sleeping there, at which point they would merrily slap on the handcuffs and book me."

"*Okaaaay,*" I said. "Then you *lied* to the police about sleeping at the inn last night."

Silence.

"You did! I'm sure they've found your sound machine and whatever it was you slept on at the inn by now."

"I packed everything up and put it in the trunk of the car this morning, actually. They'll never know."

So *that's* what she'd been doing while we were waiting for the police to arrive at the inn.

"I told them I slept in the back seat of my car at the city park," she said. "No witnesses, alas."

"Aunt Effie! Lying to the police is a crime. It's called—" I mentally skimmed my meager knowledge of criminal law.

"Obstruction of justice."

"That's it. I think you can get fined or something."

"Not only fined. I already looked it up on my phone. In New York, it's a Class-A misdemeanor. I could get thrown into the slammer for a year."

"What were you thinking?"

"I really *wasn't* thinking, Agnes dear. I was so consumed with the idea of protecting the inn—*my* inn—that I panicked. I can't afford any delays on the inn's wiring while I loaf around in a jail cell. Not with that demolition date set. No, I must avoid arrest this week at any cost. After the inn passes inspection and the demolition is canceled, *then* I'll come clean to the police." She beamed at me, perfect teeth flashing. "I can always resume work on the inn after serving my sentence. Now. I'm giving you my phone"—she passed it—"but I am begging you to be discreet about the sound machine."

I stared down at the phone's dark screen. Somehow, Effie made lying to the cops seem like the best way for her to avoid arrest. She lived in la-la land, and scarily, she was sucking me in.

"Okay, fine, I won't mention the sound machine," I said. "I'm going to tell Albright that I just have a hunch that the murderer started the rumor."

"A hunch?"

34

"That's the best I can do." I woke up Effie's phone and punched in the number from the sticky note. It went straight to Albright's voice mail, so I sent him a text: *Important clue, please call ASAP—Agnes Blythe.* "I should call Dad," I said.

"I already tried his cell and his house," Effie said. "No answer."

"Does he have *your* number?"

"I don't think I gave it to him, no."

With any luck, Dad was still on the golf course and blissfully oblivious to this mess. "Great," I said. "I have this pivotal clue, but the police won't even pick up the phone, and meanwhile, there's a murderer roaming the town trying to frame us."

"*Do* something with the clue."

"You mean . . . investigate?"

"Why not? At least until Albright calls back."

"I can think of about a dozen reasons why not, Aunt Effie." I stared blankly through the windshield. The day before yesterday, I had my life totally together. Professor fiancé. Top-notch graduate school program. Planet-friendly car. Cute apartment. And now? It was like my life had been mangled by one of those car crushers at the dump. To say nothing of my future, which had gone from being one half of a bifocals-wearing academic power couple to a big, juicy question mark.

So what did I have to lose? Quite frankly, not a whole lot.

"You know what I'm going to do?" I said to Effie.

"What?"

"I'm going to track down the source of that rumor. If I do *that*, I'll probably have identified the murderer. Okay?"

"Fine, but I've got to get to the hardware store," Effie said.

"Are you in denial about the fact that we are *under suspicion for murder*?"

"I have only one week to fix the wiring. It's a monumental task, according to Chester. I'll help you with your inquiries, Agnes, as long as you help me with the inn."

"Deal."

The rational little voice inside of my head (I picture it like a cartoon bug in a waistcoat) told me that trying to track down a murderer was, well, *idiotic*. I told the little voice to stuff it. "Let's go."

Chapter 4

Effie tossed me her purse. "Let's make a list for the hardware store. There's a pad of paper and a pencil in there somewhere." She reversed out of the parking spot. The Cadillac's cushy suspension felt like one of those kids' bouncy houses. I was queasy already.

When Effie cranked into drive, she dinged the rear bumper of a parked car. She swore under her breath and kept going.

"Stop!" I said. "You just hit that car. You have to leave your insurance information."

"What do you think bumpers are for?" Effie turned and gassed it down the street. "And it's just that this isn't exactly *my* car."

"It's a rental?"

"Ahhh . . . no. No, not a rental."

"Is this a hot car?"

I'd been joking, so when Effie replied, "In a manner of speaking," I swung on her.

"Wait a minute! What's going on here?"

"Don't look at me like that, Agnes. You don't think I'm a murderer after all, do you?"

"Maybe. You clearly have no respect for the law."

"I can't go into details about the car. Just forget about it, mm-kay?"

I rolled my eyes and excavated paper and a mechanical pencil from Effie's handbag. I clicked the mechanical pencil lead. "What's on the list?" I said in a distant, professional voice.

"Come on, Agnes, let's have fun."

"Fun? We're suspected murderers, your inheritance is about to be razed, and I have low blood sugar *and* motion sickness. No. No fun. What's on the list?"

"Voltage tester. Wire stripper. Metal fish tape. Oh, and masks."

"Masks?"

"For the dust. And there are some funny smells."

Right. Of a corpse.

Effie dictated more of the hardware store list as we zoomed into the heart of town. The sky arched blue and cloudless. Trees and beautiful old buildings were mere blurs; Effie had a lead foot.

"So who do you think killed Kathleen?" I asked, buzzing my window down.

"Put that window up," Effie snapped. "The wind will ruin my hair."

"I'm carsick!"

"I would be delighted if Paul got this car back smelling of vomit."

"Paul? Who's he?"

"A pustule."

"That clarifies so much." I didn't roll the window up, and Effie pursed her shrimp-pink lipsticked mouth. "Who do you think killed Kathleen?" I asked again.

"God knows. Everyone hated her. Do you know, when I had my little run-in with her at the supermarket, I had a full audience, and someone actually cheered me on?"

"Whoever killed her got really, really close to her in order to crank her scarf up with that washing machine wringer," I said. "That makes it seem like they knew her. It was personal. Plus, the murderer was *angry*."

"It might've been a sociopath."

"But whoever it was must have lured her to the inn at midnight, right? *That* makes it seem like it was someone she knew too."

"They say no one is more likely to kill you than someone in your own family."

Effie and I exchanged brief sidelong glances. Then we quickly looked away. *Awwwkwaaard.*

"What the hell is *this*?" Effie braked hard. White wooden barricades blocked the entrance to the business section of Main Street. Beyond the barricades, bright awnings flapped, and people milled around.

"The farmer's market," I said.

"But how will we get to the hardware store? It's down there." Effie pointed into the farmer's market.

"We'll have to walk."

"Oh, diddle," Effie said.

"I know."

* * *

We parked the car two blocks from Main, on Lake Street, which meant that our net cardio savings in taking the car from the police station was three blocks.

"We should've just walked the whole way," I said.

"It's the principle of the thing, darling."

Secretly, I thought she had a point.

We walked into the bustle of the market. Stalls of colorful fruits and vegetables, shoppers, babies in strollers, and panting dogs stretched two blocks. An accordion player squawked in front of Polly's Ice Cream Parlor. Shop doors in historic brick and stone buildings stood open to the fresh air. Tables and chairs filled the sidewalk in front of the crêperie and the Thai restaurant.

Naneda's economy rests on two things: the university and tourism. Naneda University was founded in 1865 and is a cherished safety school for overachievers. And the tourism? I get it. Naneda's a beautiful place with a rich history that includes the Iroquois Confederacy, colonial-era shenanigans, stops on the Underground Railroad, and pivotal moments in women's suffrage. Year-round visitors guzzle local Riesling and Pinot Noir, stalk the famous lake trout, goggle at fall foliage, bicycle along pastoral woodland and farm roads, and poke through antique shops. We even have tourists in winter, because although the name Naneda derives from an Iroquois word that means *you need warm clothes*, Naneda Lake somehow protects the town from the outer-space-cold blasts of winter weather that torment nearby Buffalo, Rochester, and Syracuse.

"I suppose I ought to buy some nibbles while we're here at the market," Effie said. She headed toward a produce stall.

Couldn't she focus? "Well *I'm* going to the smoothie stand to—" I stopped in my tracks. Just to the left of the produce stall,

I saw Roger. His back was turned, but I'd recognize that bald spot anywhere.

What if I threw myself weeping into his arms and told him I'd been accused of murder? I'd never played the damsel card before, but hey, maybe it would work.

The crowd parted, and I saw the woman with him. She was lightly suntanned and wearing capri leggings, flip-flops, and a pink athletic top that exposed pancake-flat abs. Her straight blonde hair was in a high ponytail, and she clung to Roger's arm, laughing.

Crud. I turned and started speed walking down the sidewalk. Had to get away. Far, far away.

"Agnes!" Effie called after me. "Yoo-hoo! *Ag-nessss!*"

I stopped. I turned.

Roger and Shelby were staring at me, their smiles slipping off.

Effie waggled a bunch of celery at me. "Agnes, come here and hold this celery for me, won't you?"

Making a point of not meeting Roger's eye, I trudged back to Effie. My orange sneakers suddenly felt as ungainly as astronaut boots.

"I forgot to ask—do you like bloody marys?" Effie dumped the dripping celery in my arms.

"She doesn't drink," Roger said in his clear, didactic voice.

Aunt Effie studied Roger over the tops of her sunglasses. "And you are—? Oh, wait. You must be Roger."

Roger cleared his throat. "Hello, Agnes."

"Hi." This was a croak.

"Agnes doesn't drink alcohol," Roger told Effie. "It gives her a rash."

"Just as well," Shelby said in a chipper voice. "Alcohol makes you *so* bloated." Her big blue eyes flicked to my middle. "I mean, it makes *everyone* bloated." She forced a cutesy smile.

I turned to Effie. "I *love* bloody marys."

"I spoke with the police about you this morning, Agnes," Roger said in a concerned-yet-still-pompous voice.

"Yeah." My eyes narrowed. "I heard. Thanks *so much* for telling them I'm erratic, because now I'm a murder suspect."

Shelby gasped.

"Remember," Roger told me, "as Ovid so famously said, 'Fortune and love favor the brave.'" With Shelby clinging to his arm, he strolled away into the crowd.

"He's vile," Effie said. She surveyed the piles of vegetables. "You can do better."

"Yeah," the girl behind the veggies said to me. "You could do better. Probably."

I felt a pair of eyes on me, belonging to a woman in mom shorts pushing a double stroller. Mom Shorts looked from me to Effie and veered the stroller in a wide arc as though we were exhibiting symptoms of the bubonic plague.

"I guess the news that we're murder suspects has made the rounds," I said. *Will* not *think about Roger and Shelby. Will* not *think about Roger and Shelby. And what is* with *this lump in my throat?*

Effie finished up her transaction with the produce stand girl. She stuffed two oranges into her handbag.

"OJ?" I asked.

"God, no. Manhattans with a twist."

"I see the smoothie stand," I said.

We went to a stand with a banner that read *Super Smoothies Save the Day!* A woman with frizzy hair and an apron was wrangling a noisy blender, surrounded by piles of bananas and kale. She switched off the blender when Effie and I stopped.

"What can I get ya?" she chirped. "You two look like you haven't been eating your kale!"

"Are you Rosalie?" I asked.

"Uh-huh."

"Don't you know who we are?" I asked.

"Can't say that I do."

"I'm Agnes Blythe, and this is my great-aunt, Mrs. Winters."

Rosalie's eyes went round. "Oh."

"*Oh* is right," I said softly, leaning over her bananas. "You've been spreading a rumor about us, and I want to know who you heard it from."

"I haven't been *spreading a rumor*," Rosalie said. "I only told Mrs. Wassmuth about what I heard, about you guys arguing with Mrs. Todd last night at the inn, because she works at the police station, and we got to talking when she came for her green smoothie."

"And who told *you* the rumor?" I asked.

"Dr. Gupta," Rosalie said. "He's telling everyone."

"Who's he?" I asked.

"You've never heard of Dr. Gupta?"

"Nope."

"He's the town gossip. He can*not* shut up." Rosalie rolled her eyes. "Everyone who goes to his office to have a cavity filled comes out knowing all the latest dish. You just lie there with your mouth open, and this guy blabs on and on. You're a captive audience. And he doesn't shut up even on his days off. He's been at the market all day today jawing to everyone."

"Is Dr. Gupta still here?" I asked.

43

"He's right over there." Rosalie pointed to the row of stalls across the way. "Mr. Popularity with the black hair and the blue button-down? That's him."

I squinted over. At a fresh-fried donut stall (because yeah, this is America, and people want donuts at the farmer's market, dammit), a small man with gleaming black hair stood inside a cluster of people. He said something and tossed his head back in laughter. The others laughed too.

Effie and I backed away from the smoothie stand.

"Let's go have a word with this Dr. Gupta guy," I said.

"Oh, look at those gorgeous plums!" Effie said, stopping at a stall called Shakti Organic Farm. Fruits and vegetables filled wooden crates, and flowers burst from metal buckets. "Such a pity they have so many grams of sugar."

"You could use a few extra calories," I said. "You can't seem to focus on the task at hand."

"Sounds like *you* could use a few extra calories, Agnes dear. Didn't you eat breakfast?"

I thought of the pile of strawberry muffins I'd inhaled. "Plenty, but then I puked."

"Now you sound like a fashion model." Effie leaned over to regard the young woman crouched behind the Shakti Organic Farm table. The woman had a pretty freckled face and blonde dreads, and she was hastily piling cucumbers into a crate. A long-haired little kid—boy or girl, I couldn't tell—stood shirtless beside her, eating a peach. Peach juice dribbled everywhere. "Three plums, please," Effie said.

"Hell no," the dreadlocks woman said, glancing up. "Get out of here, Euphemia Winters. Your money's not welcome here."

"Good gracious," Effie said. "Might I enquire why?"

"You know why, you crazy bitch."

44

"Such a shame. I do adore plums."

Effie and I hurried away from the Shakti Organic Farm stall.

"Did you see how that woman's eyes were puffy and red?" I whispered to Effie. "I'll bet she was one of Kathleen Todd's family, or a friend. She must have just heard the bad news. Didn't it look like she was packing up to leave?"

As we made our way through the crowd toward Dr. Gupta, we endured furtive glances from behind sacks of apples. Dirty looks from the fresh-baked bread stall. Pointing fingers.

"Not exactly Norman Rockwell land, is it?" Effie said.

"No. More like 'The Lottery.'"

*   *   *

We drew up to Dr. Gupta. His audience had dispersed, and he was paying for a sack of donuts. He caught sight of Effie. "Well *hello*, Mrs. Winters! Do you remember me from the supermarket yesterday?"

"Yes, although I didn't catch your name," Effie said. She whispered to me, "He's the one who cheered me on when I was having words with Kathleen Todd."

"Dr. Gupta, DDS." Dr. Gupta had a compact potbelly, huge ears, and a smile as white as a porcelain sink. "But call me Avi, you darling, you." He grabbed Effie's hand and yanked her close. "I didn't have a chance to thank you for putting the wicked witch of the east in her place yesterday at the Green Apple."

Effie tugged her hand free. "It was nothing, really. To tell the truth, it gives me a great deal of pleasure to set people like that to rights."

"Who's this?" Avi said. He gave my too-tight jeans, backpack, and celery a disapproving look. *He* was wearing small designer jeans that had—yes—ironed creases, and his blue button-down looked starched.

"Agnes Blythe. My niece, my personal assistant—oh, and the mayor's daughter."

"Oooooh," Avi crowed. "Local gentry!"

Yeah, right.

Avi said, "Your auntie, Agnes, leaped to my defense like an avenging angel yesterday evening at the supermarket. There I was, minding my own business, when that vile she-wolf accosted me in front of the Lean Cuisines. She had an axe to grind about my chicken coop, you see, even though it's well within the bounds of the historical society bylaws—I even put historically accurate gingerbread on it and that precious little weather vane from Angel's Antiques that took Doug absolutely *ages* to find—but was that enough for her? No! I even withdrew my raspberry jam entry in the contest at the county fair next weekend because I knew Kathleen—she was going to be the judge—would *never* judge me fairly. For the life of me, I couldn't figure out why everyone was always groveling to Kathleen. She had some way of making everyone do just as she wanted, and let me tell you, it wasn't *charm*. I have an alibi, of course, but if I hadn't, *I* would've *gleefully* taken a crack at strangling that cow. And"—Avi sidled closer, widening his dewy brown eyes— "don't mind the rumors, sweeties."

"Yeah," I said. "About the rumors—"

"People are just jealous, that's all, because they can't bear to have any ladies in town who've got any style." Avi's eyes flicked to my outfit. "A lady with style," he corrected, smiling up at Effie. "And the rumors—I thought you'd already *know*. Rumor has it—not that I believe this for a *second*—that you, Effie—may I call you Effie?"

"Everybody does, darling."

"Rumor has it that the two of you bumped off Kathleen Toddzilla last night because she managed to convince City Hall to raze the Stagecoach Inn at the end of the week—is it true?"

Effie made a noncommittal noise.

Avi went on, "People are saying that you were heard arguing loudly with Kathleen at the inn around midnight and that she's been found *dead*—oh, and that *you*, Agnes, having been dumped by your boy-genius professor fiancé—"

"Boy genius?" I said. "Roger is twenty-nine! He's losing his hair!"

"He *is* losing his hair," Effie said.

"Well, *anyway*," Avi said with a nervous hand-swipe over his own head, "they're saying that you're at the end of your rope because Boy Wonder dumped you for that gorgeous little Pilates instructor, Shelby, and that Boy Wonder likes Shelby because she doesn't correct people when they pronounce *escape* like *excape*."

Why was Roger broadcasting my pet peeves? *And there is no X in escape*!

"Agnes, stop chewing your fingernails," Effie said.

"Who told you all this?" I asked Avi. "We need to know."

"Let me think." Avi tipped his head. "I heard about Boy Wonder and Shelby from Allen at the dry cleaner's, and *he* heard it straight from Boy Wonder himself. He was picking up a tweed jacket with suede elbow patches, Allen said. But the rumor about the argument at the inn? I heard it from no one in particular."

"*No one in particular?*" I said. "How is that possible?"

"Well, when I went to the Black Drop first thing this morning for my steamed milk—I never drink coffee"—Avi tapped a brilliant chopper—"the shop opened a few minutes late, and everyone waiting out on the sidewalk was talking about the argument and about how Kathleen wasn't answering her phone or coming to her door."

"What time was this?" I asked.

"Eight o'clock AM sharp."

"Okay," I said, "and who was there on the sidewalk talking about the rumor?" My heart pumped hard.

"Six people," Avi said and ticked off on his fingers as he listed, "Bud Budzinski, Gracelyn Roy, Dorrie Tucker, Roland Pascal, Jodi Todd, and Susie Pak—Susie, by the way, ordered a *double Americano* even though she's coming in to see me for laser whitening this week and really shouldn't ever drink coffee *again*." Avi *tsk*ed his tongue.

"Hold on," I said. I turned to Effie. "Could I borrow that pad of paper and pencil you have in your purse?"

Effie handed the paper and pencil over.

"Okay, could you tell me those six names again?" I said to Avi. "Slowly?"

Avi repeated the names, and I wrote them down. Then he filled me in a bit on who they were. I'd seen Gracelyn Roy's poster yesterday in the library. I was pretty sure that the frumpy woman who had been hauling boxes of Pyrex with Kathleen Todd at the library had been called Dorrie Tucker.

My list ended up looking like this:

Bud Budzinski. Owner of Club Xenon nightclub/Main Street.

Gracelyn Roy. Local author.

Dorrie Tucker. Kathleen Todd's best friend.

Jodi Todd. Kathleen Todd's daughter.

Bad Housekeeping

Roland Pascal. Carpenter working on McGrundell
    Mansion repairs.
Susie Pak. Owner of Susie's Speedy Maids.

"But you have no idea which one of these people was the original source of the rumor?" I asked Avi.

"No. I was the last one to arrive outside the coffee shop, you see, and they were already talking about it. Jodi was pretty nervous since the rumor was about her mom—although of course everyone knows Jodi and Kathleen haven't spoken for *years*."

"No one seemed to be the gossip ringleader?" I asked.

"No."

"How was everyone behaving?"

"Jodi left, I assume to go and call her mom or go to her mom's house. Dorrie Tucker went all weepy and said she was going to faint, but she did the *exact* same thing at the Garden Club ice cream social in July. Just between us, she's kind of a wimp. She always asks for double Novocain when she comes in to see me, you know. Now let's see. The rest of them—Bud Budzinski, Gracelyn Roy, Roland Pascal, and Susie Pak—were all suitably shocked, but as soon as Jodi left to check on her mom, no one really had to *do* anything except wait for the coffee shop to open . . . or, yes, now I remember, Dorrie Tucker wandered off. Now I'm *so* sorry, but I've got to dash. I've got a hair appointment." Avi made a smoochy noise in Effie's direction and skittered away.

I looked at my list. "I think I should take this information to the police. Has Albright called or texted back?"

"No. Of *course* you should tell Detective Albright all about what Avi told us, although if you aren't going to mention the bit

49

about my sound machine, it doesn't really add up to much." A pause. "I can tell by the look in your eye, Agnes, that you'd also like to look into the matter yourself."

I hated that Effie could read me so easily. And what was she, some kind of scofflaw enabler? Still, I *was* itching to investigate the rumor. When Albright called, I'd tell him what Avi Gupta had told us . . . but it wouldn't hurt to satisfy my curiosity in the meantime.

Chapter 5

I led Aunt Effie the block and a half to Club Xenon, on the corner of Main and Oak. I would start my questioning there since it was close, and because I didn't know where to find Dorrie Tucker. I'd never been inside Club Xenon, but I had noticed it since moving back to Naneda. It occupied the old Davis's Department Store building.

I raised my eyebrows. Here was something new—a *neon sign*? Bright blue, although unlit, reading, *Club Xenon*. As a college town, Naneda always has a nightclub or two, but not within the historical district. "How did they get a neon sign past the historical society?" I said.

"Is neon on their no-no list?" Effie asked.

"Yep." The club was dark inside—the doors were glass—but just for the hey of it, I tried one. It opened.

"What luck," Effie said, stepping inside.

I followed. Inside, we found ourselves in a big, dim space that stank of beer and the sinus-shriveling cologne of a hundred frat boys.

"Good lord," Effie said. Her shoe crunched on shattered glass.

"Look, there's a light on back there," I whispered, pointing past the bar.

"Why are you whispering?"

"I don't know," I whispered.

"I remember when this used to be the department store, before everyone started doing their shopping at the mall in Lucerne." Lucerne was the next town over. "See the balconies? Every Christmas they were hung with swags of holly and ribbons, and on Christmas Eve, there were always carolers singing up on the top balcony."

I squinted up at the three levels of wooden balconies. It looked like a recipe for disaster to me. The kind of disaster involving Jell-O shots and sorority pledges.

We crossed the dance floor with its huge disco ball. A bar curved around two sides. Tap pulls and liquor bottles gleamed in the dim light. We went past the bar and down a corridor, passing doors marked "Guys" and "Girls." We rounded a corner, and light beamed through an open door.

"Hey! Who's out there?" a gruff male voice shouted.

Effie and I stopped in the doorway. A burly, hairy man, maybe thirty-five years old, lolled in a chair with his bare feet on a desk. Untidy papers, a chunky nineties computer, and an open package of Oreo cookies cluttered the desk. I smelled BO and citrusy perfume. A kind of stomach-turning combo.

The man narrowed his eyes at Effie and me. "What the—? You two don't look like the AC repairmen. I'm sweating buckets in here. Jesus!"

It was true. His shirt had creeping sweat stains under the arms and those little sweat speckles down the front. Oh, and he'd stripped down to his boxer shorts.

"Bud?" I said.

"Yeah. That's me. Who the hell are you? We filled the barmaid position, and anyway you're, ah, not exactly the type. And what's with the celery?" Bud glanced at Effie. "You could make an okay barmaid, I guess, if you dyed your hair."

"You'd hire *her* but not me?" I said.

"What do you want?" Bud asked. "A drink? We're closed."

"We're here to confront you about a rumor," I said.

"Agnes, darling, don't ever use the word *confront*," Effie said. "It puts people on their guard."

"Yeah," Bud said. "Listen to your grandma."

Effie sniffed.

"We heard a rumor, Bud," I said.

"Oh yeah? Fascinating. Now if you don't mind, I got work to do."

"Like eating Oreos?" I said.

"I am Euphemia Winters," Effie cut in. "Perhaps you've heard of me?"

"Oh." Understanding glimmered on Bud's Cro-Magnon features. "The mayor's aunt. Yeah, I've heard of you. And this must be Agnes, the niece who got dumped by the new genius professor up at the university. Yeah, okay."

What I wanted to know was, who the heck was spreading the rumor about Roger being a genius? Sure, he'd gotten his PhD at an ivy league school, but he didn't even know how to load a dishwasher.

"We have it on good authority that you were spreading a pretty nasty rumor about us this morning while you were waiting for the Black Drop to open," I said.

"Just making conversation. I'm kind of new to town and not exactly Mr. Popularity. These townsfolk want to pretend they live on the set of *Leave it To Beaver* even though it's a college town, and so it's got college kids who've got some steam to blow off on the weekends. Beats drinking Sour Apple Pucker in a dorm room. Which, by the way, is banned here at the club. Have you seen Sour Apple Pucker puke? It doesn't come out of the carpet."

"What does this have to do with you spreading malicious and unfounded rumors?" I said.

"Listen, cut the Judge Judy crap, all right? Everyone in this town has their dirty little secrets, trust me, and there's nothing they like better than gossiping about *other* people's dirty secrets. So shoot me if I try to warm their bitter hearts with some gossip. Just being sociable."

"That explains why you *spread* the rumor," I said, "but you still haven't told me who told it to you."

"Who told me? That little weepy marshmallow of a lady who was always glued to Kathleen Todd's side. Retired kindergarten teacher . . . what's her name? Lori or something."

"Dorrie Tucker?" I said.

"Yeah, that's it. Dorrie. She sort of stumbled on the sidewalk outside the coffee shop, and I helped her up, see, and picked up her purse. She was crying, which is why she tripped in the first place I guess, so I asked her what was the matter—come to think of it, I was pretty goddam chivalrous—and she filled me in on the facts about you two arguing with Kathleen at the inn last night and about Kathleen not answering her phone."

"Facts?" I said.

"Well, you know. The info. She didn't even say thanks to me for helping her up! It doesn't pay to be a Boy Scout with that type. Always so busy feeling sorry for themselves, they're too busy to give a crap about other people."

"Who else was there when Dorrie told you the rumor?" I asked.

"Four or five other people. I recognized Jodi, the blonde hippie chick with the dreads."

"You're talking about Kathleen Todd's daughter?"

"Uh-huh. She spazzed when she heard the news about her mom not answering her phone and then went off somewhere. The dentist was there—everyone knows him. Dr. Gupta? What a motormouth."

"Who do you think killed Kathleen Todd?" I asked.

"Who cares? She harassed half the town about stupid rules and was always siccing that Susie's maid service on anyone who doesn't reek of fabric softener. I could never figure out why anyone did what she wanted. She had this weird *hold* on people."

"Well, I thought *you* might care who murdered her, Bud," I said, "since she probably gave you hell about that neon sign you have out front. Neon, as far as I know, is crime number one in the historical society's ordinances, and your club sits smack-dab in the middle of the historical district."

Bud beetled his eyebrows, swung his feet off his desk, and lunged forward. "Is that why you're really here? Come to rough me up on account of some historical society crapspackle?"

Effie and I shrank back. This guy was suddenly scary. But what the heck? He though *we* were going to rough *him* up? A bird-boned old lady and a young woman who had several conspiracy theories about exercise equipment?

"Has the, uh, historical society ever roughed you up before?" I asked Bud.

"Hell, no." Bud sat back in his chair and rustled an Oreo from the package on his desk. "I was just joking." He took a bite.

It hadn't *seemed* like he was joking.

"You know what?" Bud said through a mouthful of cookie. "I've had enough of you two, and I got work to do." He jerked a thumb. "Out. Or I'll call the cops and tell them I'm being harassed by a couple of crazy lady murder suspects."

Another helping of the cops? No, thanks. Effie and I speed walked out of Bud's office, through the club, and outside.

* * *

"Did you smell Bud's office?" Effie asked. She paused on the sidewalk in front of Club Xenon to rummage past the oranges in her handbag for a cigarette.

"Those will kill you," I said.

"I know." She stuck one between her lips and clicked her lighter. "I'm switching to one of those electronic cigarettes just as soon as I get myself together. Things have been a little . . . hectic the past week or so."

"Because you stole that guy Paul's Cadillac." I looked down at the bunch of celery in my arms. I was pretty thirsty and beyond hungry, so I snapped off a stalk, wiped the dirt off on my jeans, and crunched into it.

"Not *because* I stole Paul's Cadillac—"

"So you admit to stealing it."

"It's not that simple, but fine. Yes. I stole it. He deserved it. Don't sidetrack me, Agnes. I still have jet lag, and I'm trying to focus."

"Jet lag? I thought you drove up from Florida."

"*Please!*" Effie puffed smoke.

I quietly chewed celery. Well, as quietly as one can chew celery.

"Did you smell Bud's office?" Effie asked me again.

"Sure. BO like a locker room. Maybe a little rancid cheeseburger or something."

"Not that. The perfume."

"Oh yeah. It did smell like perfume."

"It was Burberry Brit."

"Okaaay. Great. Bud wears Burberry Brit."

"It's a woman's perfume. A rather costly woman's perfume, and I'm dead certain it wasn't a drugstore imitation. Those always hit me at the back of the throat like Pine-Sol."

"So?"

"So Bud has been entertaining a Burberry Brit–wearing woman in his office recently."

"Who would want to touch that big, sweaty brontosaurus? Can I see your phone? I just realized we can look up Dorrie Tucker's address online."

"I cannot imagine who'd want to touch Bud," Effie said, digging in her purse for her phone. "But there are all sorts of women, Agnes, you know that, as well as all sorts of reasons why a woman might want to—or need to—touch a man, brontosaurus or no. Speaking of *men* . . . my, my." She tucked her chin to look over the tops of her sunglasses. "Here comes a big slice of home-baked heaven."

Gross. I snatched the phone out of Effie's hand, took another bite of celery, and turned to see what she was staring at.

Oh. Crud. Otis Hatch. No motorcycle and helmet this time, just faded blue jeans, a green ringer tee, and a cowboyish loping stride. His hair wafted back from his face. He carried a watermelon-sized hunk of metal. A car part, I guessed.

"He has a *Dukes of Hazzard* hairdo," I said. "Lame." *Gorgeous.* I swiped Effie's phone to life and poked the Internet icon.

"Not *quite* Dukes of Hazzard," Effie said. "Too straight. But yes, that hair would be laughable on a . . . lesser man."

"Stop leering like that, Aunt Effie! I know him!" I typed
Naneda NY white pages.

"You do?"

"Yes, and he's a—"

"Talking about me?" Otis said with a grin. "Hey, Agnes."

"No. Um. I was talking about the nightclub owner." I gulped
down celery and made a feeble gesture at the Club Xenon doors.

"Oh, yeah, Budzinski. He can be abrasive." Otis studied
Aunt Effie with smiling eyes. He hadn't shaved, and his jaw
glinted with dark-gold stubble. Darn him. "Hi, I'm Otis Hatch."
He stuck out a strong-looking hand.

Effie gave him a shake. "Euphemia Winters. Agnes's aunt."

I noticed she never admitted to being my *great*-aunt.

"Right," Otis said, nodding. "I heard Kathleen Todd died
last night and that you two found the body this morning?"

"Yeah," I said, "unfortunately." A celery string was stuck
between my teeth.

"You must be Harlan Hatch's boy," Effie said to Otis.

"Yep."

"I remember he owned the filling station out on Post Road."

"That's right. The family business. It's still there, actually.
Dad passed away a couple years ago, so my grandpa Hank and
I run it." Otis looked at me. "You ought to come out and visit
some time, Agnes. You'd like the auto shop—I remember you
were really handy in shop class back in high school."

"You took shop class, Agnes?" Effie asked in a shocked tone.

"It was either that or sewing, and I was going to learn sewing
when pigs fly." Now, of course, I wished I could sew. If only so I
could alter the waistband of these too-tight jeans. "Hey, Otis, do
you know this lady named Dorrie Tucker? Supposedly Kathleen
Todd's best friend?"

"Dorrie Tucker? Yeah, she was a kindergarten teacher at Barkley Elementary for years, and don't you remember her husband used to teach social studies at the high school?"

"No. I had Mrs. Chang for social studies."

"Oh, well I had Mr. Tucker. Bruce. Kind of a jerk, actually. Bullied the dorky kids. Dorrie was his wife."

"Was? Are they divorced?"

"No, he died last year. Heart attack. Too much good home cooking."

I inched the celery over my midriff. A memory flickered in my mind's eye: a Sharpied sign taped to a metal locker reading, *Do the Math! Agnes Blythe = Hagness Blimp.* I kicked the memory away. "Do you know where Dorrie Tucker lives?" I asked.

"On Third Street, I'm pretty sure. Well, good running into you again, Agnes, and nice meeting you, Mrs. Winters." Otis hefted the metal thing in his arms. Muscles jumped under his tawny skin; I looked away. "I'm headed to the hardware store to try to find some bolts for this baby."

"Oh, we were just going to the hardware store!" Effie cooed.

"No, we weren't," I snapped.

"Okay, well, see you around, ladies. The cops will catch the murderer soon, I'm sure—this is Naneda—but in the meantime, be careful, okay?" Otis flashed us one last big-man-on-campus grin and strode out into the street.

Chapter 6

"Young Otis Hatch is certainly a hunk," Effie said, watching him (well, watching his buns) retreat across the street. "*Yum.* Why so rude, Agnes, darling?"

"Trust me, you don't want to know. It would disillusion you about hunks forever."

"I was disillusioned *ages* ago. Even if they're asses, they're still hunks. Better than your ex Roger, who's an ass and not, well—I'm sorry to say this, Agnes—but he's really not very attractive."

"He's brilliant," I said through gritted teeth. The deep-down truth that I couldn't quite admit even to myself was that Roger had never, not even *once*, inspired the swoopy, melty feelings I got when I saw Otis Hatch. What was *wrong* with me?

Effie said, "Let's fetch the car and drive to see Dorrie Tucker."

"She lives on Third Street, which is two blocks this way." I pointed to the left. "And you parked the car three blocks the other way. If we drive, we'll be doing extra walking."

Effie was already going in the direction of the car. "I'm not *walking* to someone's house. And what if we need to make a quick getaway?"

I pictured plump, damp-eyed Dorrie hugging her box of broken Pyrex at the library. There was no way we'd need to make a quick getaway. But I followed Effie.

Once we'd buckled ourselves into the boiling-hot Caddy, I chucked the celery onto the back seat and looked up Dorrie Tucker's address on Effie's phone. "Four-oh-one Third Street," I said.

Effie angled the car out into the street. "Don't you have a phone? I thought youngsters like you were glued to your phones nowadays."

"My phone's in my backpack but—"

"I've been meaning to discuss that backpack, Agnes—"

"Let's not and say we did. My phone's out of juice, and I left the charger at my—at Roger's." The only things in my backpack were lip balm, my dead phone, and a cardigan. I hadn't even brought my wallet. I was going to have to stop by the apartment and get my stuff at some point. Maybe tomorrow.

"What were all those years with Roger like anyway, Agnes?"

"They were fine." Actually, they weren't that great. In the past six years, I had exhausted myself at my jobs, Roger had exhausted himself in grad school, and instead of making out or cuddling when we'd had the chance, we had binged on carbs and TV shows. I think the word *burnout* sums it all up nicely.

Effie slammed on the brakes at a stop sign. "You aren't in love with Roger."

"What?"

"I can tell. You're unsettled because your life is changing"— Effie gassed it across the intersection as someone screamed obscenities—"but you're secretly relieved, aren't you?"

"No, I'm not. I want him back."

"No, you don't! Not when there are scrumptious Otis Hatches strutting around in their faded blue jeans. And those were *virtuously* faded blue jeans too. Not factory faded. He faded them in his *auto body shop* for God's sake! You're *young*, Agnes. And now you're free! Enjoy it."

"You promised not to talk about Roger, so could we not?" Shouldn't Aunt Effie be crocheting toilet paper cozies instead of ogling men half her age? She *had* to be taking some kind of hormone replacements.

* * *

Dorrie Tucker's house was a perfect little jewel box of a Victorian cottage on a quiet, tree-lined street. It exuded vintage charm, unlike the house to its right, which was the same style as Dorrie's but painted purple and had rusty tractor parts and round saw blades in its garden as, I guessed, decor. Dorrie's house, on the other hand, was soft pink with cream-colored gingerbread and a sparkling leaded window over the front door. Behind the picket fence, roses bloomed sumptuously.

And there was Dorrie on her front walk, pruning a rose bush. She straightened when Effie and I pulled up at the curb.

"Is that her?" Effie whispered.

"Yeah."

We got out. Dorrie shrank back against her rosebushes as Effie and I turned down her front walk. "Yes?" she said with a wobble in her voice.

"Dorrie Tucker?" I said, brisk and no-nonsense.

"Yes?" Dorrie wore a floral shirt and stubby capris under her gardener's smock. On her feet were blue Keds sneakers, and she wore pink-flowered gardening gloves. The very picture of meek and mild . . . although the clippers she was holding looked pretty wicked.

"Mrs. Tucker, I'm Agnes Blythe. Remember me from the library yesterday?"

"Oh, yes."

"I hear you've been spreading a malicious rumor about my great-aunt and me?"

"Who, me?"

"We have it on good authority."

"It was that awful man from the nightclub who told you that, wasn't it?" Dorrie burst into tears.

Effie and I waited for Dorrie to get herself together. It didn't take long.

She sniffled. "I simply repeated the rumor to that Bud fellow as an *explanation*, you see, for the way I fell down on the sidewalk! It was so humiliating, and I felt like he was laughing at me a little even when he helped me up. I felt my"—Dorrie leaned close—"my support garment slip. *You* know, Agnes—"

Why would *I* know?

"—and I started bawling like a baby, because of—of Kathleen. I'd just overheard that rumor while waiting for the coffee shop to open, completely by accident, and I knew it wasn't true—look at you two!—but hearing the rumor had upset me *terribly*, which is why I fell and why I repeated the rumor to Mr. Budzinski."

"Uh-huh," I said. "And this was the first you heard of the rumor?"

"Of course!"

"Who did you overhear saying it?"

"That horrible, smelly Frenchman, Roland Pascal." Dorrie said *Frenchman* as though she'd gotten Ivory soap in her mouth.

She was the old-school type of Naneda resident who didn't cotton to "outsiders"—never mind that Naneda was settled by waves of "outsiders" who, oh yeah, ousted the native people from the land. So even though Dorrie was a weakling and I *wanted* to feel magnanimous toward her, I was starting to dislike her.

"Roland Pascal is the carpenter working on the McGrundell Mansion, right?" I said, recalling what I'd written on my list of suspects earlier.

"Yes. He was hired by the historical society to restore the mansion. He's living in a trailer parked in front of the mansion, you know. He's a *transient worker*, really, although I never could convince Kathleen of that. *I* wanted to hire Mr. Roberts from Lucerne. But Kathleen was, well, she was *dazzled* by the filthy little man."

"You knew Kathleen well," I said. "Who do you think killed her?"

"I can't imagine! We all *adored* Kathleen."

We did?

"She was a dear, dear friend, and I don't know what I'll do without her. Helping her with the historical society has been my guiding light ever since my husband, Bruce, passed away—I am the secretary, you see. The society gave me structure—Kathleen said I needed structure since Bruce and I never had children. Kathleen said I might as well stop being a pathetic lump and make myself useful. Now, with her gone, well, I'm just a *mess*. The doctor gave me something, of course, for the shock—nice little pills—and I was thinking of going on a Caribbean cruise. Bruce never wanted to go on a cruise, said he didn't care to be seen with me in my swimsuit, although *he* had—"

My brain was glazing over like a Bundt cake. "Okay, got it. Thanks, Mrs. Tucker." I ripped a piece of paper from the notebook in my backpack, jotted down my phone number, and passed it to Dorrie. "Here's my number. Call me if you remember any more details about the rumor." I *really* needed to get a new phone charger. Maybe Effie would drive me to Mobile Phone Mart on the edge of town. Just as soon as I grilled this gossipy Frenchman. "We'll go see what Roland Pascal has to say for himself."

"Be careful on your way out—of *those things*." Dorrie pointed with her clippers to the rusty stuff in the garden next door. "Gracelyn Roy lives there. She calls those heaps of trash art, but don't you think they just look *dirty*?"

The sculptures did look like you might need a tetanus shot if you got too close. But by golly, I'd taken a college-level art appreciation course, so I wasn't going to condemn them.

Dorrie babbled on, "Kathleen was forever trying to get Gracelyn Roy to hire Susie's Speedy Maids to clean her house up—or, ever since Gracelyn moved to town, which was only last spring anyway, but you wouldn't know it because of the way she acts like she *owns* the town—but Gracelyn outright refused and claims she only uses baking soda and vinegar to clean *her* house, thank you very much—"

"Kathleen recommended Susie's Speedy Maids to Gracelyn?" I asked.

"Of course. They're the best. Susie hires *foreign* women, of course, but I've never had anything stolen. Bye-bye!" Dorrie bent to snip at her rose bushes.

Effie and I retreated down the front walk. "Let's see if Gracelyn is at home," I whispered, "since she's on the list too."

"Fine."

Effie and I edged past the rusty tractor parts and saw blades to Gracelyn's front porch. I hit the door knocker.

No answer.

Effie and I went back to the Cadillac.

"I didn't like Dorrie Tucker," Effie said, turning the key in the ignition. "Simpering." We zoomed down the street. "Overdone."

"If she's hiding anything, it's that she's a little bit grateful that Kathleen is gone," I said. "Kathleen treated her like a doormat. I saw it for myself at the library yesterday."

"Aren't you glad I insisted we take the car?" Effie asked.

I *was* glad, but I wasn't going to admit it. "I'm really hungry," I said. "Let's stop for lunch. We could go to the Cup n' Clatter."

"That greasy pit of gossip? No. I don't mind being stared at, but not in that pitchforks-and-torches way. This town is a rumor mill stuck in overdrive. It's a wonder anyone has any secrets at *all*."

"That's the thing," I said. "In small towns like this, word travels at the speed of light once it gets out, but that just makes people extra secretive. In big cities, people walk around their apartments in their skivvies with the curtains wide open. They don't care who sees them through the window as long as they don't see them on the street. But in Naneda, people guard their secrets with their lives."

"Quite literally, it turns out." Effie shuddered. "Anyway, look, we're only a few blocks from the McGrundell Mansion. We can lunch later."

We parked across the street from the McGrundell Mansion. The mansion, once home to Naneda's wealthiest turn-of-the-century businessman, Frederick McGrundell, was now the home of the Naneda Historical Society Museum. It stood above the sidewalk on a small grassy rise, sheltered by thick-branched trees. For as long as I could remember, its geometric gingerbread trim had been in slack disrepair and painted a few shades of blue. Now it wasn't slack, and white primer splotched places where gingerbread and siding had been replaced.

A long Airstream trailer—the kind that looks like a big silver sausage—stretched along the curb. A pickup was parked in front of the trailer, but the trailer hitch rested on cinderblocks.

"Classy," I said, unbuckling.

The Airstream's door faced the sidewalk. When we reached that side, the pill-shaped door swung open. Standing in the doorway was a fifty-something, dark, handsome man with bandy legs and a burly chest. He wore a red plaid shirt, tight gray jeans, work boots, and a ruffled pink apron, and he held a wine bottle.

"Ah, it is ladies," he said. "It is as though Lord Bacchus read your minds and compelled me to take up this bottle of Pinot Noir."

Bizarre. "Are you Roland Pascal?" I asked.

"But of course."

"Good. I'm Agnes Blythe—yeah, rings a bell, doesn't it?— and this is my great-aunt Mrs. Winters."

Roland's face lit up. "Ah! Mrs. Winters! But how wonderful, for I meant to go and speak with you at the Stagecoach Inn. I understand you are the new owner." He dug into the breast pocket of his shirt—a pocket bulging with a pencil and a screwdriver—and pulled out a grubby business card. He passed it to Effie.

She took the card. "Master carpenter? Oh. No, thank you. My nephew Chester will be doing the carpentry once we get to that stage."

"But that is madness! Has the nephew any training?"

"He'll learn as he goes along."

"But how can you treat her in so callous a fashion?"

"*Her?*" Effie and I both said.

"She is an exquisite beauty, abandoned by the caprices of heartless men, left to languish. But I could bring her back to life, to beauty. Everyone would see and celebrate once more the beauty that is her birthright."

Okaaaaaay.

"Beautiful women don't need men to fix their looks," Effie said.

"And anyway," I said, "why does she have to be beautiful in the first place? Why can't she just be *healthy*?"

Roland frowned and scratched his forehead. "The inn," he said. "We speak of the inn. Please, Mrs. Winters, I beg you to reconsider—such a stunning woman must also have a stunning intellect, yes?"

"Your smooth-talking won't work on me, darling," Effie said.

"Perhaps mine won't, Euphemia—may I call you Euphemia?—but the Pinot Noir's might. It's a bottle from just across the lake."

"What's the occasion?" I asked. "The successful spread of a malicious rumor?"

"Better. The arrival of two beautiful women on my door-step, precisely when I broke work for lunch. Come in, ladies. There is plenty of wine and cheese and bread."

My stomach growled. Everyone heard it.

Roland grinned.

"I do enjoy Pinot Noir if it's not *too* fruity," Effie said and looked at me.

I shrugged. I mean, why *not* get into a possible murderer's trailer and booze it up?

Chapter 7

Effie and I climbed after Roland into the Airstream, and it was naaaaaaasty inside. As in, it reeked of garlic, cat pee, mold, and, very faintly, that blue stuff they put in Porta Potties to pretend they're sanitary. The built-in benches and tables and counters were all cluttered up with woodworking magazines, dirty dishes, ashtrays—Effie was probably loving *that*—and sawdust.

"Sit, please." Roland swept a hand across the dining booth table. Stuff crashed on the floor. Food crumbs remained on the speckled Formica tabletop.

Effie and I squeezed into the booth. Roland set out plates of bread and cheese, uncorked the bottle, and poured three generous glasses.

"Cheers," he said. "To murder."

"Mmm," Effie said. "And to rumors."

I held up my own glass even though I had no intention of drinking. "To cheese."

We clinked. Effie and Roland swirled, sniffed, and took deep, religious swallows. I reached for a piece of bread. The cheese was moldy, but cheese is supposed to be moldy, right? I smeared some on bread and got down to it.

"I hope you will reconsider my offer to restore your beautiful inn," Roland said. "To cease being modest for a moment, I am the best restorer of historic buildings in the northeastern United States."

I looked around his squalid trailer. *Suuurrre.* I took another bite of bread and cheese. The cheese was either amazingly delicious, or I was amazingly hungry.

"Modest, aren't you?" Effie said.

"I only speak the truth. I am an honest man."

"Claiming to be honest would only occur to a *dis*honest man," Effie said.

"Ah, Mrs. Winters, you have been burned by a lover," Roland said.

"No, only the tax man."

"How long have you been living in this trailer, Mr. Pascal?" I asked.

"Two years, more or less. I travel from town to town fixing old, neglected buildings. The Naneda Historical Society hired me—"

"You mean Kathleen Todd hired you," I said.

"Yes. I was working on a farmhouse in Caraway, Vermont, that belonged to an acquaintance of Mrs. Todd's. Mrs. Todd saw my splendid portfolio and knew at once that no one but I could save the McGrundell Mansion." Roland leaned over to a shelf and pulled out a photo album. He placed it on the table and flipped through photographs of woodwork and house facades displayed behind plastic film. The last page, I noticed, had a typed list of references with addresses and phone numbers. Smoothly, Roland slid this page out, crumpled it, and tossed it into a corner of the trailer. "My portfolio, yes? The McGrundell

Mansion had succumbed to carpenter ants years ago, and then dry rot set in. I have been working on her for more than three months, night and day, to save her. My work on the exterior is almost complete. Then I move to the interior. The historical society has moved all the museum's artifacts to boxes stored in the town library's basement."

Huh. That must have been why Kathleen and Dorrie had been moving those boxes of Pyrex at the library.

"Who killed Kathleen Todd?" I asked.

"God knows, but I applaud them." Roland sipped his wine. "Miserable woman."

"That does seem to be the consensus," Effie said.

"I have an alibi, naturally," Roland said, "but I would have enjoyed strangling her myself."

Can you say *eek*?

Roland went on, "She hung over me like an overseer while I was working."

"Who's your alibi?" I asked.

"You need not bother yourself with that detail."

"Okay," I said. "And you were with this *alibi* of yours at . . . midnight?"

Roland twinkled.

Ew.

Speaking of *ew*: it was weird that Roland lived in such a junky trailer if he was such a meticulous restorer of buildings. The photos in his portfolio showed immaculate, detailed work.

Roland noticed my grossed-out glances around his trailer. "You do not approve of my domestic style?" he asked.

"Um . . ."

"I am an artist, but I am also a bachelor. Kathleen Todd attempted to convince me to hire Sally's maid service—"

"Do you mean Susie's Speedy Maids?" Effie asked.

"Yes." Roland snapped his fingers. "Thank you. But I declined, for I do not desire for meddling women crawling like termites in my trailer. But I beg your pardon. It is only that I do not mince words. I am a passionate man. They say I blow hot and cold, to which I respond, I only blow hot, and *hotter*."

"Do you blow hot enough to start rumors about people you don't know?" I asked. Roland had somehow gone straight to chummy mode with Effie and me; I'd almost forgotten why we were there. "Do you blow hot enough to *murder* people?"

Roland chuckled. "I have been called a lady-killer, it is true, but I have different methods than murder. And the rumor? I repeated it merely to make conversation. It seemed a fascinating thing to speak of while waiting for the coffee shop to open its doors."

I smeared more cheese on bread. "Who told *you* the rumor?"

"Jodi, the lovely young lady with the dreadlocks. You will find her, I believe, at her fruit and flower stall in the market called Shakti Organic Farm."

That had definitely been Jodi swearing at Aunt Effie over the plums earlier, then.

Effie stood. "Back to the market, Agnes."

I smashed a last bite of bread and cheese in my mouth and stood also. I tried to swallow. Too much bread. Too dry. I coughed.

Effie thrust my wineglass into my hands. "Drink, damn it!"

"No!" I spluttered. "Water!"

Roland swung to his sink, grabbed a smeary-looking glass, and filled it with water from a jug.

"Gross!" I choked out.

"Drink! No more dead bodies!" Roland yelled.

Effie thrust the wineglass into my narrowing field of vision. "One drink won't hurt," she said in a coaxing voice.

I had no choice. The dry bread wasn't going down. I was going to puke and/or pass out. I gulped down the entire glass of wine. The bread subsided. I stood there blinking tears from my eyes. When my eyes focused, they randomly landed on something strange: Roland was still clutching the water glass, and he had those muscular worker's hands with the bulging muscle between the base of the index finger and thumb. Right on that muscle on his right hand, he had a simple tattoo of five dots, just like on dice or dominoes.

Roland caught me looking. He waggled an eyebrow.

What the *hey*?

"Are you all right, Agnes?" Effie asked.

I nodded.

"Then let's go. Thank you for the *scrumptious* Pinot, Roland, darling."

* * *

Effie whizzed the Cadillac back toward Main Street.

"I'm going to get a rash from that wine," I said. "I know it." I scratched at both of my upper arms simultaneously.

"I don't see anything."

"You're not even looking! And I swear, alcohol gives me a rash! I never drink."

"When was the last time this happened? Do you need an EpiPen?"

"Maybe." The truth was, I'd only ever drunk alcohol once, back when I was a fifteen. A raspberry wine cooler in my best friend Lauren's room, as a matter of fact. The thing was, Lauren also had a parrot, and I'm allergic to birds, so the rash *might* have been from Dollface, not the wine cooler. But I hadn't enjoyed the way the wine cooler had made me feel not in charge of my life, so I'd sworn off the stuff.

Until now, that is. A warm haze settled around me. I forgot exactly why I was so pissed off at Aunt Effie all the time, and the clench in my stomach that I'd had since Roger dumped me relaxed a notch.

"Do you want me to take you to the emergency room?" Effie said. "Because if I take a left here, the hospital—"

"No, it's fine. I usually get the rash on my, um, only on my inner elbows."

Effie didn't say anything for a second. Then, "I think you're lying to me, Agnes. You're a control freak. Control freaks hate to drink."

"Whatever," I said.

"Isn't it simply bizarre the way Susie's Speedy Maids keep coming up in our conversations with people?" Effie asked. "We only want to talk about the rumor, but it's Susie's Speedy Maids this and Susie's Speedy Maids that."

"Only in tangential ways. This is a small town. Things get incestuous."

"Ugh. You can say *that* again. God, what I wouldn't give to be sipping Chartreuse in a sidewalk café in Paris right now."

"Well, why aren't you?"

"Agnes, you requested that I not speak of Roger, and I am in turn requesting that you not ask about the recent events that compelled me to return to this gossipy backwater, mm-kay?"

"Fair enough."

Effie parked, and we plodded—well, Effie strutted and I plodded—back to Main Street.

The farmer's market was wrapping up. Stray veggie leaves and smushed fruit littered the asphalt. Vendors loaded folding tables, awnings, and empty crates onto pickup trucks. I balled my fists and pumped my legs in my too-tight jeans; I was getting worked up. I had convinced myself that Jodi was the murderer and the origin of the rumor, and that made me really, *really* mad.

When I reached the spot where Jodi's stall had been, it was empty.

"Oh, diddle," Effie said, pulling up next to me. "She's gone."

I felt like karate-chopping a board in half, like in the movies—that's how jacked up I was. "Could I have your phone?"

Effie passed me her phone. "Detective Albright still hasn't gotten back to us. Oh, and program your phone number in there while you're at it."

I added my number to Effie's contacts, and then I did a map search for Shakti Organic Farm. Nothing. I waved at a guy who was loading buckets into a truck with *Hernandez Flowers* on the side. "Hi," I said. "Quick question."

"Yeah?" the guy said, giving his Yankees cap a wiggle.

"Do you know where Shakti Organic Farm is located?"

"Matter of fact, I do, because I went out there to deliver some used hydro supplies just last week. You go out on Route 20 toward Lucerne, take a left on Route 14A, go a few miles, and then take a right on Douglas Road. There's a black mailbox full of bullet holes at their turnout, about two miles up. Hard to miss."

Bullet holes? *Ummmmm . . .*

"Jodi left real early today, anyway," the guy said. "She said something happened to her mom."

"Thanks," I said. I turned to Effie. "Want to go to Jodi's farm?" I would have asked to borrow the Cadillac, except that my driver's license was in my wallet at my ex-apartment, and also, I didn't really want to tool around in a stolen car.

Effie glanced at her wristwatch. "I really must get to the hardware store . . . But after that, yes."

*   *   *

I felt jumpy stepping through the doors of the hardware store, and I trailed after Effie and her shopping cart expecting to bump into Otis at every turn. The jumbly shelves and bad lighting even tricked me into thinking—for one belly-dipping second—that a strange man in the power tools aisle was Otis.

This was a familiar feeling, this blurry searching/hoping/ dreading. The thing is, in the years since high school, I'd dreamed about Otis Hatch. A *lot*. Not sweet dreams, but one breathless recurring dream in which I jog through ill-lit high school hallways, tears streaming down my face, looking frantically for Otis. Looking for the beautiful, kind Otis who I'd loved so hard before that awful betrayal of the Sharpied sign on the locker. Looking for the Otis who had been my trusty lab partner in AP Chemistry, the Otis who'd cracked me up with his easy wit and impressed me with his kindness to everyone he interacted with. The Otis who, as it turns out, didn't really exist.

When Effie finally thrust a paper sack of purchases in my arms and led me out of the hardware store, I breathed a huge sigh of relief.

"—and then after that, we'll go to Jodi's farm," Effie was saying.

"Wait," I said. "After what?"

"You haven't been listening! I saw you looking around in there, Agnes, and I know exactly who you were looking for, too."

"No, you don't," I said in a crabby voice.

"Did you date?"

"Date who?"

"Otis."

"No!" No, we hadn't dated. We hadn't even hung out, actually, outside of school activities. We'd had completely different circles of friends. Never in a million years would I have been invited to a party with the athletic, popular kids, and we'd sat with our own friends in the cafeteria. But every day of senior-year chem class, sitting next to Otis at our shared bench, had been pure bliss. We had both gotten an A+ each semester.

"I was *saying*," Effie said, "the cashier said Chester was in the hardware store half an hour ago and that he'd expressed an intention of going to the brew pub next door. We must roust him out—he is supposed to be working on the inn's wiring *now*."

"Yeah, Chester may not have been your best choice for an electrician."

"He was my *only* choice, Agnes, because he's working for free, on spec. Who could say no to that? Ah. Here we are. The Pour House. Can't you get a business license in this town if the name isn't a pun?"

"I think puns entitle you to a tax break," I said.

Unlike Club Xenon, the Pour House was a drinking establishment that clicked with Naneda's own fantasy about itself. Its brick exterior had been recently pressure-washed, and the hand-painted sign called to mind an English pub. The dim interior boasted more clean exposed brick, a big fireplace, and a long, gleaming mahogany bar. Since it was barely past noon, the only patrons were two old dudes hunkered over beers in a booth and, at the bar, a young woman and a stumpy young man.

"Chester?" I said, squinting at the stumpy young man. I'd just seen him at Dad's last Sunday dinner. We'd had a little spat about who got to eat the last slice of orange spice cake with cream cheese frosting, until Cordelia had suggested we split it. Somehow splitting it had not been a satisfying resolution.

"It *is* your cousin," Effie said to me. She settled herself on a barstool next to Chester. I climbed onto the stool next to Effie. "I thought you said you were going to start rewiring the inn today, Chester," Effie said. "We don't have much time."

"Can't." Chester swiveled on his stool, away from the young woman. Chester battles the same doughy Blythe genes that I do. He has a pleasant round face, curly brown hair, and intelligent hazel eyes, but that day he was sprouting an unfortunate soul patch. "Last time I checked, the police were still there. If I start ripping things apart, they'll think I'm helping hide evidence for my homicidal relatives. Oh yeah, and did you forget that I'm not a licensed electrician?"

"What?" Effie cried. "You didn't tell me that! You said you had no *end* of experience."

"I do," Chester said. "But no license."

"But—"

"Calm down." Chester sipped his beer and leaned in. "I can still do the work, okay? We just don't want anyone *seeing* me doing the work. Then, when I'm finished, we'll have the city electrical inspector come in, get his stamp of approval, get the new certificate of occupancy, and we're in the clear."

"And if your wiring job *doesn't* get approved?" I said.

"It will. But if you guys are so worried about it, why don't you go to the city code-compliance officer and have him hold off on the demolition? Kathleen Todd is dead, and she's the one who bullied him into setting that date for razing the inn, right?"

"The code-compliance officer is responsible?" Effie said. "I spoke to him just two days ago. Karl Knudson. He was the one who explained to me that the inn was condemned simply on account of the ancient wiring. It's odd, you know—when I originally spoke to him, he didn't seem to think the wiring was such a big issue. Talking to him again isn't a bad idea."

"You're welcome," Chester said.

I snorted.

Chapter 8

The young woman next to Chester swiveled on her barstool. She was small and sturdy like a gymnast, with smeary aqua eyeliner that made her look haggard, although she probably wasn't more than twenty-five. Pink residue scummed the inside of her empty glass. "Hey, be nice to Chester," she said to Effie and me. "He's an all right guy." She sounded sloshed. "Barkeep! How about another of these fruity things?" she shouted toward the door behind the bar.

"Just a minute!" a man yelled back.

"Aunt Effie, Agnes," Chester said, "this is Kimmie."

"Hi," I said.

"Charmed," Effie said.

Kimmie pointed at Effie. "You look like a grandma in a soap opera, and you"—she pointed at me—"omigod, *you* look just like Velma from *Scooby-Doo*."

"Shouldn't we get going?" I grumbled to Effie. "I'm dying to talk to Jodi about that rumor."

"What rumor?" Kimmie asked. "I love rumors."

I loudly cleared my throat.

Effie ignored me and said, "The rumor that Jodi Todd has been propagating about us, dear."

"Kathleen Todd's daughter? The younger one with the dreads who was, like, totally getting screwed over by her mom?"

Wait. *What?* Hello, possible motive.

"Ah, delightful," Cousin Chester murmured. "So exotic, so simple. Kimmie, my dear, in a past century, you would've been a milkmaid." He caressed Kimmie's Kona-tan shoulder.

"I liked you better before you started in with the poetic talk, Chester," Kimmie said.

"But I'm wearing my janitor coveralls," he said. "You said they were sexy."

Chester *was* wearing his janitor coveralls. He worked night shifts at the middle school.

"Well, I changed my mind," Kimmie said.

"I see," Chester said in a hurt voice. He slapped some cash on the bar, said to Effie, "I'll see you later at the inn," and flounced out of the bar.

I should mention that Chester studied nineteenth-century British literature at Dartmouth, but he has a tough time holding down jobs because he spends most of his energy hitting on girls who can't stand him.

"Where is the bartender?" Effie asked, tapping her nails on the bar.

"Bartender?" I said. "What about how Jodi was getting screwed over by her mom?"

The bartender appeared and asked what we would like.

"I'll have a vodka martini," Effie said. "Extra olives."

"I'll have another of these fruity things," Kimmie said, shoving her glass across the counter.

"All right," the bartender said. "But Kimmie, this one's going to be a virgin, all right?"

Kimmie giggled. "Oh, *Luke*."

Luke got to work. The blender whirred. The shaker clacked. Two drinks were set before us, and then Luke went off to tend to some other customers who'd come in.

I turned sideways on my stool to face Kimmie; Kimmie shrank back. "Okay. How was Jodi getting screwed over exactly?" I asked.

Kimmie chewed her beige-glossed lip. "Kathleen Todd has—had—two daughters, right? Megan, she's the older one, and Jodi. Jodi runs a stand at the farmer's market—some hippie name—oh yeah, Shakti Organic Farms, I think? Megan's a rich bitch. Drives a Range Rover. She gets her nails done, like, twice a week at Tracy's Nail Heaven."

"Fast-forward to the part about Jodi being screwed over," I said. "What did you mean by that?"

"I shouldn't have said anything. Boss will be so mad."

"We won't breathe a word to your boss," I said.

"Mr. Solomon is super touchy about privacy."

"Mr. Solomon, of Solomon and Fitch?" I said. That was the law firm above the stationery store just down the street.

"Yeah. I'm Mr. Solomon's paralegal."

"You said something about Kathleen Todd?" Effie prompted.

"I really shouldn't say."

Effie lowered her voice. "Luke made your drink a virgin, the old meanie." She poked Kimmie's drink.

Kimmie sighed. "I know."

"You look sad, darling."

"He cuts me off."

"I don't think I should have this martini after all," Effie said, "because I might need to drive . . ." She hadn't yet taken a sip.

"*You're unconscionable*," I hissed.

"Here, Kimmie," Effie said. "Take it."

"Okay!" Kimmie said, stretching out a hand.

Effie whisked the martini out of her reach. "Ah-ah!" She shook a finger. "Not until you tell us about Kathleen Todd's will."

I am the great-niece of a she-wolf.

"Okay." Kimmie licked her lips. "Kathleen was going to sign her will next week, and I helped Mr. Solomon prepare the final version, and everything was going to the older daughter, Megan, and Jodi wasn't going to get, like, anything."

"Kathleen Todd didn't already have a will?" Effie asked. She slid the martini toward Kimmie.

Kimmie took a deep swallow. "I guess not. Which is, like, weird, since she actually seemed like she was pretty rich. You wouldn't know it from meeting Jodi, though. She and her boyfriend Jentry are granola types. My friend Chuck went to a party at their place once, and he said it's really rundown because Jodi and Jentry are, like, total do-it-yourselfers. Homesteaders, sort of." Kimmie gulped the rest of the martini and struggled off her barstool. "You know what? I just totally remembered that I have to go do something, like, right now."

"Oh, I'm sure you do," Effie said.

Kimmie slung her purse over her shoulder and clomped out on superhigh cork wedges.

"Come on," I said to Effie. "Pay up, and let's go to Jodi's farm. I want to see this thing through."

"I do realize this wild-goose chase is a *very* therapeutic distraction from Roger and his fitness bimbo, Agnes, but it's lunchtime, and I really did want to drink a martini."

"*That's* going to be your lunch? A martini?" Effie hadn't touched the bread and cheese in Roland Pascal's trailer.

"I always order extra olives."

I slung on my backpack. "How are you not dead? Come on."

* * *

Shakti Organic Farm was about ten miles outside of Naneda. Ten miles gave me plenty of time to think things through and cool off, with the AC blasting and all the windows down too, since Effie was at the coffin nails again.

Two million years ago—give or take—massive glaciers scoured what is now western New York like an OCD germophobe. The result was a row of long, narrow lakes in a sprawling landscape. Effie and I drove through a patchwork of lush forests, vineyards, and farmland picturesque enough to make me fantasize about becoming a Mennonite dairy farmer.

Yeah. That fantasy lasted about three seconds.

"If Jodi was getting written out of her mom's will, that's a classic motive for murder," I said. "I seem to remember that being a motive in an episode of *Magnum, P.I.*, anyway."

"I'd forgotten all about that show! I *loved* Magnum's sexy moustache. I suppose you had the hots for the little sidekick fellow—what was his name?"

"Higgins. And no, I did *not* have the hots for him."

"What is your hypothesis?" Effie asked. "That Jodi found out about her mother's will sometime late yesterday, lured her to the kitchen porch of the inn, and in a rage, strangled her?"

"Basically. Except, who says Kathleen was lured? She may have been followed."

"True, but why would she have gone to the inn?" A pause. "You do realize that if Jodi is the murderer, we are going to her

84

rather remote home to tell her we know that she's a murderer, at which point she may, oh, I don't know, strangle us too and bury us in her organic compost heap?"

"You're right. Maybe this *is* a bad idea. We can't just go to her house and confront her."

"*I* know—we'll be sweet." Effie flashed her teeth.

She didn't look sweet when she smiled like that. She looked like the love child of an antique doll and a crocodile handbag.

"I hate to admit it," I said, "but that was a good idea Chester had about going to the code-compliance officer and asking him to reconsider the demolition date for the inn."

"It was. Why don't you call and make an appointment?"

"It's Sunday."

"Don't procrastinate, Agnes."

I used Effie's phone to call City Hall. City Hall was basically shut down for the weekend, but I kept dialing random offices until someone finally told me that the code-compliance officer, Karl Knudsen, would be back in at nine o'clock Monday morning.

"Thanks," I said and hung up. I relayed the info to Effie. "Look! There's the mailbox with the bullet holes. Slow down."

Effie braked and turned into a dirt driveway. We were stopped by a shut stock gate. Birch trees obscured the property. Signs nailed to trees read,

Posted
Private Property
Hunting, fishing, trapping, or trespassing
for any purpose is strictly forbidden.
Violators will be prosecuted.

"Okay, turn back," I said.

"You're a chicken!"

I sighed, climbed out of the car, and pushed open the stock gate. The hinges screeched.

I got back in, and we jostled up the long, twisty dirt drive—a quarter mile, maybe. Weeds on the middle strip dragged and thumped across the Cadillac's underbelly, which made Effie smile and say, "I *do* hope Paul enjoys destroyed suspension."

A pooched-out old farmhouse came into view, and then a small outbuilding and a big red barn. The barn's paint looked patchy, but its roof glittered with solar panels. A fenced pasture sprawled behind the barn, dotted with cows. A fruit orchard and patches of vegetables and flowers stretched to the side of the pasture. A banged-up white pickup sat in front of the house.

I heard a squawky sound beyond the purr of the Cadillac's engine, and as we drove closer, I realized it was a couple of dogs barking.

Effie parked behind the pickup truck and switched off the engine.

"Um, those sound like really big dogs," I said. These weren't little yips; they were *booms*. "In the barn, maybe?"

Effie patted her handbag. "I have pepper spray, if it comes to that."

Woo-boy.

We mounted the front porch, and I knocked on the door. While we waited, I looked around. Busted red tricycle, chock-full kitty litter box, saggy corduroy sofa. Cute.

"No one's home," I said.

"But the truck is here."

"Who says they have only one vehicle? Kimmie mentioned that Jodi has a boyfriend. And look—no car seat in the pickup, and Jodi had a little kid on her lap at her market stall, remember?"

"Wonderful deduction," Effie said dryly.

Actually, I was pretty proud of my deduction. I squinted over at the barn (my glasses don't perform well at distances longer than the length of a library shelf). A person—a guy, a pale skinny guy wearing all black—was *running* from the outbuilding and into the barn through a side door. I recognized him: he was the morose teen I privately thought of as Gothboy, who bagged groceries at the Green Apple.

What was he doing running around this farm? *Creepy.*

Effie must not have seen Gothboy, because she was striding across the matted dirt drive that lay between the house and the barn. "Yoo-hoo!" she called. "Anybody home? Hello?"

My sneakers felt like they were superglued to the porch. *"Aunt Effie,"* I said.

She didn't hear me.

"Aunt Effie!"

"Chop-chop, Agnes," she called airily over her shoulder.

She was ten yards away from the barn. Eight. The barking grew louder, and I realized that the dogs weren't in the barn, but in the outbuilding.

Effie was six yards away, still *yoo-hoo*ing.

I had no choice; I couldn't let my old auntie, whose bones were probably like sticks of chalk, confront anyone on her own.

I was going in.

I jogged to catch up. "I think we'd better go back to the car," I huffed and puffed, reaching Effie's side.

"Nonsense. You said not half an hour ago that you want to see things through." She reached for the handle of one of the big barn doors.

"Yeah, well, that was before I knew this would involve a Stephen King farm and a pack of rabid dingoes. You can't just open someone else's barn!"

Too late. Effie had cracked the door. It wasn't dim and murky inside; it was blazing white-hot with suspended lights. Hundreds—maybe thousands—of tall, frondy green plants were lined up on long benches.

"Oh, crud," I whispered. "That's pot."

"Ah, reminds me of Morocco, nineteen seventy—"

"Let's skip the trip down memory lane and shut the door and get the heck out of here." Effie seemed to be mesmerized. Do people get cannabis flashbacks? "Come *on*, Aunt Effie!" I grabbed her arm and pulled.

Off to the right, a door swung open on the outbuilding. A second young man slid out, and so did a couple of pointy, black dog heads, barking away. Dobermans. For real. The man leaned on the door and sort of squashed the dogs back inside the outbuilding. He latched the door. The dogs kept barking.

"Ummmmm . . ." I said softly.

The man held a shotgun diagonally across his body, like a militia guy on TV. He had a buzz cut and a narrow, mean mouth, but he could've been handsome. He was about my age, slim and muscular-looking in his jeans and wife-beater.

"Didn't you see the signs?" he yelled over the barking. "This is private property!"

"We were looking for Jodi," I said. My voice sounded raspy. "Are you Jentry?"

Bad Housekeeping

He sneered a little; I took it as a yes. "Jodi's not here. Someone murdered her mom." He was reading the lettering on my T-shirt with undisguised contempt. "Sorry to disappoint you, *Band Camp*. Now I suggest you two get the hell off my property before I have you arrested for trespassing." He hoisted the shotgun.

My belly went loop-de-loop. But could I keep my mouth shut? Nope. Because I *hate* it when people think I'm dumb. I said, "That's not basil in there."

"Don't know what you're talking about." Jentry did that menacing *clunk-CLICK* thing with his shotgun.

I took a step back. "Because, you know, I totally thought it was rosemary. It smells exactly like rosemary, doesn't it, Auntie? This here's my old auntie. You wouldn't shoot an old lady, would you?"

"I am *not* an old lady," Effie said. "Where are your manners, Agnes?" She looked at Jentry. "How old would you say I was?"

"Get out of here," Jentry said, "or I swear to God I'll kill you." He aimed at the ground between himself and us. *Splat*. Dirt chunks exploded. My eardrums buzzed, and Effie screeched and took off running. Not toward the car, though. She was headed to the back of the house.

I hoofed it after her, dodging cow pies and dirt clods.

"Hey!" Jentry took a couple more potshots.

Effie rounded the corner of the house, and I was two steps behind. A tire swing dangled from a large, leafy tree. Aluminum lawn chairs slumped in overgrown grass.

Effie stopped, panting. "Look at my shoe! It's ruined. I stepped in something."

"Who cares about your stupid shoe?" I was wheezing, half-bent, but I did smell something, and it wasn't cow pie. It was

Doberman poop. "Pee-eww! Why did you run back here instead of to the car?"

"I don't know. I wasn't thinking clearly." She wiped the sole of her shoe clean on the ground.

"Hey, look." The farmhouse's back door was wide open to a porch with a big white chest freezer. The kitchen was visible—dingy cupboards, avocado-green stove. "It's completely trashed in there."

"We really ought to get going."

True. I stole a peek around the corner of the house. "Oh no. Here he comes. And he's wearing his Mister Pissy face."

We scampered around the back of the house, down the front driveway, and dove into the Cadillac. After some fumbling for her keys, Effie got the engine going, and we jounced down the rutted drive in reverse.

I had a clear view of Jentry emerging from behind the house and hefting his shotgun. Then Gothboy came loping out of the barn, and *he* had a shotgun too.

"Hurry!" I cried.

"I *am*." Effie was driving with her neck corkscrewed to see out the back.

Jentry took aim.

"*Duck*!" I screamed.

We ducked a fraction of a second before our windshield crackled into a spider web of fissures.

"What a *psycho*!" I yelled.

Effie peeked up just enough to get us around a bend in the driveway and out of sight of the house. She did a five-point turn, jerking between drive and reverse, and then she roared the rest of the way down the drive, past the stock gate, and burst out onto the main road.

Chapter 9

I struggled upright. Foam padding oozed from a singed bullet hole in my headrest. "Oh my gosh," I whispered. "He was really going to do it."

The Cadillac zigzagged as Effie burrowed in her handbag. Luckily, no one else was on the road. She fumbled a cigarette from the pack. "Light this for me, would you, darling?"

"How?"

"With this." She tossed a BIC lighter in my lap.

I stuck the cigarette between my lips and lit up. My hands were shaking. "If I get addicted to nicotine because of you, I'll kill you." I puffed the tobacco to life, coughed, and passed the cig to Effie. "Did you see all the solar panels on the barn roof? I read that those grow lights—for the pot, you know—take a ton of electricity, and that's one way the police find these farms: massive electricity bills. So the solar panels are a way to get off the grid."

Effie nodded, a little spastically. "And that paralegal Kimmie said that Jodi and Jentry are do-it-yourselfers, which gives them a simply marvelous excuse to keep everyone away from their farm."

"Yeah," I said. I was still struggling for breath. I'd had more cardio that day than I'd had in the previous three months combined, but I realized part of my wheeziness was from good old-fashioned fear. I'd never been shot at before. Obviously. I sneaked a look behind us. No white pickup on our tail . . . yet. "Jentry might've strangled Kathleen. He's violent. He could've done the dirty work, and then Jodi started the rumor at the coffee shop this morning. They have a motive—to make sure that Kathleen didn't sign her will and disinherit Jodi."

"Do you suppose Jentry will attempt to hunt us down?" Effie glanced in the rearview mirror.

"Maybe." Holy hamburgers. I couldn't *believe* this was happening.

A shrill chirping emanated from Effie's handbag.

"That must be Detective Albright calling," she said, fumbling for her phone. "Or your father."

I prayed it was Albright. I was dreading talking to Dad. My whole life, I'd always wanted him to be proud of me. I was only six when Mom died of cancer, but that was old enough to have been aware of his devastation. I remember thinking, *It's up to me to make this guy happy again*. Now I know you can't really do that for another person, that we're all responsible for our own happiness, but I still carry around this self-imposed burden, this backpack weighted with guilt and grief. I couldn't let Dad down. I just *couldn't*.

Effie tossed me her phone, and I recognized Albright's number. I took a deep breath and tapped *answer*.

"Remember, darling, be discreet," Effie whispered.

"Hello?" I said into the phone.

"Miss Blythe, this is Detective Albright." It sounded like he was driving too. "You texted that you have an important clue to relay?"

"Yeah." In a rush—and discreetly omitting Effie's sound machine—I explained to Albright how I had a hunch that the murderer had been the one who started the rumor about Kathleen having a fight with Effie and then not answering her phone or her door. Meanwhile, Effie sped along country lanes smoking, and I grew carsick.

There was a long pause when I'd finished. Then Albright said, "And what do you think the purpose of starting such a rumor would be?" He suddenly sounded like a therapist. The leading question, the warmly condescending tone . . . Was he doing some kind of criminal psychology test on me? Like, maybe he wasn't even taking my theory seriously but was using this as an opportunity to profile my psychosis?

"Um, to frame my aunt and me for murder?" Jeez, that sounded so feeble. I sounded like someone concocting stuff to divert attention from myself. I sounded . . . guilty. What if Jentry really pressed trespassing charges? His farm was clearly marked with private property signs, and we had gone through that closed gate. Plus, Effie and I were driving around in a stolen car.

Dad. This would kill Dad. He had high cholesterol already, and this could tip his poor lumbering heart over the edge.

"Is there anything else, Miss Blythe?"

I'd meant to tell Albright about Jentry shooting at us, and about Jodi being written out of Kathleen's will, and about the pot farm. But I heard myself blurting, "Nope! That's all! I'll let you go!" And I punched *end call*.

Oh, no. What had I done? I had the vague idea that neglecting to mention things to the police was almost as bad as lying to the police, when it came to obstruction of justice.

I was half hoping that Effie would protest and tell me to call Albright back to tell him about all those other things. But she didn't. On the contrary, her bony shoulders relaxed as she cruised down the road.

I narrowed my eyes. "Why are you relieved?"

"I'm not," Effie said in the airy voice I'd already learned to be deeply suspicious of.

"*Why?*" I said. "Spit it out."

"Nothing, really, except that . . . It just so happens that the Naneda police chief has, well, a bee in his bonnet about me, so I'm glad you didn't mention anything that would result in another trip to the police station."

"Spill," I said. Effie was turning out to be quite the problem auntie.

She zoomed around a bend, very nearly swiping a row of mailboxes. "Well, you see, the police chief—Ken Gwozdek—have you met him?"

"Sure. He was appointed by Dad." Ken Gwozdek is pretty much a walrus, complete with whiskers, midriff rolls, and the surly attitude. "What's the bee in his bonnet about?"

"He blames me for his parents' divorce. He's very hurt about it."

"What? Ken is, what, over fifty years old? And didn't his parents divorce in, like, the seventies?"

"In eighty-one."

"Omigod. You *did* break up his parents' marriage?"

"No. No, I did not break up their marriage. They were already separated when I came to stay in Naneda for the summer—that was when my mother was dying, and I was here to help her, and I needed comfort. And Scottie—he was Ken's dad, but you probably don't remember him—he needed comfort too. So we provided comfort for each other."

"At the Motel 6?"

"No, at my mother's house."

"You're the *femme fatale* of Naneda!"

"I'm human, Agnes."

"Why does Police Chief Gwozdek think you broke up mommy and daddy, if you didn't?"

"Oh, because they didn't get back together after that summer. Not that they ever would have. They hated each other."

"Okay, great," I said. "Then we should *definitely* avoid any more trips to the police station. At least until we have concrete proof that Jentry and Jodi had a motive to kill Kathleen. I mean, right now all we have is hearsay about the will."

"Proof of a motive? How are we going to get *proof*?"

"Well," I said, "if—theoretically—we managed to take a peek at Kathleen's will—"

"Take a peek at the will?"

"I know it sounds crazy. But listen. Jentry doesn't know who we are—at least, not yet—so he can't find us as long as we lie low, and this is a stolen car, so he can't trace it to you even if he did see the license plate."

"What if we tipped off the police—anonymously, I mean—about that marijuana operation?" Effie said. "Then they would arrest Jentry, and we'd be safe."

"No way. Even if the police couldn't for some reason trace the tip back to us, Jentry would."

"But he'd be arrested."

"Maybe, but not necessarily. And maybe not that creepy Gothboy—you saw him at the farm, right?"

Effie nodded.

"And," I said, "not Jodi."

*   *   *

Effie dropped me off at Dad's. Dad and Cordelia were both out—thank goodness—and I had the place to myself. Amid the colonial furniture, swagged drapes, and brass knickknacks, the idea of a pot farmer shooting at me seemed impossible.

Also impossible-sounding was the two-pronged plan Effie and I had hatched during the rest of the car ride back, which went something like: number one, make an appointment to see Mr. Solomon the lawyer under false pretenses and, once in his office, somehow manage to locate and read Kathleen Todd's unsigned will; and number two, visit the code-compliance officer at City Hall and beg him to reconsider razing the inn. Effie was making the appointments. All I had to do was hope that Jentry didn't murder me in my sleep so that I could show up at the Stagecoach Inn in the morning, ready for more insanity.

I was eating lemon meringue pie straight from a Tupperware pie keeper in the fridge when Cordelia came home and caught me in the act.

"Oh," I said through a mouthful. "Hi." I suctioned the lid back onto the pie and shut the fridge.

"I heard about Kathleen Todd," Cordelia said, setting grocery bags on the counter. "And about you and your great-aunt?" This was an accusatory question of some kind that I had no intention of answering.

"Yeah, crazy, huh?"

"Your poor father has been just *frantic*, you know. He started calling me a few hours ago from the golf course because Police Chief Gwozdek called him and told him about Kathleen and you and your great-aunt. He said you weren't answering your cell phone. Where have you been?"

"Oh, out and about. The farmer's market. The um—" I swallowed. "The Pour House."

"Drinking during the day?" Cordelia pursed her lips. "Well."

If only she knew what *else* I'd been up to. "Where is Dad now?"

"At his office in City Hall. He said he should be there in case he was needed. People don't get *murdered* in Naneda. We need his strong leadership at a time like this. Now you go and call him and tell him you're all right."

"Okay." Oh, the guilt. I headed for the door, still holding my fork because putting it in the dishwasher would be like confessing to having hoggish manners.

"Oh, and Agnes," Cordelia said, "Roger called earlier."

I stopped in my tracks. Hope curled in my heart like a wisp of smoke. "What did he say?"

"He only said he wants you to call him."

"Oh." There was a telephone in the kitchen, but I went to the one in the entry hall. I dialed Roger's cell.

"Roger?" I said when he picked up.

"Agnes. I'm glad you called."

Really? Was he going to tell me he'd made a mistake and that he couldn't play G.I. Joe to Shelby's Skipper any longer? That it's *brains* that count, not toned bellies? That—

"I've boxed up all your belongings. I'm going to leave them in the mudroom so you can pick them up at your leisure."

Roger pronounced leisure like *leh-zhur*. I'd once found that refreshingly correct. Now it seemed dumb.

"That way," he said, "we can avoid any . . . unseemly encounters."

"Um, okay . . ." Hope was replaced by the urge to scream.

"But I do look forward to working as your academic advisor. We can start by fixing some of those stylistic problems you have in your scholarly writing."

"Just make sure my contact lenses and phone charger and wallet are in those boxes, okay?" I slammed the phone into its cradle. I hesitated, and then I dialed Dad at the mayoral office.

No one picked up. Maybe he was already headed home. I went upstairs for a shower.

Did Roger think I had a rhinoceros-thick skin? Yeah, maybe he did. Maybe I'd always been so busy playing it sardonic and smart with him that I'd never shown my sensitive side.

Or maybe he was just a total jerk.

In the bathroom, I washed the stupid pie fork I'd brought all the way from the kitchen and put it on the sink. I peeled off my too-tight jeans and band camp T-shirt, and then, all of a sudden, I felt paranoid. I did one of those spy-movie peeks out the bathroom curtains, half expecting to see Jentry's white pickup truck down in the driveway.

Nope.

After my shower, I collapsed on my pink princess bed and fell instantly to sleep.

* * *

Dad woke me up at dusk to tell me that Aunt Effie was on the phone. "And you'll be having dinner here tonight?" he asked.

"I was planning on it."

"Great." Dad forced a smile, but his eyebrows were knitted. We were going to have a heart-to-heart about me being a murder suspect.

Every parent's dream, I'm sure.

I waited until Dad left, and then I got up and went to the upstairs hall telephone.

"Yeah?" I mumbled into the receiver.

"I managed to get us an appointment with the attorney Solomon for ten o'clock tomorrow morning," Effie said.

"Someone was at his office on Sunday?"

"He has an answering service. So we can go tomorrow and try to see that will."

"Oh. Good." It was beyond trippy to be talking about this, especially while staring down at the fuzzy chick slippers that I'd had since I was twelve.

"And after that, we'll go and see the code-compliance officer," Effie said. "But come to the inn earlier in the morning, if you can, to help Chester with the rewiring. The police said they're all done photographing and fingerprint dusting and all that, so we're good to go."

"I'll head over after breakfast," I said and hung up.

Dinner was lasagna, green salad, and margarine-soaked garlic bread. His high cholesterol was one hundred percent Cordelia's fault.

Dad didn't broach the topic of murder until we were both on our second slab of lasagna. "Sounds like you and your great-aunt Effie got into a little bit of a pickle today," he said, trying for a lighthearted tone.

"Yeah. Someone started a pretty nasty rumor about Aunt Effie and me, and unfortunately, the police are buying into it."

"I know you were here last night, Agnes, but the police do have sworn testimony that you, er, *threatened* Kathleen Todd at the library—"

"I'd just gotten dumped by my fiancé! I wasn't really feeling like Little Miss Rainbows and Unicorns, and she was so *rude*."

"Okay, Agnes, okay." Dad patted the air with his hands. "I don't believe for a minute that you did anything wrong, but the fact is, you threatened to wring her neck, and, well, her neck was wrung. So what I want to do is hire a lawyer—"

"*What?*" I screeched.

"As a precaution. For you and for Aunt Effie."

"Hiring a lawyer would blow this whole thing out of proportion! The police are still in their preliminary bungling stage. Pretty soon they'll unearth a suspect with a real motive, and then they'll forget all about Aunt Effie and me. Please, Dad. Don't hire a lawyer. Not yet. It's bad enough that I'm suddenly living with my dad again and sleeping in my pink bed and wearing clothes left over from my adolescence. Having daddy intervene on my behalf . . . it's just too, I don't know, too *demeaning*. Besides, you're the mayor. It'll make you look bad if you get involved."

"I'm already involved, Agnes."

"Let me be an adult, Dad. Please. I'm twenty-eight. Let me deal with this by myself."

"You really should have a lawyer present if the police question you again."

"I know."

"By the way, Aunt Effie never told me where she's staying while she's in town."

Luckily, I was chewing garlic bread, so all I could say was "Hmgh."

"I sure hope she's not staying at the inn, because technically, she could be arrested for trespassing."

"Glamorous Aunt Effie staying in *that* dump? Pfftt!"

"I heard a strange rumor—although I don't like to give rumors any credence—"

"She's staying at some fancy B and B on the other side of the lake. I forgot the name."

"And she hired a *licensed* electrician to do the rewiring work?"

"Is there any other kind of electrician?" I smothered my guilt for lying to Dad with more garlic bread and then said, "So . . . who do you think killed Kathleen Todd?"

"Well, her husband is dead, and she didn't have a gentleman friend that I know of. She had her two daughters, and she was close with the older one, Megan—Megan married a doctor, and her house is always featured in the historical society's Holiday Home Tour fundraiser. The younger daughter, Jodi—well, I think she was a bit of a disappointment to her mother. She didn't go to college, and she had a child out of wedlock. Kathleen had all the members of the historical society wrapped around her little finger, and she had a way of getting people to do what she wanted for the most part, but she *did* step on toes by enforcing the historical district ordinances pretty aggressively." Dad looked at me closely. "You're not . . . you're not poking around in this, are you?"

"What? *Me?* No." I scoffed.

"Good. Because I can't help remembering how much you loved those Nancy Drew books when you were younger."

"Huh."

Dessert was the remains of the lemon meringue pie I had worked on earlier. Cordelia didn't say anything about how I'd broken into the pie, but I could tell she was annoyed because she gave me a Weight Watcher's–sized slice. She also informed me with a smile that she'd found the fork in the upstairs bathroom in case I was wondering, and she was of course *not upset in the least.*

Uh-huh.

To make matters worse, when Cordelia walked out of the dining room with a trayful of dirty plates, Dad's eyes lit on her butt. Cordelia swayed her hips a little, and as she passed through the swinging door to the kitchen, she tossed him a flirtatious look over her shoulder.

I sneaked a peek at Dad. He was smiling down into his pie.

Oh, *Gawd.* Say it ain't so.

* * *

I said an awkward good-night to Dad. Before going upstairs to bed, however, I fired up the computer in his study and looked up the New York State trespassing laws on the Internet.

What Effie and I had done, going onto Jentry and Jodi's clearly posted private property, was considered trespassing in the third degree. It could carry up to ninety days in jail.

That would ruin Dad. Totally ruin him.

While I was online, I also Googled *five dots tattoo hand.*

The results page popped up. I blinked.

Five dots on the hand, like Roland Pascal had, was a common French prison tattoo. Well, what do you know. Charming Roland Pascal was, in all likelihood, an ex-con.

The sad thing was, if I got arrested and convicted of criminal trespassing, I'd be an ex-con someday too.

I carefully deleted the browser history on Dad's computer before going upstairs to bed.

Chapter 10

After breakfast the next morning, Cordelia drove me to the Stagecoach Inn in her impeccable Mazda sedan—it was *so* impeccable, I worried that I was dribbling muffin crumbs on the freshly vacuumed floor mats. I felt like a teenager getting a ride to the mall from mom.

"It's not my place to say it," Cordelia said, hunched over the steering wheel as she maneuvered around some sort of auto part abandoned in the inn's driveway, "but your great-aunt, well, she may have bitten off more than she can chew. If she wants to go into the hospitality business, why doesn't she just buy a Comfort Inn franchise?"

Yesterday, I would have heartily agreed. But now? I looked at the hulking gray inn. "Great-Aunt Effie marches to the beat of her own drum," I said. "I can't picture her even setting foot in a Comfort Inn. But this place? Well, if she did somehow manage to bring it back to life, it would be pretty special. And it would be so *her.*"

Cordelia's lips puckered. "I don't think she can do it."

I opened the car door. "We'll see. Thanks for the ride, Cordelia."

"Oh, and Agnes?"

"Yeah?"

"Just be *careful* around your great-aunt, okay?"

"Sure." I nudged the car door shut.

I let myself through the inn's front door and went back to the kitchen, where I heard voices.

"Oh dear," Effie said when I walked in. "What are you *wearing*, Agnes?"

"Clothes?" I stumped over to the paper cup of coffee on the counter that said *Agnes* on it in marker.

Cousin Chester, across from Effie at the kitchen table, snickered. "Looks like wearable birth control to me."

"Children, enough," Effie said. "Auntie's got a headache."

This is the problem with going back home and hanging out with your family. Everything seizes up in a time warp where we're all the most unflattering versions of ourselves.

Unflattering, you ask? Okay, how about this: I'd dug into my high school wardrobe again since I hadn't had the foresight to launder the outfit I'd been wearing when Roger had booted me out of the apartment. I wore gray sweat pants (not cute yoga pants, oh no—the baggy, gray Rocky kind, high-waisted and with a tendency to wedge in crevices) and a green T-shirt that read *Naneda High School Debate Squad!!!!* The number of exclamation marks was directly inverse to the actual excitement of being on the squad. I suppose the T-shirt was overcompensating.

"Guess what," I said once I'd swallowed half of my coffee. "Roland Pascal is an ex-con."

That got their attention. Effie lit up. Donut crumbs stuck to Chester's soul patch. I told them about the five-dots tattoo.

104

"You should tell the police," Chester said.

"No way." I gestured with my coffee cup at Chester. "Does *he* know about our investigation?" I asked Effie.

"Yup," Chester said. "Ill-advised. Adorably madcap. You'll wind up dead."

"Okay, well Aunt Effie and I are still persons of interest in their murder investigation, and now we're an inch away from being arrested for criminal trespassing. The less we interact with the police, the better." Actually, since Effie was sleeping at the inn and driving a stolen car, she had *three* potential criminal charges hanging over her head.

"Should we ask Roland about it?" Effie said.

"Um, *no*?" I said. "Because he's an *ex-con*? Anyway, Jentry is our man, right?"

"Probably. Let's get to work, shall we?"

Aunt Effie gave me a tour of the inn, starting with the stuffy attic that smelled like rodent. Next, she whisked me through the dozen shabby guest rooms on the second floor.

"See how spacious?" she said, sweeping her hands around a corner room. "Just picture it with the hardwoods refinished and an antique four-poster bed with luxurious linens. Custom drapes. Thick rugs. Oooh—those scrumptious thick spa robes. Local artwork on the walls. We'll have an authentic-looking gas fireplace installed in each room, and fresh flowers every day, and claw-foot tubs and marble tile in the private bathrooms—"

"Um, *what* private bathrooms?" I asked.

"Well, a little remodeling is in the cards—but can't you just *see* it, Agnes? Restful. Elegant. Pure vintage class and charm."

My imagination hurt, but I *could* picture it. What I couldn't picture were all the steps necessary to get from point A to point B.

"Come downstairs," Effie said.

As she led me along the upstairs hallway, I glimpsed a room containing Louis Vuitton trunks and a camping cot spread with a sleeping bag. Her room. It seemed so sad and weird that I pretended I hadn't noticed it.

We went down the supercreepy, cobwebby back stairs to the lofty public rooms on the main floor. First stop: the long, narrow, glassed-in porch overlooking the lake.

"This will be the restaurant, of course," Effie said. "Tables along the row of windows, see? It'll be world-class, a culinary destination. We'll feature locally sourced foods, and of course the local wines, and the menu will be seasonal and absolutely *exquisite*. We'll need to hire a chef, naturally. I must start looking into that immediately. Now. Come along through here—these French doors lead to the sitting room."

In the sitting room, water stains blotched the floorboards, dangerous-looking wires dangled where a chandelier once must have been, and the flocked green wallpaper stank of mildew.

Aunt Effie seemed blind to the room's trashed-out appearance, though. She almost purred as she pointed out the elaborate millwork along the tops of the walls, the pocket doors, and the—admittedly lovely—view of the lake through tall, dirty windows.

"We'll have cocktail hour every evening in here," she said, "and this will be the place for weddings—just in front of the fireplace, I think—when it's cold outside. In good weather, people will want to say their vows on the lawn."

I read once that people will spend more money restoring an old building than it would take to build a new one from scratch. Maybe salvaging a wreck of a building is a metaphor for salvaging the wreckage of our own lives. It's like we're telling ourselves, *See? It* can *be done. It's never too late.* I'm not sure if it's tragic or inspirational.

"Now down to brass tacks," Effie said. "The inn was last wired in about 1917, with knob and tube."

"1917?" I said. "It's a miracle it never burned down."

"I know. It all has got to go. Chester said we're lucky because the fuse boxes—and *only* the fuse boxes—were replaced with breaker boxes in the late eighties and will still be up to code. We would have required a city permit to replace those, and, well, I doubt the city would have granted it. Now. Chester is in charge, Agnes, which I know will be difficult for you, but please do as he says, mm-kay?"

"I like what I'm hearing," Chester said, strolling in.

I glared.

"I'll go and make drinks," Effie said and left.

"Drinks?" I said to Chester.

"Yeah, baby. This is Great-Aunt Effie we're working for."

I looked around. "By the way, what exactly is the potty situation here?"

"If you don't mind rust-colored water, the plumbing is perfect. Okay, Agnes, as my minion, it's your job to watch and learn, all right?"

"I want to kick you."

"Refrain." Chester crouched by an antique-looking outlet low on the wall, pulled out a screwdriver, and removed the cover plate. "The good thing about this job is that we're not connected to city power, so there's no danger involved. Even minions can do it. We're going to remove all the old outlet boxes and wiring from the walls." He pried the metal outlet box free—it was nailed to something—and then yanked on a black wire. It came snaking out. "I already cut this one up in the attic."

107

"That actually looks like it might not be *un*fun," I said.

"You mean, it looks like fun."

I shrugged. I wasn't going to go *that* far.

"These wires are supposed to be attached to the knobs and tubes—which are sort of wire-holders made of porcelain because porcelain doesn't conduct electricity—inside the wall. But I'm finding that for the most part, the wires are no longer fastened to the knobs and tubes. Which makes everything way easier." Chester turned on alterna-rock radio on a boom box, and we got to work on two separate outlets.

Effie brought us drinks after a few minutes.

"What's this?" I asked, frowning down into the plastic mug. "Orange juice?"

"Screwdriver, dear," Effie said.

"At this hour?"

"This *is* the hour one drinks screwdrivers, Agnes."

"Juice still has carbs when it's mixed with alcohol, you know."

"I beg to differ. Anyway, I thought we both needed a bit of courage before going to see Mr. Solomon, and I did notice that the wine yesterday did *not* give you a rash. You're cured."

I set the drink on the floor.

"You're such a fuddy-duddy, Agnes," Chester said.

"Am not."

"Are too."

"Am not." I took a long swallow of screwdriver and wiped my mouth on the back of my hand. "There. Happy?"

"Yeah, because now you've splashed screwdriver all over your debate squad shirt."

"You're such a jerk, Chester!"

Chester, singing along to alterna-rock, pretended not to hear me.

"Here," Effie said, "take the shirt off, and I'll rinse it and hang it on the clothesline—there's one in the side yard."

"Are you serious?"

"Chester is your cousin, dear."

True. And I was wearing a high school–era sports bra. So I peeled off the shirt, and Effie took it away.

Hey, the screwdriver was actually kind of nice, because I didn't care about the flesh bulging up around my sports bra elastic. Dragging out the old wires was gratifying, and the wire was piling up on the floor, and the music was blasting, and I was just thinking how Chester wasn't really *that* annoying as long as he wasn't talking about some unattainable woman, when a throat-clearing sound burst my bubble.

I was on a ladder, my arms upstretched to pull old chandelier wires. I turned my head.

Otis stood in the doorway looking as hot as ever, and there I was in my sports bra and Rocky sweat pants. Cool. Real cool.

"Oh, hi, Otis," I said over the music, taking the nonchalant, so-what-if-I'm-one-third-nude? approach, which is actually hard to do when your glasses are filmed with plaster dust.

"Hey, Agnes." Otis smiled. "So you got roped into this project too?"

"Yeah, just chipping in." I willed my belly to dissolve.

Although, the funny thing was, Otis didn't seem to give a hoot about my belly. He just kept on smiling into my eyes.

"Did you fix it?" Chester said, heading over to Otis. Otis held a metal apparatus in his hands. Was he always lugging apparatuses around?

"Like new," Otis said.

I tried not to notice Otis's tanned biceps. Yes, I know, women may have evolved to be attracted to muscles as a way to select mates with better survival odds. But this is the twenty-first century. The wise thing these days is to find a little nerd like Bill Gates if you're interested in survival odds.

"I, um, just remembered, um, a thing," I said, climbing down from the ladder.

The guys didn't seem to have heard. They were talking about the metal thingie. Excellent. I hustled toward a different door than the one the guys stood in.

"Hey, Agnes," Otis called.

I pretended not to have heard. I ducked through the door and shut myself inside. It was a closet. A pitch-dark closet. *Dammit.*

"Agnes?" came Chester's muffled voice. "That's a closet."

I popped out. "Yeah, I know. I, um—" I made a vague gesture toward yet another door. "I'll be right back." I took to hustling again.

"Agnes," Otis called after me, "I wanted to ask if you were going to be at the Pour House tonight to hear the Varmints." This was Naneda's almost-famous folk-rock band. "If you are, maybe we could meet up and have a drink or something."

"Nope," I said over my shoulder, "definitely not. I have to work at a book signing at the library and then, um, sleep. Sorry!" I dodged through the door, which led, thank goodness, not to another closet but to a back hallway.

* * *

I found my way to the kitchen and stumbled out to the backyard. I spotted my T-shirt flapping on a clothesline. I was stuffing myself into it, even though it was still damp and smelled like vodka, when I heard Effie's *yoo-hoo.*

I popped my head through the shirt's head hole. Effie was on the kitchen porch and decked out in sunglasses, white slacks, and a silky orange blouse. "You weren't thinking of running away just because a gorgeous man asked you on a date, were you?"

"Otis did *not* ask me on a date. Wait. Were you eavesdropping?"

"Darling, this is my property. It's just as well that you've stopped working, because it's time to go see Mr. Solomon."

There was the sound of a large, well-tuned engine churning toward us. Effie and I watched as a sparkling-white Mercedes SUV crunched to a stop in front of the garage. The windows were tinted, and the sign on the driver's door said, *Susie's Speedy Maids*. The door swung open, and a small woman hopped to the ground. It seemed a long, long way down for such a small lady.

"This must be Susie Pak," I whispered to Effie. "Did you know she was coming?"

"No."

"Hey!" Susie barked, power walking toward us through the weeds in a white velour tracksuit. Her black hair was pulled into a severe ponytail, and layers of moisturizer and sunscreen glossed her unlined fifty-something face. Her tiny feet were shod in pristine white sneakers with gold laces.

"Hi," I called. "What's up? Are you Susie Pak?"

"Yes, and this place is disgusting!"

"It's not that bad," I said.

Effie said, "Oh, I do agree. An absolute pigsty. And you haven't even seen the inside—would you like to? I have a few minutes before my niece and I have to dash for an appointment."

"Yes," Susie said.

Effie led the way inside. Why? No idea. I guess she was house proud. Susie craned her neck when we passed through the kitchen porch, taking it all in—the antique washing machine, the patch of linoleum floor that screamed *dead body was here*.

"Cheese and crackers," Susie barked, taking in the kitchen. "Filthy!"

"Yes," Effie said, reaching for her cigarettes. "My great-nephew referred to it as *skanky*." She lit up.

"You can't smoke when you're running this as an inn," Susie said, fanning a hand in front of her nose. "It's against the law."

"Let's just call this my last hurrah."

"Could we help you with something, Susie?" I asked. I disliked her flitting eyes and wrinkled nose. She seemed simultaneously judgy and prying. "We're kind of busy with, um, demolition."

"If it was up to me, I'd demo the entire building and start again," Susie said. She poked gingerly at boxes on the counter. "A nice clean motel, that's what I'd put here. These old places never get really clean. There's always those little cracks in the woodwork and between the floorboards, and who knows what's inside the walls. Anyway, *I'm* really busy too. I'm always busy. Don't even *talk* to me about busy. Got ten maids out every day now, getting some real good business out in Lucerne because Becky Fritz—from Becky's Cleaning Service, you know—broke her leg. My business plan is, poach all her clients."

"You're ruthless," Effie said.

"It's business," Susie said. "That's why I'm here, Mrs. Winters. I wanted to offer you a discount on your first cleaning of this dump." She passed Effie a business card.

"We're not really in the cleaning stage yet," I said. "Kind of the opposite."

"Yeah, I see that," Susie said with another nose scrunch. "But I offer every newcomer to town a discount on their first cleaning."

"Is that how you drum up new customers?" Effie asked.

Susie shrugged. "Sometimes. Other times I give a free cleaning. Once people have a cleaning from Susie's Speedy Maids, they're hooked. No going back." Her eyes narrowed. "You want a free cleaning, is that it? No free cleaning for this dump. Only a discount. Ten percent."

"Goodness, your offer is *incredibly* generous," Effie said in a dry tone, "but as Agnes said, we aren't quite ready."

Susie crossed the kitchen and peered down the entry hall.

"What a snoop," I muttered.

"Pardon me?" Susie called.

"Nothing."

"You got a security system in here?" Susie said. She was in the entry hall now, rattling a sash window. "Look. Someone could just wiggle this window open."

Effie said, "Yes, well, I think the events of two evenings ago confirmed rather nicely for all of Naneda that the Stagecoach Inn is *not* secure, Ms. Pak."

"There was a break-in last night," Susie said. She marched toward the front of the hall. "Megan Lawrence's house."

Effie and I exchanged surprised glances.

"Megan, Kathleen Todd's daughter?" I asked.

"Yeah. They broke in while she was sleeping—somehow got past her security system and trashed the place."

"Did they steal anything?" I asked.

"She didn't say. I'm on my way over there now to give her a Presto-Clean estimate."

It didn't look like Susie was on her way to Megan's house; it looked like Susie was checking the bannister for dust. And she found it.

"Yuck," she said, looking at her begrimed fingers. "You really need a cleaning, but I'm not so sure I could offer you the ten percent discount. There might be a surcharge for nasty."

"You're so very busy digging though everyone's dirt, aren't you?" Effie said.

Susie blanched. "What are you talking about?"

"Their *dirty houses*, darling. What did you think I meant?" Effie swung open the front door. "Perhaps you could have a look at the front porch on your way back to your car, to give you a better sense of the magnitude of the cleaning."

Susie stepped out the door wearing an uncertain expression.

"And we will certainly think of you, Ms. Pak, when the time comes for a cleaning. I'll text you Agnes's phone number." Effie kicked the door shut with her pointy snakeskin bootie. "What a little monster," she whispered to me and passed me Susie's business card.

Chapter 11

Effie drove the four blocks to the Solomon and Fitch office on Main Street, and then we circled around looking for a parking spot. Effie had patched over the bullet hole and cracks in the Cadillac's windshield with silver duct tape, which reduced my visibility and, I was pretty sure, could get her pulled over.

We parked three blocks from the office. Yeah, I know.

We softly talked over the plan as we walked. Main Street was pretty quiet, although the Cup n' Clatter and Flour Girl Bakery were busy as usual.

"First," I said, "we need to figure out where Kathleen Todd's unsigned will is in his office—it's got to be in there somewhere, right?—and then we'll distract him somehow and take a peek."

"If we do succeed in viewing this will," Effie said, "and it does indeed cut Jodi out of the inheritance, how are we to present this proof of Jentry and Jodi's murder motive to the police?"

"Let's just worry about that later," I said. I'd actually lost sleep over that one. The more Effie and I nosed around in other people's business—and on other people's property—the bigger the risk that the police could arrest us for . . . something.

"How will we distract Mr. Solomon?" Effie asked.

"Solomon's a *man*," I said.

"Oh, you mean—?" Effie gave my sweat pants a quick yet meaningful glance.

"Not *me*. He's about a hundred years old! No. *You*."

Effie patted her hair. "Fine."

* * *

It looked like our plan was a good one, because when the secretary showed us into Mr. Solomon's office, his withered little face lit up at the sight of Effie. I guess she was one hot tamale with the over-seventy set.

"Hello, ladies," Solomon said faintly. He was a tiny hunched-over guy in a gray suit, with a comb-over and huge glasses with black plastic frames.

Effie slunk over to his desk with a Marilyn Monroe hip churn and wide eyes. "Good morning, Mr. Solomon," she said in an odd, breathy voice. "Thank you *so* much for agreeing to see me on such short notice. I'm ever so grateful. I need *help*, you see."

Solomon shrank into his leather chair, but he stared up at Effie like she had a halo.

I didn't know if I was old enough to watch this.

"Please, sit." Solomon gestured to the chairs in front of his desk. He looked at me. "Who is this?"

"My niece and personal assistant, Agnes. She may be privy to anything that is said here."

"All right, then." Solomon steepled his liver-spotted hands. "How can I help?"

"Well, I'm drawing up a will. I've got considerable assets, and I just don't know where to *start*. It's all so confusing. Should

I leave everything to Agnes, here? To a charity? What would happen if I didn't even bother drawing up a will? I've just got *so* many questions. I heard that you worked with Kathleen Todd on her will, and I believe my circumstances are quite similar to hers."

Solomon's eyes flicked to a wooden filing cabinet off to the side and then back to Effie. Effie glanced at me. I made a miniscule nod: *got it.*

"I'm not certain your circumstances *are* similar to Mrs. Todd's," Solomon said. "Have you any children, Mrs. Winters?"

"Well, no, but—oh!" Effie's hand flew to her eye. "Oh dear—ouch! I've got an eyelash caught in my—" She bolted to her feet. Her handbag swung, narrowly missing my head. "It is *terribly* painful! Oh, Mr. Solomon, would you be an absolute darling and help me—ouch!"

Solomon was on his feet, if not in a flash, then as swiftly as his likely arthritic joints would allow. He hobbled over to Effie. "Allow me to look, Mrs. Winters."

Effie batted her lashes and rolled her eyes up. But the problem was, in those snakeskin booties, she was maybe seven inches taller than Solomon, so he couldn't get a good look.

Effie scrunched her eyes shut. "This is *so* embarrassing, Mr. Solomon, but would you escort me to the washroom? I don't think I can see well, and I really—oh, this is so painful! It's my new mascara—silly me, I really oughtn't bother with—"

"You're a beautiful woman, Mrs. Winters." Solomon hooked his arm through Effie's. "Cosmetics might be gilding the lily in your case, but you're certainly not *silly*." They went out, Solomon bent and creaky, Effie clinging to his arm.

Mental note: tell Effie that her acting is more over the top than Disney's *Hamlet on Ice*. Jeez.

As soon as they'd gone, I hurried to the filing cabinet. The top drawer had a typed label: *A-M*. The second drawer said *N-Z*. I yanked open the second drawer and flipped through the files.

Todd, Kathleen, one of the typed folder tabs said. *Yes!* I shimmied the file out. There was only one sheet of paper inside. "Last Will and Testament of Kathleen Patricia Todd," it said on top.

I did a little victory jog in place. The Rocky sweat pants were a nice touch.

I scanned the document. It was pretty simple, and it hadn't been signed. However, everything was *not* going to Megan, like the boozy paralegal Kimmie had said. No, Kimmie had it backward. Every last bit of Kathleen's estate was going to Jodi Christine Todd.

Whoa. Jentry and Jodi would have wanted Kathleen to sign this will. Not to die. Which meant Jentry and Jodi didn't seem to have a motive for murder, after all.

I slid the will into the folder, replaced it in the filing cabinet, and got back in my chair. Effie and Solomon came back in, and then I had to twiddle my thumbs through the rest of Effie's fake consultation. At last, we got up to go.

"When we were in the washroom, the darling asked me to the Lake Club dance," Effie said to me as we trotted down the stairs and out onto Main Street.

"Are you going to go?"

"Of course! The Naneda Lake Club dances are the best place to meet men around here. You should come too. It's next month."

"No thanks. And, um, you're going to go to meet men? What about Solomon—you know, your *date* to the dance?"

"Well, he wouldn't be able to dance."

"So he's a stepping-stone?"

"I wouldn't step on the little dear. Bones would crunch."

"Well, your romantic conquests aside, I saw the will. It's bad news for us."

Effie stopped on the sidewalk. "What do you mean?"

I glanced around. No one was within earshot except for a golden retriever tied to a bike rack. I told Effie that the unsigned will left everything to Jodi, not Megan. "That's the *opposite* of a motive for murder," I said.

"Maybe Jodi wasn't aware of the contents of the will."

"Maybe. But I have the feeling we were barking up the wrong tree with Jentry and Jodi. Yeah, they have a pot-growing operation, but maybe it's not connected at all to Kathleen's death."

"*Diddle*," Effie sighed and pulled out the inevitable Benson & Hedges. "Now what? You're not quitting the investigation, are you?"

"Heck no. At least, not until Detective Albright tells us he's found better suspects than you and me."

"Then what next?"

"I'm not sure. I need to think it through." I looked down at my sweat pants. "And I *really* need to get some other clothes. Could we stop by my apartment—I mean, my old apartment—after our stop at City Hall? Roger informed me that he packed up all my stuff and left the boxes in the mudroom of our building."

"Festering little scab. Yes, of course."

* * *

At City Hall—a gracious three-story brick building on the edge of downtown—we found Karl Knudsen's office in the public works department. There wasn't a receptionist in sight, so Effie rapped on his door.

"Come in," he called.

Effie and I entered a cluttered cubbyhole of an office.

"Mr. Knudsen, *so* lovely to see you again," Effie gushed, shaking his hand over his desk.

Karl, a rangy, stooped man with glasses and a silver ponytail, pulled his hand away. "Hello, Mrs. Winters."

"This is my niece and personal assistant, Agnes Blythe," Effie said. "*You* know, the mayor's daughter?"

"Oh. Right." Karl moistened his lips.

"I'm here to ask you to be an absolute knight in shining armor and reconsider the demolition date for the inn," Effie said. "I do realize the building has been condemned for three years now, but it has been in *my* possession for only a few weeks, and I fully intend to bring it up to code and then restore it completely—"

"No," Karl said in a flat voice. "The demo has been scheduled. That's final."

Effie blinked. "But I mean to spend every last cent I have to fix whatever—"

"I'm sorry, Mrs. Winters, but you can't just come waltzing in here at the last minute and expect me to pull strings for you. The inn's days were numbered before you inherited it from your cousin, and yeah, it's a real heartbreaker that you have big plans for it, but I'm going to have to say no." Karl removed his glasses and chewed one of the earpieces.

"No," Effie repeated. "*No*? Just like that? What can I do to make you change your mind?"

"Nothing. Now if you don't mind, I've got work to do?"

Out in the hallway, I said to Effie, "I wonder why he's so inflexible. What's it to him whether or not the inn is razed?"

"It was only the day before yesterday that Kathleen Todd convinced him to set the demolition date. Something's fishy."

"He seemed nervous," I said. "Did you see him gnawing on his glasses?"

"Perhaps he's worried about displeasing the mayor's daughter and aunt."

"Maybe. So what are you going to do?"

"Get the wiring up to code by the end of the week. I really don't seem to have any other options."

Rewiring the entire inn so quickly seemed like an impossible task, especially with Chester at the prow, but I kept my lips zipped.

*   *   *

My old apartment building was a converted Victorian mansion inside the Naneda historical district. Effie stayed in the Cadillac, idling at the curb and smoking, while I went to the mudroom to get my stuff.

There weren't any boxes. Only the same old rakes and other yard odds and ends that were always there. I went to the car, asked Effie for her phone, and called Roger.

"I'm very busy, Agnes," he said. "I'm on my way to a faculty meeting."

"You sound smug," I said.

"Sour grapes, Agnes, sour—"

"I was just in the mudroom, and there aren't any boxes."

"I put them there myself. I think I pulled a muscle in my—"

"Then where are they?"

"I don't know. Now I really must—"

I punched the *end call* button. It felt really good. Except—where in the *H-E* double toothpicks was my stuff?

The landlady, Millie, lived on the main floor. I buzzed her doorbell.

"Agnes," she said when she opened the door. She wore a yellow bathrobe and held a squirming cat.

"Hi, Millie," I said. "I guess you heard that Roger and I broke up?"

"Yes, dear. I'm so sorry. It would have been a coup for you to have snagged that one. He's so clever!"

Puke. "Okay, well anyway, he said he left some boxes of my stuff in the mudroom?"

Millie stroked her cat. "Oh. Oh dear. I thought those boxes were for charity. Bobby next door hauled them off to the Goodwill this morning."

"The Goodwill?"

"Yes. The donation center in Rochester."

"Thanks, Millie." I trudged back to the Cadillac.

"Well?" Effie said.

"All my earthly belongings have been hauled away to the Goodwill in Rochester."

"How sad."

"You don't sound very sad. My wallet and contact lenses were in those boxes! And my cell phone charger and all my books and clothes. I don't always wear sweat pants and ugly T-shirts, you know." I glared down at my *Naneda Debate Squad!!!!* shirt. There were a couple muffin crumbs stuck to my midriff. They must've been there for hours. Stylish. I started picking them off.

"I'm certain you had some lovely pieces in your wardrobe, Agnes, but you're going through a breakup, so perhaps you should embrace the sense of change and tweak your appearance."

I popped the muffin crumbs in my mouth. "This isn't the makeover montage in a chick flick. This is my *life*."

"Suit yourself. Otis Hatch seemed to enjoy you in those sweat pants, anyway."

I clapped a palm to my forehead. "Just *drive*."

"Where?"

"To Mobile Phone Mart, for starters. I need a new phone charger. Oh, wait. Never mind. My wallet has been donated to the Goodwill."

"I would be happy to advance you your first paycheck, Agnes."

Inwardly, I groaned. Accepting an advance meant working to the end of the pay period—however long that was. We hadn't discussed it. "Okay," I said. "Thanks."

While Effie drove, I used her phone to call the Goodwill donation center in Rochester. The man on the line told me that no one was allowed to go through the boxes of donated stuff, but I convinced him to let me have a look by telling him the boxes had been stolen. I hung up. "I have an appointment to rummage through a mountain of junk in Rochester at three o'clock," I told Effie. "Could you give me a ride? Please?"

"Detective Albright told us we can't leave town."

"He'll never know."

"In that case, I'd be delighted to take you," Effie said.

Chapter 12

Effie drove us to the Mobile Phone Mart in the small strip mall on the edge of town. I bought a new phone charger with the wad of cash Aunt Effie had pushed into my hand. Then I insisted we stop at the sandwich shop next door for lunch. I bought a foot-long turkey and Swiss sub, Diet Coke, and barbecue potato chips. Aunt Effie bought a bottle of water and a salad in a plastic box. We took our trays to the furthest booth in the back.

"Okay," I said once I'd eaten a few bites and buoyed my blood sugar. "Let's take another look at the suspect list." I pulled the list from my backpack and smoothed it on the table.

Bud Budzinski. Owner of Club Xenon nightclub/Main Street.
Gracelyn Roy. Local author.
Dorrie Tucker. Kathleen Todd's best friend.
Jodi Todd. Kathleen Todd's daughter.
Roland Pascal. Carpenter working on McGrundell Mansion repairs.
Susie Pak. Owner of Susie's Speedy Maids.

"We have talked to everyone except Gracelyn Roy and Jodi," I said.

Effie poked a flesh-tone tomato wedge with her fork. "I heard they put fish genes in tomatoes nowadays so they don't freeze. Didn't anyone tell them it makes the tomatoes taste like fish?" She pushed the salad away. "Jodi can't be *completely* eliminated, you do realize. She could have a nonfinancial motive, and we don't even know if she has an alibi or not."

"Still, a top priority should be talking to Gracelyn Roy. We know next to nothing about her. Lucky me, I'm helping out at her book signing thing at the library tonight, so I can try to corner her there." I tossed a potato chip in my mouth. "On the other hand, while I was waiting in line at the phone store, I realized—duh!—that Kathleen's other daughter, *Megan*, has the motive."

"Brilliant. Let's get out of this horrible place—I always feel so *exposed* under fluorescent lights—and go see Megan." Effie picked up her handbag and stood.

"Not so fast," I said. "I'm still eating." I squirted an extra mayo packet into my sandwich.

Effie sank back into her seat. "Megan wasn't at the coffee shop yesterday morning. She's not even on your suspect list."

"Yeah, I was thinking about that. It's possible that Jodi heard the rumor from Megan early on. After all, they're sisters."

Effie looked at her wristwatch. "We really ought to get going, Agnes, if we want to stop at Megan's house before the drive to Rochester."

Translation: I am out of my natural habitat in this greasy plastic booth, and I'm getting jumpy. "Fine. I'll finish eating in the car."

"Oh, good. Smear some of that mayonnaise on the uphol-stery for Paul's benefit, mm-kay?"

*   *   *

I looked up Megan's address on Effie's phone, and we drove to her house. We pulled to a stop at the curb. It was a pristine white Dutch colonial with black shutters and a lawn like a minigolf course. The hedges had been clipped into perfect cubes and spheres. The front door shone glossy red. A brass door handle and kickplate gleamed.

"Dad told me that her husband is a doctor," I said by way of explanation.

"My second husband was a doctor. A plastic surgeon." Effie absently touched her pert nose. "Doctors make wonderful husbands."

"I heard they make awful husbands. Always having flings with the nurses and writing themselves prescriptions for painkillers."

"Yes, but they're hardly *ever* home."

"I've thought of what we can tell Megan. Remember how Susie Pak said Megan's house was broken into last night? We can say the inn was broken into last night too, and we want to compare notes—figure out if it was the same person, something like that."

"Agnes, my dear, you're an absolute genius."

We went to the front door and rang the bell. A dog yipped inside. A minute later, a very young, harried-looking woman in jeans, sweat shirt, and a glossy brown ponytail opened the door, holding a snarling gray-and-white Maltipoo. "Mrs. Lawrence isn't home," she said.

"And who are you?" Effie asked sweetly, peering around her.

"The housekeeper."

"When will Mrs. Lawrence be back?" I asked.

"Maybe in an hour. She's at the funeral home seeing to funeral arrangements for her mother. What do you want?"

"We're friends of Megan's," I said.

The housekeeper took in my sweatpants and T-shirt. She didn't seem convinced. The Maltipoo growled. "Shush, Baby-boo," the housekeeper said.

"We'll come back later," I said. Effie and I went back to the car.

The drive to Rochester took about forty minutes, and by the time we reached the Goodwill donation center, I was pretty sure I was addicted to nicotine. The people at the donation center showed me the avalanche of junk and boxes they had received so far that day. It was enough to fill three garages.

I poked through for about twenty minutes. I didn't see any of my stuff, but I *did* get stabbed by a 1980s ski. Defeated, I went back to the Cadillac. It was going to be a massive pain to replace my driver's license and credit cards.

Effie and I drove back to Naneda, and since I had to do the Gracelyn Roy book signing at the library, I stopped by the Stagecoach Inn only long enough to get my bike. We agreed to try to corner Gracelyn together at the library later and ask her about the rumor. We'd have to put off talking to Megan Lawrence till the morning, since Effie needed to help Chester dink around with the wiring.

"Or I could see her by myself this evening," Effie said, "while you're working at the library—"

"No!" I blurted.

A pause. "I didn't know it *meant* so much to you, Agnes," Effie said.

I hadn't known, either.

Dad's house was empty. The only message on the answering machine was about Cordelia's hair appointment. I plugged my phone into my new charger in my room, grazed for a while in the kitchen—steering clear of the cherry pie Cordelia had left on the counter like bait—took a shower, checked my e-mail, watched *Murder, She Wrote* in the den (not as inspiring as I'd hoped, since there was only, like, one suspect), and at six forty-five, I set out for the library on my bike.

When I arrived at the library, dusk was falling, and the library's big windows glowed yellow. Figures darted around inside. I stashed the bike in the rear parking lot by the recycling bin and went in.

"Agnes! Get over here!" Chris the Slug shouted. He held a clipboard, and he had a serious case of camel toe going on with his khakis. "Where have you been?"

"I'm only a couple minutes late," I said. "By the way, I wanted to ask you why you thought it was necessary to snitch to the police about my run-in with Kathleen. That was super jerky."

Chris fluttered his eyelids. "How could I *not* have? You threatened to strangle her, and she was strangled."

"Wow. Well, if you think I'm a murderer, are you sure you're comfortable with me serving hors d'oeuvres to the guests tonight? I mean, I might stab one of them with a toothpick or something."

"Go. Change. Now." Chris pointed toward the rear office. "Your uniform is back there."

"Uniform?" I glanced down at the outfit I'd cobbled together: too-small gray cords, black turtleneck, and penny loafers, high school edition. "Isn't this okay?"

"No, it's not," Chris said coldly. "Please. Ms. Roy will be here any minute, and I don't want her to think we're a bunch of amateurs."

"We *are* a bunch of amateurs."

"I hired a professional caterer."

I went to the back office. A folding table was spread with trays of finger foods sealed under plastic wrap. A woman in a hairnet and one of those white food-service smocks had her back to me. She was fiddling with a package of paper napkins.

"Hi," I said.

Hairnet grunted without turning around.

Okay. Not the chatty type, then.

A black-and-white polyester dress hung on a door. Mine, presumably. I grabbed it and went to the staff bathroom to change.

The first *oh crap* moment came while I was zipping it up. I had to suck in everything like a hamster squeezing through a hole. When I let my breath out, I felt the pressure of my midriff against the zipper and seams. Impending explosion of nuclear proportions.

The second *oh crap* moment was when I looked in the mirror. It was one of those vaguely stripperish maid's uniforms with the low-cut bodice, too-short hemline, and white ruffly apron. It had probably been designed by some scuzzy guy with an adidas tracksuit and five o'clock shadow. I stashed my own clothes on top of the bathroom cupboard and got cracking with the hors d'oeuvres.

Hairnet handed me a tray of bite-sized pigs in a blanket, and I took it out into the foyer. The library foyer was filling up. Most people congregated around a table at which Gracelyn Roy roosted. I recognized her from all the posters. Red curly hair. Dimples. Ample figure in a chambray dress. Pink cowboy boots. Her table was stacked high with books. I couldn't see how I was going to have a private chat with her about the rumor.

I drifted around, offering pigs in a blanket. The crowd around Gracelyn grew thicker and thicker. Soon, all the pigs in a blanket were gone. I went back for another tray. Hairnet passed me miniquiches.

I was down to two quiches when someone behind me said, "Hey, I kind of like tiny quiche."

I swung around. "Otis!" I steadied the tray. "You *like* miniquiches? The filling-crust ratio is completely off."

Otis plucked one from the tray. "But look. It has bacon on it." He popped it in his mouth, which should've been gross, but he had such nice white teeth that it looked awesome, like a miniquiche ad.

I frowned. Feeling this, well, this *tug* toward Otis was the last thing I needed. Oh—and I had *completely* analyzed it: the tug was only my subconscious revisiting the sensation of first love. Why, I hadn't figured out yet. Maybe a side effect of my budding nicotine addiction. But it wasn't like I was *falling for* Otis again. Gawd, no.

"You know, Otis, this is the fourth time I've seen you in the past few days, and every time, you've just *showed up*."

Otis's eyes twinkled. "The only way to make sure our meetings *aren't* by coincidence is to plan them out ahead of time. Which I tried to do by inviting you to see the Varmints with me tonight, but you turned me down. Change your mind?"

"All I want to do is sleep."

Otis helped himself to the last miniquiche. "I've never seen you in a dress before. You look cute."

Sensitive topic. Must change. "You're a fan of Gracelyn Roy?" I asked.

"Nope." Otis wiggled the book tucked under his arm. "But my grandma is, and since she's got bingo tonight, I said I'd bring her book to get an autograph." He showed me the cover. *Barnyard Upcycle.* "Whatever *upcycle* means."

"It means recycling a thing into something better."

"Oh, like when people BeDazzle old jeans?"

"More like when people make old jeans into bridesmaids' dresses. Does your grandma enjoy handicrafts with rusty tractor parts?"

"In theory, yeah, I think she does. She grew up on a farm. Taps into something for her."

"Nostalgia. Marketing genius." Awkward silence. "So," I said, "how's your brother Garth?" Garth had been one year behind us in school, the high school football god and Mr. Popularity.

"Garth?" Otis's eyebrows lifted. "He's doing all right. He owns an RV dealership over in Lucerne, has two little kids—he married Debbie, remember her?"

"The captain of the cheerleading team?"

"Yep."

"A match made in heaven."

Otis quirked his lips. "They still talk about high school a lot. Reminisce, you know. It was the high point of their lives. But I'm kind of surprised you want to know about Garth after, well . . ."

"After what?"

Otis shrugged. "Nothing. Water under the bridge."

What was Otis talking about? *He* was the one who had caused me to stay home due to sheer mortification for the last two weeks of senior year. Not Garth.

I thought of the day at the end of senior year, when our AP Chemistry class had taken a field trip to the Corning Museum of Glass. This was the one time Otis and I had spent time together outside of our chemistry classroom. We had shared a seat on the bus ride down and eaten lunch together while exchanging little inside jokes that only we got. In the afternoon, we had somehow become separated from the herd and wandered into an exhibition of nineteenth-century glass sea creature models. Otis had stopped me in front of an amazingly lifelike glass octopus. He'd been smiling about something, but his face had gone grave, and he'd been moving closer to me . . . and then our class had burst noisily into the room, and he'd pulled away.

He had been about to kiss me. Had I done something to make him feel rejected? Or maybe I'd had bad breath? I just didn't know. We'd sat together on the bus ride home, but things had grown awkward. Less than a week later, I found the Hagness Blimp note on my locker.

"Are you okay, Agnes?" Otis asked. "You look . . . tired."

"Gee, thanks," I said.

"No, I just meant—"

"You know what? I *am* tired. I'm completely exhausted. I have had three of the weirdest days of my life back to back, and it just won't end." I studied Otis. He was *way* too handsome, of course, but he knew everyone in town, and he happened to be really smart. I'd heard he'd gone to Rochester Institute of Technology for mechanical engineering, and that's a really good school. So as we stood there in the crowded library foyer, I told him—whispering, of course—about my sleuthing adventures.

By the time I'd finished, Otis's eyebrows were furrowed. "This sounds really dangerous, Agnes. Are you sure you don't at least want to report Jentry shooting at you to the police?"

"*No.* Aunt Effie and I are persons of interest, and we were *trespassing* on Jentry's farm when we saw his pot crop, and Detective Albright thinks that—you know, this is just great. I told you all that because I trusted—"

Otis spread his hands. "Okay, okay. Sorry. No police. Got it."

"Narc," I said, mustering a weak smile.

"Me? No way." Otis grinned. "I'm a bad boy. I've got a wife-beater on under this shirt."

My gaze coasted a little way down his blue button-down with the sleeves rolled up. *Jeez.* Two days with Great-Aunt Effie, and I was already acting like a junior cougar on the prowl.

"Just promise me you'll steer clear of Jentry," Otis said. "He's unbalanced."

"Have you met him?"

"Not really, but this is a pretty small town. Everyone has a reputation, right?" Otis caught my eye. "Although, sometimes reputations are unfounded."

Wait. Was he talking about Jentry's reputation, or his own?

I looked away. I just *had* to remember that Sharpied sign on the metal locker: *Do the Math! Agnes Blythe = Hagness Blimp.* Even though it had been more than a decade since all that had happened, it stung like a fresh paper cut.

Otis lightly touched my arm. "Be careful—and call me if you ever need help with anything, okay? Here, let me text you my number." He pulled out his phone, and I told him my cell number. "I don't want anything bad to happen to you."

The trilling *tee-hee* of Aunt Effie cut through the hubbub. I was more than glad for an excuse to bolt. "That's Aunt Effie, nice seeing you," I mumbled to Otis and wedged myself and my empty quiche tray into the crowd.

Chapter 13

"Why hello, Agnes, darling." Aunt Effie stood out from the blah book-signing crowd in her candy-yellow sheath dress and sky-high black pumps. Her legs looked like swizzle sticks, her makeup was geisha-perfect, and her shoulder bag was so big, it looked like it might tip her over. Next to her stood Dr. Avi Gupta. "Aren't you serving champagne?" Effie asked.

"You sound hurt," I said.

"It's a matter of basic thirst."

"That," Avi said, "and the need for a little anesthesia. My eyes actually *hurt* from all this chambray and plaid."

"Are *you* a Gracelyn Roy fan, Dr. Gupta?" I asked.

"God, no. I'm just here to soak it all in. Everyone wants to know the latest gossip about the murder, which is why so many people have turned up for the signing. Naturally, Gracelyn thinks it's all about *her*, but she always thinks that. She's got the ego of a steroid-jacked body builder—and, between you and me, the molars of a horse. But didn't you notice everyone's sneaking peeks of you and the chic vision that is your auntie?"

"*Great*-auntie," I said. "I've got to get back to work or Chris will have a conniption."

"What about the champagne?" Effie said.

"There *is no champagne*."

"I brought some," Avi said. He held up his leather satchel. Well, let's be honest: it was a man-purse.

"You gorgeous little man, you!" Effie breathed. They sneaked off together, and I went into the back office for more hors d'oeuvres.

I came out with a tray of barbecue nuggets. It was a good thing I had my uniboob-causing sports bra on, because it was starting to seem like some of the gents in the lobby had had something to drink other than ginger ale, the way they were leering at me. Slap on an ill-fitting polyester French maid's uniform, and suddenly you're looking pretty dang hot. Throw some barbecue nuggets into the mix, and you're a sex goddess.

As I wove my way past Gracelyn Roy's table, I heard her speaking in low tones to a guy in designer jeans and a pink polo shirt with a popped collar, a shaved head, and a nose ring.

"This *is* what my fan base looks like," she whispered to Popped Collar.

He said something I couldn't hear. Then Gracelyn said, "Well, we could hire actors, right? At least for the front row? Because—" The rest was lost in the chatter.

I kept going, but I was frowning. Because Gracelyn's cute hick accent had all but disappeared while talking to Popped Collar.

Edging away from Gracelyn's table, I had to hold my tray of barbecue nuggets aloft to get through the bodies. I couldn't see very well, so I smashed right into . . . Roger. Bleh.

"Oops. Sorry." I backed away from him, stepping on someone else's toes. I didn't want Roger to think I was foisting myself upon him. Even if I technically *had* foisted myself upon him.

"Agnes. Hello."

"Barbecue nugget?" I proffered the tray.

"No, thanks. I'm eating healthfully now." His eyes flicked to Shelby, who was right up in the first tier of Gracelyn groupies. Her face was aglow as she flipped her long blonde hair. "Shelby just loves Gracelyn Roy."

"I'll bet she does."

"God, Agnes, why do you have to be so *negative* all the time?"

"I'm not being negative!"

"Your tone clearly indicated that you think Shelby's admiration for Gracelyn Roy is ridiculous."

"Well, isn't it?"

Roger flushed. "That's beside the point."

"Okay, and what *is* the point? That you wouldn't have dumped me if I'd somehow summoned up my inner cheerleader?"

"Would that have been so difficult?"

"Yes, as a matter of fact, it *would* have. Do I look like a freaking cheerleader to you?"

"You could if you tried."

My blood was boiling. "I cannot believe what I'm hearing! You're a *professor*, Roger!"

"I'm still a red-blooded man."

"You know, Roger, you're right. Maybe we don't belong together. But it sure would've been nice of you to tell me all this stuff earlier. Like, during the years I supported you financially while you were in grad school? Do you even realize that you've dropped an atom bomb in the middle of my life? That I'm starting over at square one in my dad's house, broke, alone—"

"I didn't ask to fall in love with Shelby." Roger cleared his throat. "Although, of course, perhaps I *was* slightly understimulated in our relationship."

"*Understimulated?*"

"In layman's terms, bored."

"*Bored?*" I saw red. The room seemed to sway. I took a sticky handful of barbecue nuggets from my tray and stuffed them in Roger's breast pocket. Then I wiped my fingers down his shirt, leaving four reddish-brown streaks.

"I see," Roger said. "You are trying to seem *not boring.*"

"Go to hell!" I shoved away through the throng, banging people's elbows with my tray. My eyes were doing that hot and squinchy thing. I couldn't face Chris the Slug or Hairnet. She probably wouldn't even let me back into the office before these stupid barbecue nuggets were gone.

The stacks. It would be quiet there.

I went into the library's north wing, dumped the tray of barbecue nuggets in a trash can, and kept going. Behind nonfiction was a small reading area made up of leather chairs, next to the utility closet doors. I slumped into one of them. I stared at the wall through the blur of tears. What had happened to my life?

"There she is!" This was Avi Gupta's chirpy voice.

"Darling!" That was Effie.

Fantabulous.

They clattered over. Effie was holding a copy of *Barnyard Upcycle.*

"We saw everything with Roger and that bimbo," Avi said. "Ugh. She's just like Barbie's little sister—what was her name?"

"Skipper," I said. "I know. But with some chipmunk DNA."

"Exactly. She's a mutant. And anyway, those abs of hers will stretch out like a hammock when she gets pregnant. After that, Shar-Pei city and no going back. I also heard that last year she dated a *much* older married man from Rochester—"

"Roger said I'm understimulating," I blurted.

"*He's* understimulating," Effie said. "He could make an airline magazine shrivel up from sheer boredom."

Avi dug in his man-purse. "Here." He thrust a half-full bottle of champagne at me. "It'll do you good."

Normally I would have said no way. But I took the bottle and gulped some champagne down. It made me want to eat cheese.

I heard shuffling heavy footsteps on the other side of the stacks.

"Chris!" I whispered. "Hurry!" I hurled myself to my feet and yanked open the utility closet door. "Get in!"

Effie, Avi, and I pushed ourselves into the dark closet, and I pulled the door shut. We waited there, holding our breaths, as the footsteps drew closer and closer . . . and then receded. Chris hadn't found us.

"What is this place?" Avi said. "A mildew spore-breeding facility?"

Someone snapped on the light. We were standing in a largish closet with shelves of cleaning products and library supplies— binding tape, book glue, containers of bar code stickers—and, on the floor, several cardboard boxes of old magazines.

Effie bent and picked one up. "*Good Housekeeping*, May 1967. No wonder it smells funny. It's dripping with housewife's angst."

"Kathleen Todd donated all these magazines to the library," I said, "and Chris was too afraid of her to get rid of them."

"Really? These belonged to Kathleen?" Effie studied the magazine in her hand with more interest. "Maybe I'll just take a few. Perhaps they'll shed some light on our murder victim."

"That's stealing," I said.

"On *CSI* they call it *profiling*," Avi said, taking the champagne bottle from me.

Effie stuffed three or four magazines into her large shoulder bag. Then she waved her copy of *Barnyard Upcycle*. "Gracelyn's bio says that she grew up dirt poor in the Adirondacks and that her father was a professional possum trapper and that her mother sold homemade wild-berry jam to make ends meet."

"Possum trapper?" I said. "There aren't possums in the Adirondacks."

Effie frowned down at the book. "That's what it says."

"She's padding her hick resume," I said. "Did you happen to hear her talk?"

"Better. I spoke to her one-on-one and asked her about the rumor."

"And?"

"And she said yes, she heard it at the Black Drop, but she couldn't recall from whom."

"Great. More evasion."

"I gave her your telephone number and told her to call if she thought of anything."

"Why not *your* phone number?"

"I don't like giving out my number. I enjoy my privacy."

"Gracelyn's accent," I said. "Isn't it over the top?"

"Mm. Sounds like a reject from *The Beverly Hillbillies*."

"I know, it sounds fake, right? I swear she dropped the accent when she was talking with this guy earlier."

"Which guy?"

"The guy in the pink shirt with the popped collar."

Avi said, "Oh, he's the TV producer from Hollywood. Cute, isn't he? Gracelyn is in talks for her own show. She's going to be *huge*."

That made sense. Gracelyn's accent was all about developing her brand.

"Something else about her seems so very *off* to me," Effie said. "She could be the murderer."

"*Shh!*" I whispered.

"Don't worry, sweetie," Avi said to me. "Your auntie told me absolutely everything."

I made laser-beams-of-annoyance eyes at Effie. She told *the town gossip* everything about our investigation? "I can't believe you did that," I said.

Avi smirked. "Your auntie told me you bear a grudge against her, Agnes, which makes you extra-impatient with her. I'm simply *dying* to hear what that's all about. She won't—"

"You guys have been *talking* about me?" My head felt like it was about to pop.

"I thought it wasn't right for me to mention the precise nature of your grudge to Avi," Effie said. "I thought you should be the one to tell it."

I have no idea why this angered me so much. It was the last straw, I guess. Or maybe it was the champagne. I swung to Avi and told him all about the husky teen model incident.

When I finished, Avi blinked. "What's wrong with that?"

"That's what *I* thought, darling," Effie said to him.

"Do you have any idea what that did to my self-esteem?" I raged.

"But Agnes, you were—and are—so very pretty. And models come in all shapes and sizes."

"You've got great teeth too," Avi said.

"She got that from my side of the family," Effie told him. "I starred in a Pepsodent commercial in sixty-three."

"Teenage girls don't want to be called husky!" I yelled.

Effie and Avi stared at me. Finally, Effie said, "I'm sorry, Agnes. It wasn't meant as an insult. Please forgive me."

I swallowed. I took a deep breath. "Okay," I said. Weighty silence. Avi chugged champagne. "Okay, Aunt Effie. I forgive you." Just like that, sixteen years of resentment rinsed away. "Now can we get out of this closet?"

* * *

Effie promised to meet me in the library parking lot after the book signing so I didn't have to ride the ten-speed back to dad's house. She was acting supercontrite and subdued. It was unnerving, to tell the truth.

When I arrived in the dark parking lot, she was sealed up in the driver's seat of the Cadillac and smoking with her eyes closed. The duct tape on the windshield glinted in the light of a streetlamp. I rapped on the window. Smoke and Rachmaninov billowed out when she opened the door. Maybe her secret to preservation was, like a cured sausage, smoke. "There you are," she said.

"Did Avi go home?"

"Ages ago. He has three root canals to do first thing in the morning."

"Ew. Could you pop the trunk?"

Effie popped the trunk. While I was trying to figure out how to stuff my bike into the trunk, I heard voices. It was Gracelyn Roy, having a hushed parting conversation with Popped Collar on the steps of the library. They were glancing around and

talking in low tones. I mashed the bike in the trunk but left the
door open. The bike lolled halfway out.

I got in the passenger seat. "I can't close the trunk."

"I'll drive carefully."

"*Omigod*," I said on a lung-emptying exhale. I didn't inhale.
Too freaked out.

"What's wrong, Agnes?"

I pointed across the parking lot.

"Oh, my." Effie's cigarette froze in midair.

Light from the library bounced off of a beat-up white pickup
truck, a silhouetted man with close-cropped hair at the wheel.

"Evidently the sloth is Jentry's totem animal," Effie said. Her
tone was carefree, but I saw her cigarette cherry tremble in the
darkness.

"And why is he staring at us?"

"Is he? It's difficult to say."

"Of course he is!" Jentry's eye sockets were in shadow, but
he was definitely turned in our direction. Adrenaline spurted
into my bloodstream. My fingers twitched. "Let's get out of
here. It's fairly obvious that he and his boom stick want to finish
what they started at the farm yesterday."

Effie started the engine. "Nonsense. He wouldn't shoot us in
town, surrounded by houses."

"Hold on," I said. "Gracelyn's leaving."

Gracelyn seemed to have said good-bye to Popped Collar.
They walked down the steps together and retreated to their separate cars.

Popped Collar zipped out of the parking lot in a black
BMW. Gracelyn followed in an antique purple pickup truck.
But while the BMW went right, Gracelyn turned left out of the
parking lot.

"Let's tail her," I said.

"Why?" Effie was already in drive.

"Um, because she's one of our murder suspects? And she isn't heading home right now? She lives on Third Street next to Dorrie Tucker, but she's heading east."

"What about Jentry?"

"We're not going to stop, okay? Let's just see where Gracelyn stops and then keep on going."

"Fine." Effie's headlights washed across Jentry in his pickup, and I saw a flash of his face. He was definitely staring at us.

Yikes.

We left Jentry behind and tailed Gracelyn's pickup at a block's distance. Effie smoked placidly as she drove. I kept looking out the rear window, but no headlights tailed us. Which was a relief, but the panicky relief of, say, the last puppy in the box. Like, *Phew! I'm safe! For now . . .*

We hadn't followed Gracelyn far—five blocks through leafy residential streets—when Gracelyn parked. Across the street from the McGrundell Mansion, as a matter of fact.

"What's she doing *here*?" I whispered. "This is very weird. Should we stop?"

"I thought we weren't going to stop."

"Yeah, well, I don't see Jentry around, so it's probably safe." Truth was, even though I was creeped out by Jentry, I was also about to spontaneously combust with curiosity. And curiosity was winning.

Effie slid to a stop halfway up the block and switched off the headlights. "Maybe she's going to steal something from the McGrundell mansion. I never trust redheads."

"The mansion's totally empty while Roland Pascal works on it—*oh*. Look."

Gracelyn had climbed inside Roland's Airstream trailer and shut the door.

"Oh-ho," Effie said, tamping out her cigarette in the overflowing ashtray.

"You don't think Gracelyn and *Roland*—"

"Why not? He's a ladies' man. She's a lady."

"They could be accomplices in murder." I shoved open my door. "I want proof that they're an item."

"What about Jentry?" Effie called out her cracked door.

"Stay in the car if you're worried."

Effie got out of the car.

We went down the dim sidewalk. Televisions flickered blue in house windows. I heard the clatter of pots and pans being washed somewhere, and a cat yowled.

Roland's Airstream was all lit up, but the curtains were closed. I stood on tiptoe and peered through a crack in the curtains. An involuntary *urk* came out of my mouth; Roland and Gracelyn were engaged in a very athletic embrace. They were crashing around, Roland fumbling with Gracelyn's bra hooks and Gracelyn digging around in the front of Roland's trousers.

"They're at it," I whispered to Effie.

"At what?"

"*It.* So I guess that's our proof. Let's go so I can wash my eyes out."

"I want to see," Effie whispered.

"Trust me, you don't."

Effie peered through the crack.

Something hard yet bouncy hit the base of my skull. My glasses went flying. Pain jangled, stars exploded, and I dropped to the sidewalk like a sack of potatoes.

"*That's for snooping, you fat dork,*" a man snarled.

144

I heard another sickening *thunk*, and Effie cried out. I heaved myself to sitting. My elbow screamed with pain.

A lean figure was jogging away down the sidewalk, a bucket swinging in his hand. I was too blind without my glasses to make out any details, but I knew it was Jentry.

Effie lay crumpled in the gutter.

"Aunt Effie!" I crawled over to her. "Are you okay?"

She sat up slowly and rubbed the back of her head. Her usually sleek hair tufted like a rocker's. "My. Quite the front hand on that one."

"It was Jentry."

"No surprise."

"I didn't know he was following us." I found my glasses and put them on. The frames were bent. *Dammit.*

"What did he hit us with?"

"A plastic bucket with something heavy inside. Maybe dirt. It must've been handy in his pickup."

"Then, on the bright side, as long as he's hitting us with buckets, he's isn't shooting us with shotguns."

"That's incredibly comforting."

Chapter 14

Once we'd locked ourselves into the Cadillac, Effie lit a Benson & Hedges first thing.

I could've used a slice of pie. I guess everyone has their vices. "Let's go to the police about Jentry," I said. My heart was still wringing itself, and I peered between strips of duct tape on the windshield, scanning the neighborhood.

"I thought you weren't—"

"It's getting way too creepy!" I gingerly touched the back of my skull. No bump, but it felt tender and throbby. "Do you know what he said to me right before he hit me? 'That's for snooping, you dork.'" I left out the *fat* part. Forgiveness or no, discussing the teen model thing had brought up a bunch of sore feelings.

Effie started the engine. "Perhaps we should report the assault to the police and risk the consequences."

I nodded.

We drove through the dark streets. Every pair of headlights I saw made my neck tense, but we didn't see Jentry's pickup again. "This Gracelyn-Roland tryst is pretty darn interesting, if you ask me," I said. "Gracelyn loathed Kathleen—at least that's what Dorrie said. Kathleen had a problem with Gracelyn too." I explained how Kathleen had ripped Gracelyn's poster off the door that day at the library. "Roland also seems to have hated Kathleen. He complained about her micromanaging his work."

"Mmm." Effie blew smoke.

"Don't you get it?" I said. "Gracelyn and Roland are lovers. Gracelyn and Roland both hated Kathleen. And—remember?— Roland hinted that he was with a lover at midnight the night Kathleen was murdered. So *Gracelyn and Roland are each other's alibis.* Which means, technically, they could've been accomplices in murder. Heck, maybe they started that rumor at the coffee shop *together.*"

"Good God, you're right."

*   *   *

White lights shone from the first-story windows of the police station. The rest of the building was dark. I glanced at the dashboard clock as Effie parked. Almost nine thirty.

Detective Albright wasn't there. "He's got a bowling tournament in Lucerne," the secretary said.

"Is there someone else we could speak to?" I asked. "It's urgent."

"Police chief's here."

Effie spun on her heel and clicked toward the doors.

"Euphemia Winters!" a man's voice boomed.

Effie was gone.

Police Chief Gwozdek stood in a doorway and adjusted his saucer-sized silver belt buckle. He looked me up and down. "Every time your great-auntie comes to town, she stirs up a whole mess of trouble," he said. "We'd all be better off if she just stayed away, don't you think, Agnes? And I sure hope you two aren't up to more mischief. Your dad will be so disappointed in you, after all he shelled out for that fancy college of yours."

Effie was right. No way was Gwozdek going to treat us fairly.

"I just, um, remembered something that I, uh, forgot," I said and hurried out after Effie.

"Wait just one goldarn minute, young lady!" Gwozdek yelled after me.

I ignored him.

I found Effie in the Cadillac and got in.

"He was going to give us the little lady treatment," Effie said.

"What?"

"You know, like John Wayne. Treating us like lobotomy patients because we haven't got boy parts."

"Oh, yeah. 'Don't worry your pretty little head' and all that?"

"Exactly." In the buzzy yellow light of the streetlamps, Effie looked delicate. Her bright lipstick was almost worn away.

I felt a surge of protectiveness. "Forget Gwozdek. We'll tell Detective Albright about Jentry and risk the trespassing charges, okay? And if you're worried about being treated fairly, well, we can keep trying to crack this thing ourselves. We've got leads, right? We're probably ten steps ahead of those idiot police. We might even know stuff they don't, like the fact that Roland Pascal is likely an ex-con, and I'm not so sure they know about Kathleen's will."

"But it has gotten dangerous. Aren't you frightened?"

I thought of Jentry's shotgun and Roland Pascal's prison tattoo. We were in it deep. For real. With no quick fix and zippo help from the police. "Honestly, maybe I'm a little scared. But it doesn't make me want to stop. It makes me really *pissed off.*"

Effie's lips twitched up. "I really do like you, Agnes Blythe."

"Ditto, Auntie."

* * *

Dad and Cordelia were bundled in their robes in the breakfast nook with cups of tea when I let myself into the kitchen.

"Oh. Hi," I said. I willed myself not to wonder *why* they both had their robes on. But when you will yourself not to think of something, you think of it. So, *yuck*.

"Agnes, are you all right?" Dad said, concern in his voice. "You look a little stressed out—and is that dirt on your pants?"

"There are some veggie sticks in the fridge," Cordelia called.

"Off to bed!" I speed walked all the way upstairs.

* * *

I woke up the next morning to the tinkling of my cell phone. My *own* fully charged cell phone. Beautiful, beautiful sound. Except—I smushed on my glasses and looked at the screen—it was Aunt Effie.

I poked *answer*. "Yeah?" I mumbled.

"Chester and I are outside waiting for you in the car."

"What time is it?"

"Nine thirty. What better time to visit Megan Lawrence?"

"Why is Chester coming?"

"We're stopping at the supermarket because Chester is infatuated with one of the checkers there."

"Give me five minutes."

I dressed in another high school special from my closet: a long, shapeless floral dress with about twenty buttons down the front. Maybe that doesn't sound too bad, but let me assure you, it looked like the polar opposite of terrific once I'd tied my orange sneakers on. I looked like the least favorite wife of a cult leader.

I splashed water on my face, brushed my hair and teeth, bent my glasses' frame mostly back into shape, and grabbed three muffins on my way through the kitchen. I heard Cordelia vacuuming the living room, and Dad had already gone to work. I was only too happy to avoid talking to Dad. His kind, ponderous presence made me feel not only guilty about all the fibs I'd told him but kind of like a teeny-bopper sneaking off to see her bad-boy flame. Except that instead of a James Dean look-alike in a Corvette, I had Aunt Effie and Chester in a Caddy.

Outside, the day was blue and gold. I tasted fall in the air. The Cadillac idled in Dad's driveway, looking pretty worse for wear with dirty wheel wells and that duct-taped windshield. Chester was hogging the front seat, so I got in the back.

"Why *thank you* for bringing me a muffin," Chester said, stretching a hand around the seat.

I passed a muffin over.

"Can you see your brain when you roll your eyes like that?" Chester asked through a mouthful. "If so, I say hi."

"Well, the inn is most definitely haunted," Effie said as she vroomed out of Dad's driveway.

"What do you mean?" I said.

Chester said, "Superstitions are for kids and hippies, Auntie."

"I know what I saw," Effie snapped.

"What did you see?" I pictured one of those swirling movie poltergeists. But Aunt Effie wouldn't be afraid of a poltergeist; they looked like clouds of cigarette smoke.

"It moved my cigarettes."

"The *ghost* moved them?" I said.

Chester looked back at me and rolled his eyes.

Effie went on, "And while I was searching the inn from top to bottom for my cigarettes, I started hearing strange noises. Creaking floorboards. Little rustles."

"Aren't you scared to sleep in a building where someone was murdered?" I asked.

"The only thing I'm *scared* of, Agnes, is being a scared old lady."

"When did all this ghost stuff happen?"

"The noises were around midnight."

Okay, I was getting creeped out.

"*Then*," Effie said, "I found the cigarettes on the windowsill in the dining room. *I* didn't put them there. Why would they be there?"

"So what we have here is an insomniac phantom who smokes," I said. "Eerie."

"Fine. *Don't* take me seriously."

"Why don't you stay at Dad's, Aunt Effie?" I said. "His house is big, and I'm sure he'd be glad to—"

"*No.* I'm not running away from a *ghost*, for God's sake."

*   *   *

Once again, Megan Lawrence's housekeeper answered the door with the snarling Maltipoo in her arms. She told us that Megan was out.

"Where is she this time?" I asked.

The housekeeper studied Effie and me. Chester was waiting in the car. "Are you some kind of private detectives or something?"

"What?" I tried to make a *that's so silly!* laugh, but it came out like a goose honk.

"What happened to your windshield?" the housekeeper asked. "Did someone *shoot* at it?"

"Listen," I said, "we're Megan's friends, and we'd like to see her."

The housekeeper lifted her eyebrows at my floral tent of a dress. "Mrs. Lawrence is getting a mani-pedi. She should be back in an hour."

"Thanks," I said.

Effie and I returned to the car.

"Isn't it strange that Megan is getting her nails done?" I said, buckling myself into the back seat.

"Why? Look at her house. She's a rich housewife. She probably lives at the nail salon and the spa."

"Yeah, but her mother was just murdered."

"Maybe she hated her mother," Effie said.

"True. And maybe she chipped her nail polish while cranking her mom's scarf in that washing machine wringer."

"Do you guys realize how you *sound*?" Chester asked.

* * *

We needed to kill time, so we stopped by my bank, but they wouldn't issue me access to my account until I got a new driver's license. Sigh. In the parking lot, I crossed paths with Susie Pak as she was power walking to her Mercedes SUV.

"Hi, Susie," I said. Here was one of our six Black Drop murder suspects we hadn't learned much about yet. "How are you?"

"Busy!" she barked. She beeped her Mercedes unlocked and climbed in.

Next, Effie drove me to the pharmacy, but they were sold out of my kind of contact lenses. So I was stuck with my slightly bent glasses for a few more days.

We stopped at the Flour Girl Bakery and then the Green Apple, where Aunt Effie bought vegetables and cigarettes, and

Bad Housekeeping

Chester tried to impress a tattooed checkout girl by purchasing a two-pound tub of body-builder protein shake mix. The girl didn't seem impressed.

I looked around for Gothboy but didn't see him bagging groceries. Effie and Chester were already heading out of the supermarket; I lingered at the tattooed checkout girl's register.

"Excuse me," I said to her, "could you tell me when the bagger with the sort of Goth hair and makeup will be in?"

"Pete?" she said. "He was fired."

"Really?"

"For selling weed out by the delivery dock. The manager caught him in the act."

"Did the manager call the police?" I asked.

"Naw. It's just weed, you know?"

"Do you know where Pete lives?"

The checker looked me up and down and lowered her voice to a whisper. "Are you looking to score?"

"Uh, yeah. I am." I thought about claiming to have glaucoma but nixed the idea.

"Pete's always selling at Club Xenon."

Oh *really*. "Thanks," I said and hurried out of the supermarket.

In the car, I told Effie about Gothboy selling weed at Club Xenon. "*Jentry's* weed, I assume."

"Of course," Effie said. "Do you think Bud knows about it?"

"That's the million-dollar question," I said. "Aunt Effie, this could be *the* crucial piece to the puzzle. Here's a theory: Jentry and Gothboy are supplying Club Xenon kids with weed, and Bud knows about it—maybe he's taking a cut, maybe he's just turning a blind eye, but either way, it's criminal. Then Kathleen Todd finds out about the drug deals somehow, so Bud or Jentry kill her."

153

Chester said, "There are about sixteen missing pieces to your puzzle, Agnes."

"No, no," Effie said, twiddling her fingers, "I think Agnes may be onto something." She swiveled in her seat to regard me through her sunglasses. "The question is, how do we look into this?"

"Well, for starters," I said, "we go to Club Xenon and try to take photographs of drug deals."

"Wow, sounds *super*safe," Chester said.

Effie said, "I'm glad you think so, Chester, because you're coming with us."

"Me?"

Effie nodded. "For backup."

*   *   *

We headed back to the inn to while away another thirty minutes before trying to visit Megan Lawrence again. No sooner had Effie and I dumped our shopping bags in the kitchen—Chester had gone off to sulk and/or work on the wiring—than someone rattled the kitchen's screen door. "Hello?" a man's voice called.

Effie and I locked eyes. "*Albright*," I whispered. What did *he* want? Were we really going to tell him about trespassing on Jentry's farm and about Jentry clobbering us with a bucket? Would Jentry really follow through with his trespassing charges threat? There was no time for discussion.

"Come in, Detective," Effie called. "How was your bowling tournament in Lucerne?"

Albright stepped into the kitchen. "Why, thanks for asking, Mrs. Winters. I did really well, as a matter of fact. My team is progressing to the semifinals."

"Oh, well *done*," Effie said. "Please, sit. Would you like some coffee? A scone, perhaps? They're from the bakery on Main Street."

"Flour Girl Bakery?"

"That's the one."

"Then I don't mind if I do." Albright sat and looked around. "Mrs. Winters, you aren't living here in this condemned building, are you? Because you could be arrested for—"

"*Living* here?" Effie touched her throat. "God, no. I told you, I've been sleeping in my car. The first night, it was at the city park, but that felt so tacky, so . . ."

"You're sleeping in your car here on the property?"

"The *driveway* isn't condemned, darling."

"That's true." Albright took a couple bites of scone. "Well, I guess you know why I'm here."

"Nope," I said.

"Police Chief Gwozdek told me you two came to the station last night under mysterious circumstances and then fled?" Albright pulled out a notebook and flicked through the pages. It was jam-packed with handwritten notes, and I couldn't help thinking what an eye-opener it would be to have a peek. Effie caught me looking at the notebook. Her eyebrow lifted. We were thinking the same thing. Never mind tattling to the police; this was a golden opportunity.

"We—*I*—just wanted to say hi," I blurted. "To you."

Albright's round brown cheeks glowed. "Me?"

"Um, yeah."

"You ought to try bowling, Agnes," Albright said. "Lots of nice guys at the alley. *Single* nice guys."

Effie said, "Not to change the subject, but I did want to ask you your expert opinion, Detective Albright, about installing a bowling alley right here at the inn."

"Oh, yeah?"

"I was thinking we just might be able to fit a lane or two in the dining room—it's quite a long room. Would you have a look and tell me what you think?"

"Sure, I guess I could spare a couple minutes."

"It's just through here. Oh, and have another scone"—Effie pressed a scone into Albright's hand—"or two."

Albright eagerly followed Effie out of the kitchen, a scone in each hand. And—score!—he'd abandoned his notebook on the table.

As soon as they were a safe distance away, I grabbed the notebook.

Crapola. Albright's handwriting was epileptic chicken scrawl. I flipped through but couldn't decipher much. However, I *did* make out a page of notes about Dorrie Tucker. Albright had been having a good handwriting moment while interviewing her, I guess. I picked out *widow, kindergarten, distraught, best friend, avid gardener,* and *asked if police aware of a Rolodex belonging to Kathleen.*

A *Rolodex*? Who used Rolodexes anymore?

Footsteps out in the hall. I dropped the notebook on the table like it was hot.

"Geewillikins, I forgot my notebook," Albright said, trundling in. He was down to one scone. He grabbed the notebook. "I hope you don't mind me mentioning that you look really . . . *nice* in that dress, Ms. Blythe."

"Umm . . . this old thing?" I said.

"Don't forget what I said about bowling."

"Oh, she won't," Effie said from the doorway.

We waved Albright off. When he was gone, Effie turned to me. "Did you see anything in the notebook?"

"Yes. Not a lot—his handwriting is awful—but he'd written something about Dorrie Tucker asking him if the police knew about a Rolodex belonging to Kathleen."

"A Rolodex? How quaint."

"We should ask Dorrie about it."

Chapter 15

It looked like Megan had returned from the nail salon when Effie and I parked once more outside her house, because a lacquer-black Range Rover hulked in the driveway.

Effie refreshed her lipstick in the rearview mirror, and we went to the front door and rang the bell.

"Are we still going to say we want to compare notes about house break-ins?" I whispered.

"I can't think of anything better."

A woman I took to be Megan answered the door. "Yes?" she said. She was a younger, smaller version of Kathleen Todd, with the same ash-blonde hair and WASPy good looks. She wore costly looking black yoga pants and a fitted black hoodie.

"Hello, Mrs. Lawrence," Effie said. "I am Mrs. Winters, and this is Mayor Blythe's daughter, Agnes."

"How *dare* you come here?" Megan swung the door toward us.

"Wait," I said, stopping the door with my sneaker. *Ow.* "We're here, neighbor to neighbor, because we heard your house was broken into a few nights ago."

Megan's mascara-crisped eyes narrowed. "Yes, it was."

"Well, my inn was broken into as well," Effie said.

"You mean that rotting heap of code violations where you murdered my mom?"

"I did not murder your mother, Mrs. Lawrence," Effie said. "Surely you don't believe that."

"Well, neither of you look like you have enough strength," Megan said, "and Mom did an hour on the elliptical every single day. I just wish Mom had been able to buy that inn when she'd wanted to. Then none of this would have happened."

"She wanted to buy the Stagecoach Inn?" I said.

"Yes. But that old guy who owned it flat-out refused."

Good going, Uncle Herman. "Why would your mom want to own the inn?"

"To tear it down, obviously. I don't know how she managed to make that code-compliance officer finally see reason."

"We wanted to compare notes with you about the break-in," I said. "We were thinking of starting a neighborhood watch type of thing. We even got the mayor on board." I cringed inwardly. I'd never been one to throw Dad's job title around. "Could we come in?"

"Oh, all right," Megan said. She opened the door and let us in. We followed her through an entry hall and dining room straight out of a Crate and Barrel catalog. Her feet were bare, her toenails tropical-punch pink. Girlish, citrusy perfume swirled in her wake.

We emerged into a huge kitchen with white custom cabinets and jumbo stainless steel appliances. French doors looked out onto the backyard, where the housekeeper was watering potted plants. The Maltipoo frolicked with a pink ball on the grass.

Megan circled around a huge, marble-topped island and perched on a stool. She didn't invite us to sit, so Effie and I hovered.

"First of all," I said, "could I get your phone number?"

"What for?"

Effie said, "For the neighborhood telephone tree."

"Oh." Megan rattled off her number, and I punched it into my contacts on my own phone.

"Why didn't you go to the police about your break-in?" Megan asked. She folded her hands, which sported a fresh French manicure and flashing diamond rings.

"Oh, we did," Effie lied. "But I think it's ever so important to create a community network about these things. We can't have the riffraff taking over, can we? Naneda simply isn't *that* kind of town. Now tell me, what happened?"

"Dr. Lawrence—my husband—is in Cleveland at a conference about some new antidepressant drug," Megan said. "I armed the security system. I always do. But the intruder somehow got past it and went through a bunch of our stuff—the desk in Dr. Lawrence's home office, the antique roll top in the living room, and some of the drawers in the kitchen."

Of *course* Megan called her hubby *Dr. Lawrence*. Blegh.

"How terrifying," Effie murmured. "Especially so soon after losing your mother."

"You know what hurts the most?" Megan said. "The Madame Alexander doll collection Mom started for me when I was born is never going to be complete now. She gave me a new doll every birthday. I have them in display cases upstairs."

Honestly, that may have been the creepiest thing I'd heard all day.

"Oh, Mom! I'll miss you!" Megan fanned her teary eyes in the manner of overcome beauty pageant contestants.

"That is a lovely manicure," Effie said to her. "I do think it's important to pamper yourself when the going gets tough. Will your husband return for the funeral?"

"He said he couldn't get away from the conference."

Sounded like a real charmer.

"You must have other family here to help," I said. "Your sister lives nearby, right?"

Megan looked like she wanted to scowl, but her Botoxed forehead wasn't going to let that happen, so crinkles appeared on the sides of her nose instead. "My sister? Let's just hope she and her scuzzy boyfriend skip the funeral."

"What about your mother's family?" Effie asked.

The tiniest wince flickered at the corners of Megan's eyes. She was hiding something. Something about her mother's family. "Mom was an orphan. We don't know any of her family. She grew up in an orphanage in Western Massachusetts. She never talked about it. It was like her life really began when she met Daddy."

"And where did she meet your father, dear?" Effie asked.

"She was a secretary at the insurance company's main headquarters in Rochester—Daddy was an executive for an insurance company. It was love at first sight."

"What insurance company did he work for?" I asked.

"Sentinel Insurance."

"Do you know Bud Budzinski?" Effie said out of the blue.

I stared at her. What the *heck*?

Megan's glossed upper lip curled. "*What?* No, I do *not* know Bud Budzinski. And you know what? I think it's time for you two to leave."

Effie and I made a beeline toward the front door.

"I think you're here to snoop!" Megan yelled after us. "And I'm going to call the mayor's office and tell them you've been telling lies about starting a neighborhood watch!"

Well *crud*.

* * *

"Why did you bring up Budzinski out of the blue like that?" I asked Effie in a sour tone, buckling myself into the Cadillac. "She was just starting to warm up to us, but *now* she's going to call Dad's office! All that stuff about Kathleen being an orphan and stuff—that could've been important!"

"I'll tell you why." Effie affixed her sunglasses to her face and started the engine. "Did you smell Megan's perfume?"

"How could I not? It was like a napalm cloud."

"Didn't it smell familiar?"

"It smelled like a migraine."

"It was Burberry Brit. The same perfume we noticed in Bud's office at Club Xenon."

"So?"

Effie shrugged. "Perhaps it's nothing. Or perhaps Megan and Bud are having an affair."

"What? *Gross*." I rubbed my temples. I wasn't sure whether or not a Megan-Bud affair imploded my theory about Bud and Jentry killing Kathleen over the pot deals. It definitely stirred up a *new* theory, which was that Bud killed Kathleen for his lover, Megan. About the will.

Why was this all so freaking *complicated*? It was like a Rubik's Cube—one with nonremovable stickers.

I said, "Let's go ask Dorrie Tucker about that Rolodex, okay?"

"Fine."

Bad Housekeeping

At the first stop sign, I saw the white pickup truck in my side mirror.

"Don't look now, but Jentry's back," I said. Suddenly, I felt like puking.

Effie gassed it through the intersection.

"Don't try to get *away* from him," I said. "I'm sick of this! Turn around and chase him. We can get him to stop and demand—"

"He's violent! Who knows how many shotguns and plastic buckets he has crammed in that pickup truck!" Despite her protests, Effie did a U-turn in the middle of a four-way stop—a sedan and a pickup truck blasted their horns—and then we were zooming straight at the pickup. But Jentry cranked out his *own* U-turn and vroomed away. He was hunched down behind the wheel with a baseball cap pulled low over his eyes. He hadn't wanted us to see him.

"Diddle *daddle*." Effie stepped on the gas and U-turned again. My stomach churned. We sped down a residential street lined with parked cars. We were gaining on Jentry—the Caddy's engine was a beast—but suddenly, he did a two-wheel turn and vanished into an alleyway.

"Don't let him get away," I shouted.

Effie screeched into the alleyway. Garbage and recycling bins cluttered the edges. The pickup rolled neatly through, but Effie smashed and bumped into the bins.

I twisted around to see out the back. "Come *on*. This isn't the demolition derby!" Rolling bins and refuse scattered in our wake. Dogs woofed behind fences.

"Do you want me to catch up to Jentry, or do you want me to win the good citizen award?"

"Both!"

"You're too demanding, Agnes. If you'd only lower your expectations, you'd feel so much better."

The pickup reached the end of the alleyway and turned left. We followed.

The pickup raced to another four-way stop, but even though there was already another car in the intersection, it roared straight through. Brakes screeched, and a horn beeped.

"*No,*" I said, grinding my foot instinctively into the floor mat.

"Yes," Effie said. She gunned it.

I screamed and squeezed my eyes shut. The adrenaline floodgates burst. The Cadillac swayed in an S-curve through the intersection. More beeps, brake screeches, a man bellowing obscenities.

By the time we were across the intersection, Jentry had disappeared, and sirens wailed in the middle distance.

Effie slowed to a crawl. "Dorrie Tucker's house?" she said, smoothing her hair.

"Sure." I pried my fingernails from the seat's upholstery.

Effie drove at a tortoise's pace. We passed by a police car, lights flashing, headed the other way.

"So here's a question," I said once my adrenaline buzz started to taper off. "Why was Jentry trying to get *away* from us? Why didn't he want to be seen? You saw his baseball cap, right?"

"All men are secretly frightened of women, Agnes."

"He didn't seem frightened when he was blasting his shotgun at us or when he was whacking us with that bucket. Trying to get away from us, that makes it seem like he's sort of *keeping tabs on us,* you know?"

"But why?"

"I guess he's afraid we're going to blab about the pot farm."

164

"If that were the case, he'd be sticking to outright intimidation, wouldn't he?"

"Well, if he wants to keep tabs on us, then he doesn't want us dead, right?"

One thing had become crystal clear: I needed to buy my own car. Like, yesterday. I told this to Effie.

"What's wrong with this car?" she asked, rolling through a stop.

"Other than the duct-taped bullet hole in the windshield, nothing is wrong with the car. It's the *driver* that's the problem."

"You could go to Otis's shop—he sells used cars at the auto body shop, doesn't he? I'm certain he'd give you the bargain of the century. You'll probably need to change out of that dress for the best deal, though. Maybe back into those sweat pants—"

"Let's leave the sweat pants out of it."

* * *

When Dorrie Tucker opened her front door, she was wearing an apron with little pink kittens printed all over. The scent of warm sugar and vanilla swirled out.

"Hi, Mrs. Tucker," I said. "How are you?"

"*Fiiiiine. . . ?*" Dorrie said in a questioning tone.

"Smells great," I said. "Cookies?"

"Oatmeal raisin."

"For Kathleen's wake?" I asked.

Dorrie's eyes glistened, and she dabbed them with a corner of her apron. "No. For the historical society meeting."

"There's going to be a meeting right after the chairman was killed?" I asked.

"Chair*lady*," Dorrie said coldly. "And yes. In fact, because I was the society secretary, I have been appointed as interim chairlady. There is too much business to simply stop our weekly meetings, you know."

"What sort of business?" Effie asked.

"If you give people an inch, they'll take a mile," Dorrie said. "Just this morning, I visited that awful Budzinski fellow at Club Xenon to give him his final warning to remove his garish neon sign."

"Is he going to remove it?" I asked.

Dorrie closed the door a few inches. "What was it you wanted?"

"I just had a quick question for you," I said. "When I called Kathleen to apologize for being so rude to her at the library that day—"

"You apologized?"

"Well, sure."

"Agnes is a little lady," Effie said.

"*Anyway*," I said, "when I called, Kathleen mentioned that she was too busy to meet in person because she was looking for a misplaced Rolodex." Possibly my lamest lie to date.

Dorrie's cheeks trembled. "I'm sure I don't know anything about a Rolodex, Miss Blythe. And why do you ask?"

"Oh. Um, the police asked *me* about the Rolodex, actually, and I thought you might know about it since you and Kathleen were best friends."

"But why are you two asking questions? Our boys in blue are working on the case, and doing a fine job too. Last thing I knew, you two were their prime suspects—was it *you* who broke into my house last night?"

"Wait," I said. "Someone broke into your house last night?"

"If I were you, I'd mind my own beeswax, young lady." Dorrie slammed the door.

"Agnes, dear," Effie said, "who taught you to lie so badly?"

Chapter 16

We got back in the car, and I directed Aunt Effie to a pizza place out on Route 20. It took some convincing, but I pointed out that it had a salad bar—salad was the only food Effie ever seemed to eat—that it was frequented more by travelers than by gossipy townsfolk, and that Jentry wasn't likely to find us there.

We settled ourselves onto vinyl chairs and ordered.

"So Dorrie's house was broken into too," I said after a few bracing sips of Diet Coke. "That makes three break-ins: Dorrie, Megan, and you."

"Mine wasn't a break-in, sweetie. It was a ghost."

I rolled my eyes. "Fine. But Dorrie and Megan? And don't forget that Jodi's kitchen at the farm looked like it had been ransacked too. I'll bet someone—the murderer, maybe—is looking for something."

"For the Rolodex."

"Huh," I said. "Yeah. Could be. I guess this eliminates Dorrie, Megan, Jodi, and Jentry as murder suspects, right? I mean, if their houses were broken into *by* the murderer . . ."

"No. One of them could have *staged* the break-in at their own home to cover their tracks."

True. Shizap. "Don't people keep addresses in Rolodexes?" I asked.

"They *used* to, before computers and smart phones."

"So Dorrie wanted to know if the police had seen Kathleen's address collection?"

"She denied any knowledge of the Rolodex, Agnes."

"I'm sure she was lying. She was so defensive. I mean, who slams doors like that unless they feel threatened?"

"Bitches do, darling."

I sipped more Diet Coke. "Oh, and did you notice how Megan was all sentimental about her mom? She doesn't seem to be aware that her mom's unsigned will was going to cut her out of everything."

Effie snapped her fingers. "What if Kathleen wrote Megan out of the will *because of* the Budzinski affair? To punish her."

"You know, that's a really good theory."

"Don't sound so surprised, sweetie."

I dug my phone out of my backpack. "What did Megan say was the name of her dad's insurance company?"

"Sentinel Insurance."

I Googled Sentinel Insurance on my phone and pulled up the number for the main headquarters in Rochester. I dialed. While it was ringing, Effie said, "Why are you calling?"

"Didn't you think Megan's story about her mom being an orphan was a little weird?"

"Not especially."

"Well, I did. That thing she said about her mom's life starting when she met her dad. It sounded like something from a soap opera—as in, *fake.*"

"That's how things were in the seventies, I'm afraid."

"Like a soap opera?" I pictured a bunch of people in bell-bottoms and wrap dresses talking about amnesia and long-lost twins.

"No, I mean, many girls didn't feel like they had a purpose in life until they were married."

"Okay, well, I still want to—hello?" Someone had picked up at Sentinel Insurance.

After twenty minutes of getting the runaround—I was pretending to be a newspaper reporter—I finally got connected to someone who had access to the company records from the seventies. Kathleen had worked there as a secretary, yes, for almost two years back in 1975. She'd quit to marry John Todd. Her maiden name was Brown, and she'd attended Pressley Secretarial College in Syracuse. "Thanks," I said. I hung up and told it all to Effie.

"I'd keep it down if I were you," Effie said. She sipped her water. "Mr. and Mrs. Bingo Night are all ears."

I glanced over to the next table. Two seniors slumped over crossword puzzles with that too-still look that eavesdroppers get. "I'm going outside for a second," I said.

Standing outside and poking at my phone, I found the number for a place called the Pressley Program in Syracuse and, mentally crossing my fingers, called.

Yes, it was formerly the Pressley Secretarial College, the chirpy guy who answered told me.

"Great," I said. "I'm an investigative reporter for the *Boston Herald*, and I'm writing about the murder of Kathleen Todd in Naneda."

"I saw that on the news," the guy said. "Strangled, right?"

"Yes. I'm trying to track down some information about her past, and I learned she attended Pressley Secretarial College in the early seventies. Her maiden name was Kathleen Brown." This sounded plausible! I was starting to feel rather awesome, despite the onset of hypoglycemia. "Is there any way you could confirm this for me?" I really wanted to know about the orphanage Kathleen had supposedly grown up in, but baby steps.

"I can try. Our database is actually superupdated because one of the instructors has students log in old records as part of a data entry course."

"Great."

The guy mumbled to himself, and I heard computer keys ticking for a minute or so.

"This is weird," he said. "The database is updated all the way back to 1967, but I don't see a Kathleen Brown listed anywhere."

"Really?"

"Let me try some different spellings."

I waited.

"Nope," he finally said. "Only a Katharine Murphy. And she graduated in 1969."

"Rats," I said. "That was a good lead."

"I could try to look into it some more," the guy said eagerly. "I always wanted to be an investigative reporter. Maybe you could give me some tips on how to get started. It would be great to have connections with the *Boston Herald*."

I winced. "Sure!" I said. I gave him my number. "What's your name?"

"Eric Tanaka."

"Okay, Eric, you dig around some more and give me a call if you find anything. In the meantime, I'll see what's going on with internships at the *Herald*."

"Really? Awesome!"

"Yep. Awesome," I said dully. I hung up. My upper lip felt damp. What kind of horrible person had I become? Stomping on the dreams of youth.

When I went back inside, a steaming sausage-and-black-olive pizza was waiting for me. After wolfing down a slice, I told Effie about how there was no record of Kathleen Todd in the Pressley Program's database.

"Oh, really?" Effie forked up some lettuce.

Maybe she was hallucinating ghosts at the inn because all she ate was rabbit food. Just a thought.

"But the insurance company confirmed that that's where she'd gone to school?" Effie asked.

"Well, that's where she *said* she'd gone to school. Maybe she lied to them."

"Surely they would've checked with the school before they hired her."

"Not necessarily. She was probably really pretty when she was young. Maybe they just hired her on sight. I've heard what things were like back then."

"Another possibility is that she *did* attend Pressley but under a different name."

"But there wasn't even a Kathleen in the database."

"Which would indicate that she was quite invested in the name change. You've really got skeletons in the closet when you change not only your last name, but your first."

"Do you think Kathleen was another ex-con?"

Effie speared a cucumber slice. "She certainly had cold eyes."

171

"Maybe we should, you know, break into her house and have a look around."

"That would be foolhardy, Agnes. We're already dodging trespassing charges."

I shrugged. I couldn't tell what was foolhardy and what wasn't anymore.

Effie pointed at my dress with her fork. "We've got to do something about your disguise for tonight."

"Disguise? For Club Xenon? *No.*"

"You've got to wear club clothing. Should we drive to the shopping mall in Lucerne?"

"No malls. They make me tired. My friend Lauren's vintage shop would be okay. I need to catch up with her, anyway. It's long overdue."

* * *

After we finished lunch, Effie and I drove to Lauren's shop on Main Street. Lauren had gotten a fine arts degree at an obscure college in Vermont and then returned to Naneda and started up Retro Rags.

The storefront was conservative enough, in keeping with the town's historical flavor. Inside, however, the walls were birthday-cake pink, and wild vintage clothing and accessories burst from gold-painted armoires. The oversized chandelier was constructed of mannequins' legs and blazing lightbulbs.

"Agnes! Hey!" Lauren said. She was sitting on a stool behind the counter, a thick paperback book in her hand. I made out the dragon and castle on the cover. Lauren inhales fantasy novels. "You've been avoiding me."

"Not on purpose," I said. I led Effie over. "Lauren, this is my Great-Aunt Effie. Mrs. Winters."

"Nice to meet you," Lauren said. She was a tall, translucent-fair redhead with a prominent nose, glasses, and Jane Russell lipstick, and just then she looked a little nervous.

"Call me Effie—and don't mind the rumors about me. Only half of them are true." Effie flicked expertly through a rack of blouses.

Lauren gave me a stern look over her cat-eye glasses. "Why didn't you stop by and tell me about Roger and, oh, I don't know, *how you discovered a dead body*? I heard those things from *customers* because you're not taking my calls."

"I had to get a new cell phone charger."

"I called your dad's and talked with Cordelia."

"She never told me you called!" *Cordelia*. "And things have been kind of . . . crazy." Understatement of the decade.

"Roger is . . . well, honestly, Agnes, I never liked him."

"*Now* you tell me?"

"You can't tell people you don't like their boyfriends until after they break up," Lauren said.

"Everyone knows that," Effie said.

Lauren went on, "I took a Pilates class with that blonde strip of Sizzlean once."

"You did?" I said. Lauren was effortlessly skinny, and she claimed that her vintage clothes wouldn't fit right if she put on muscle mass.

"I had a coupon from Downtown Daze." Lauren shrugged. "It was awful. People aren't supposed to roll up and down like Fruit Roll-Ups."

"Tell me about it." Secretly, I wouldn't mind having a six-pack. Even a two-pack would be pretty great. But I will admit this aloud only if suspended over a pit of red-hot coals.

"Are you going to be okay?" Lauren asked me. "I heard you could be a person of interest in the murder case?"

"Yeah."

"If you ever murdered someone, Agnes, you'd plan it out so you never got caught."

Lauren knew just how to compliment me. "Anyway, thanks to Roger, all my clothes have been sent to the Goodwill center in Rochester, so I need some new clothes."

Lauren clapped her hands. "Yay! *Finally.*"

I went limp like a cat dressed in doll's clothes. For the next forty-five minutes, I allowed Effie and Lauren to choose outfits for me while I stood in my underpants and sports bra behind the flowery-gold changing room curtain. Luckily, Lauren didn't have fluorescent lightbulbs back there. She knows a woman doesn't need to commune with her lumps just because she wants to try on a skirt. Effie and I filled Lauren in on our murder investigation, falling silent whenever other customers came in.

By the time we were done, I had three cute day dresses and one silk cocktail dress that looked like something a femme fatale from 1971 would have worn to a drunken pool party, with red passionflowers and a plunging neckline. This could only be worn, according to Lauren and Effie, with the strappy gold pumps that Lauren gave to me as a "gift" since she knew I'd refuse to buy them. I had a fifty-fifty shot of being able to walk in them. I never wear heels.

"Could I come tonight?" Lauren asked. "*Please?* I've never set foot in Club Xenon—it's just full of Greek system kids from the university, I heard—but this detective stuff sounds like a hoot."

"Sure," I said. "Just to warn you, my cousin Chester might be there, and as you know, he can be El Creepo with the ladies." Lauren knew Chester; he'd been only three years ahead of us in school.

Lauren's eyes narrowed. "Chester? I can manage him."

*   *   *

A huge steel rent-a-dumpster had been parked at the back of the inn when Effie and I returned. Chester was in the kitchen, covered in grime and making a sandwich.

"Hi," he said, smearing mustard on bread. "Guess what the rent-a-dumpster guy told me?"

"What?" I said.

"Susie Pak's house was broken into last night."

"Are you serious?" I said. "How does he know?"

"Because he's Susie's nephew, that's how."

"That makes four break-ins!" I said.

"Three," Effie corrected. "Mine was the ghost, remember?"

I spotted a bag of sour-cream-and-chive potato chips on the counter and stress-ate a handful. "Okay, so what's the common denominator with the break-ins?"

"*Duh*," Chester said. "They all knew Kathleen Todd?"

I shook my head. "This is a pretty small town. Everyone knows everyone, or at least knows *of* everyone. What if it's about that Rolodex?"

"Explain," Chester said, piling baloney on his sandwich.

I explained about the Rolodex mentioned in Albright's notes.

Chester snorted. "So someone is desperate to get their hands on Kathleen Todd's Christmas card list?"

I shrugged. "For all we know, that Rolodex is full of drug clients' names and numbers. Tonight we might be staging the biggest bust in Naneda's history."

"That sounds *awesome*, Agnes," Chester said, "but you licking sour cream and chive powder off your fingers is kind of ruining the Vice Squad effect." He went off with his sandwich.

*   *   *

Chester and I spent a couple hours hauling old wires and chunks of plaster out of a bunch of rooms and chucking them into the rent-a-dumpster. Effie sorted through stuff upstairs. Then it was time for a coffee break.

Effie fired up her laptop at the kitchen table. "I keep thinking about how Roland Pascal is an ex-con," she said. "That *must* be relevant, don't you think?"

"You mean, like he's linked to Jentry and Gothboy's drug business?" I sipped the vanilla latte Effie had brought me from the Black Drop.

"Or he's behind the spate of house break-ins. Let's see about that last town in which he said he was working." Effie lit a cigarette. "What was it again?"

"Caraway, Vermont," I said. "You have Wi-Fi on your computer?"

"Chester installed it—it's somehow running through my cell phone."

"*Yeah*, Agnes," Chester said, making yet another sandwich at the counter. "I'm *handy*. Oh, and I texted Otis Hatch to see if he wants to come to Club Xenon tonight—"

"Don't!" I cried.

"—so you can have two men looking after you."

"*Jerk*," I muttered.

"Why, thank you," Chester said.

"Children, *please*," Effie said.

Fifteen minutes of Googling turned up no spate of break-ins in tiny Caraway, Vermont.

"It might be a good idea to try to get ahold of Roland Pascal's portfolio," Effie said. "We could call his references."

"That reminds me," I said. "Remember how Roland ripped out the page of references and crumpled it up when he was showing us the portfolio?"

"No."

"You were probably busy with your wine. Anyway, he did. Suspicious, if you ask me. There must be something—or someone—on that list that he didn't want us to notice."

"Well then, we can't call his references. They're probably at the recycling center by now."

"Not necessarily. Roland doesn't clean. I'll bet that crumpled list is still in the corner of his trailer where he left it. Okay, I'm going to call Susie Pak. I want to know why she didn't tell us that her house had been broken into when I ran into her at the bank this morning." I found the business card Susie had left the previous morning and dialed.

"Why would I tell you that?" Susie said when I got her on the line. It sounded like she was driving. "Why should I talk to you at all after you refused a ten percent discount for Susie's Speedy Maids? Buh! You two are snoops, that's what I think!" Silence.

"She hung up on me," I said, staring at my phone.

"Susie Pak is angry about something," Effie said.

"It's her ex-husband," Chester said. "She used to be married to this famous chemistry professor at the university, but they divorced maybe three years back. That's when she started Susie's Speedy Maids."

"Susie drives a very expensive car," I said.

"Yeah well, there was alimony."

"Mmm," Effie said in a buttery, approving way.

"Maybe it's only her ex-husband that Susie's so ticked off about," I said. "But maybe it's something else."

Chapter 17

After putting in a couple more hours hauling junk at the inn, Chester gave me a ride back to Dad's in his beyond-crappy Datsun. I planned to have a shower and dinner and then rest a little before Effie picked me up to go to Club Xenon at ten. I could only pray that Otis wasn't really going to show up too. That many people over twenty-five at the club, and the college kids would stampede for the exit.

Dad and Cordelia were both out. I knew this because the security system was still armed when I let myself into the kitchen. Their being out was a major relief since I was pretty sure Megan would have made good on her threat to tell Dad that Effie and I were pretending to set up a mayor's office–endorsed neighborhood-watch thingie.

I showered, ate some leftovers, and then stretched out on the leather couch in Dad's den to watch TV. Fifteen minutes into *The Real Housewives*, I dozed off. The housewives were soothing. They made me feel like *my* life wasn't such a disaster.

I bolted awake to the earsplitting blips of the burglar alarm. My heart chugged hard. I squished my glasses back onto my face, stood, and looked around blearily. The fire poker. Yeah.

I grabbed the brass fire poker and tiptoed to the doorway that connected the den to the living room. The living room was empty, so I tiptoed through that too. I went down the center hall, peered into the dining room, and—*aha*. The dining room French doors that led out to the back patio were wide open. Curtains billowed, and rain sprayed in. I shut the doors, locked them, and then went to the kitchen to disarm the security system. The phone rang. It was the security company asking if everything was okay.

"I think so," I said. "I think the wind blew some French doors open and set off the alarm."

I was *pretty* sure that had been the case.

* * *

It was pouring rain by ten o'clock. I got dressed and went downstairs. My clubbing outfit was hidden under a shapeless trench coat I'd excavated from the hall closet. The gold pumps were the only clue that something was going down—if anyone had been home to see them. I stood at the kitchen counter, buried in the raincoat and scarfing down confetti cake until I heard a honk outside. I shoveled in the last bite, put the fork and plate in the dishwasher, and rearmed the security system. I grabbed my backpack and dashed through the rain.

It was about one hundred degrees inside the Cadillac and smokier than a burning building. Chester was at the wheel, wearing a fedora. Effie was in the passenger seat in a white fur coat.

"Do you have a camera?" Effie asked me.

"I have one on my cell phone. All charged up and ready to go."

"Does it have a flash?" Chester asked.

"Yup."

We were seriously doing this. *Woo-boy.*

Chester parked two blocks from Club Xenon.

"Don't you think we should park closer?" I said. "What if we need to make a quick getaway?" I thought of Bud's caveman-whose-bison-drumstick-was-stolen face.

"Give me a break," Chester said. "This is Naneda. Small-town USA?"

"Then why are you wearing that ridiculous fedora?"

"*I'm* ridiculous?" Chester said. "You're the one who looks like a flasher."

"*All* right," I yelled. "I've just about had it with—"

"*Children,*" Effie said.

Chester and I fell silent. The three of us slammed the car doors and trudged down the wet sidewalk, chins tucked in coats to keep out the slanting drizzle.

"This rain is going to absolutely *ruin* my fur," Effie said.

"I cannot believe you're wearing poor little dead animals," I said.

"It's vintage, darling. Vintage fur doesn't count. These little animals have been dead since the Nixon administration."

The yoga studio and the cupcake shop were dark as we passed, but the front windows of Guido's Italian Ristorante poured light onto the slick pavement. Even though I'd just wolfed down a hunk of confetti cake, I couldn't say no to a little pasta voyeurism, so I looked in as we trooped by.

My heart shriveled. Roger and Shelby were bent over glasses of wine, heads dipped, fingers woven tight, smiling.

"They remind me of the dogs in that stupid Disney movie," Chester said. "Come on." He grabbed my arm and pulled me down the sidewalk. "You can't let Roger see what he's doing to you, Agnes. He doesn't deserve the satisfaction."

"He's not *doing* anything to me."

"Oh no? You look like your self-esteem just turned into pink slime."

"Fine. I feel like screaming and throwing stuff, okay? But it's not because I want him back. Our relationship sucked. There was no passion, and frankly, I *hate* discussing French critical theory. But . . ."

"You *do* want him back, so *you* can dump *him*," Chester said.

"How did you know that?" I walked a little faster.

"It's what every dumpee wants, darling," Effie said.

I gave myself a mental shake and blotted Roger and Shelby from my mind. I was (maybe) about to do a drug bust. Eat *that*, Roger.

"Okay, guys," I said to Effie and Chester as we drew closer to the club, "we go in, get photos of deals if we see them, and also try to figure out if Bud is aware of pot dealing in his club. Then we get the heck *out*."

"That doesn't sound like much fun," Effie said. "I want a drink."

"I was thinking of dancing," Chester said.

"Fine," I sighed. "But only a *little*. We have a job to do, and we have to do it well."

"That's from *The A-Team*, right?" Chester asked Effie.

"I thought it was from *Rocky and Bullwinkle*," she said.

The bass line of a dance track pulsed out of Club Xenon, and college-aged kids huddled over cigarettes on the sidewalk. The neon sign was all lit up.

"Look at that," I said. "Looks like Dorrie Tucker couldn't convince Budzinski to cease and desist with the neon sign after all."

"I'm not surprised," Effie said. "Dorrie probably has as much persuasive power as a plush toy. No oompf to her."

"She goes to Skeeter's Shooting Range," Chester said. "So does Susie Pak. I saw them both back when I temped as a receptionist there. So maybe Dorrie has *some* persuasive power."

"*What?*" I said. "Dorrie Tucker and Susie Pak shoot guns?"

"Yup. Vulnerable single ladies need to pack heat. It's the American way."

We filed through the double doors.

Inside, Club Xenon reeked of spilled beer and cheap aftershave. *Ah, youth.* Blue-and-purple lights pulsated. The place was ant farm–full, since the university's fall semester was starting the next day. Almost everyone was on the dance floor or milling in sweaty packs around the bar, but there were seats and tables on the balconies.

I elbowed Effie. "We should go up to a balcony," I said over the music. "Good vantage point."

Effie nodded. We bought drinks and went upstairs. All the balcony tables were taken. Effie rectified the situation by telling a clump of drunken college boys to scram.

"Jeez, Auntie," Chester said, sliding into the low U-shaped couch.

"What?" Effie said. "They're young. I've got bunions."

I stripped off the trench coat, took a tentative sip of the drink Effie had ordered for me—a yellow concoction with a sugary rim—and coughed. While Chester was slapping my back, a familiar face caught my eye, down on the edge of the dance floor. "*Omigod*. It's Gothboy." I pointed. "This is almost *too* easy."

Gothboy stuck out like a vampire bat in a petting zoo. Most of the crowd wore jeans and T-shirts—or, in the case of the frat boys, polo shirts—and everyone was smiley and laughing. But Gothboy's pale-powdered face glowed in the strobe lights, and his dark sweep of emo hair and all-black outfit disappeared each time the lights pulsed.

"He's really creepy," I said. "Just standing there."

"Look," Effie said, "someone's approaching him."

Two girls with long, swingy hair and sparkly tops approached Gothboy. I scowled inwardly. Those girls were just two more incarnations of Shelby—two-thirds human and one-third *My Little Pony*. Mere mortals like me couldn't compete.

"Oh-ho," Chester said. "A little transaction, perchance?"

It was tough to see in the blinky light, and people kept criss-crossing in front of Gothboy and the girls, but it sure as heck looked like the girls gave Gothboy something, and then Gothboy passed *them* something. Something really small. The girls left.

"It's true," I whispered. "He's selling drugs. Let's go get some pictures." Effie stood, but Chester stayed seated and seemed to shrink under his suit and fedora. I followed his eyes.

Lauren.

"Hey, guys!" Lauren said, approaching our table. She was ready for the foxtrot in a beaded flapper dress, with a long black clutch tucked under her arm. Her lips were crimson, and her eyelashes looked glued on.

"Hey," Chester croaked.

"Hi, Lauren." I slid out of the seat so Lauren could be next to Chester. I hoped he'd pee his pants from fright. "Effie and I will be back in a minute."

Effie and I both polished off our drinks, I grabbed my backpack, and we teetered down the stairs. On the way, we passed the hallway that led to the bathrooms and Bud's office. A line of girls snaked out of the bathroom. Two of them were crying. Just like a middle school dance.

"I hope you don't need the loo," Effie said to me.

"Nope."

"Good. And I've got my Depends on."

"*What?*"

"Kidding, darling."

We reached the outer perimeter of the dance floor. "Where the heck did Gothboy go?" I asked Effie over the deafening music.

"I don't see him, but it's very crowded. Let's sit at the bar—I see two free stools—and keep looking. My right bunion is really acting up tonight."

We settled on two stools surrounded by steamy bodies. Effie expertly flagged down a bartender and ordered us martinis. I scanned the shadows around the dance floor for the white smudge of Gothboy's face.

A college-age guy sidled up on Effie's other side. "Hey," the guy yelled to her over the music. He bobbed his head in time.

Effie raised her eyebrows.

"I freaking love this song," he yelled. Bulked-up muscles strained the sleeves of his baby-blue polo. His curly hair was gelled, and he had a slightly turned-up leprechaun's nose. Handsome, in a jocky way. Oh yeah—and about twenty-two years old.

The bartender slid a martini to Effie and one to me. "Twenty bucks," he said.

Mr. Jocky slapped a twenty and two singles on the table. He winked at Effie.

"Oh dear," Effie said. She took a deep swallow of her martini.

"So, you come here a lot?" Mr. Jocky asked her.

"No," Effie said.

"Well you should. There aren't enough hot girls who come here." More head-bobbing to the music.

Effie looked at me in disbelief. I shrugged. Who knew? Maybe the guy forgot his contact lenses. Or maybe he had a grandma thing. It happens.

"Agnes," someone said by my ear.

I swiveled. "Otis. Hi." My belly fluttered. *Darn it all.*

"This place is a zoo," Otis said, "and it makes me feel so *old*." He glanced around the bar area. "I feel like I should be marching these girls back to their moms. Jeez. I never saw so many belly button rings in my life." He smiled down at me. "You look really cute in that dress."

I hid my confusion with a slurp of martini. Red warnings flashed in my mind: *System Alert. System Alert. More Booze Not Good Idea.*

And because sometimes I'm a total idiot, I ignored the warning.

* * *

Otis ordered a beer and then said, "So Chester told me you're here to try to take some photos of, um"—he glanced around and leaned in really, really close—"*some deals?*"

His warm breath tickled my ear and spurred a domino effect of buzzing nerves all the way to my toes. "It's happening," I said. "We saw Gothboy doing a transaction with some girls. I've lost track of him. You know what he looks like, right?"

"The little makeup dude who bags groceries at the Green Apple? Yep."

Bad Housekeeping

Otis and I watched the crowd together. Effie was still trying to fend off the conversation of Mr. Jocky, who didn't seem to notice that Effie was over seventy, nor that her body language screamed *Beat it*.

Otis's beer arrived. "Cheers," he said.

"Cheers." We clinked.

And something new zapped me: The whole time I'd been with Roger, why hadn't I ever enjoyed a drink now and then? Why hadn't I ever gone dancing? Why hadn't I ever had a bit of freaking fun or worn lip gloss or high heels? I guess I'd thought on some level that Roger was *preventing* me from doing all those things. But it wasn't true. *I* was the stick-in-the-mud. *I* had prevented myself from loosening up.

This was a depressing revelation.

Chapter 18

"Agnes?" Otis said over the chatter and hammering dance music. "Are you okay?"

"Yeah." I shoved my glasses into position. I glanced away, to look at anything but Otis and his swim-team bod, and saw in the flashing purple light a college-aged guy and girl place pills on their tongues and wash them down with alcohol.

"Omigod," I whispered to Otis. "I just saw those kids over there popping pills."

"Where?"

I pointed. No need to be discreet in this madhouse.

The pill-popping pair were gyrating onto the dance floor in that self-conscious way kids have.

"Well, I can't say I'm surprised," Otis said. "I mean, it's a nightclub, and college kids take drugs, even in idyllic Naneda."

All true, yeah. But I'd come to the club that night looking for pot deals. Harder drugs were not part of my investigation.

"Excuse me," I said to the bartender when he passed by.

He stopped. "Yeah?" Another Mr. Jocky, although this one had intelligent eyes.

I leaned toward him over the bar. "I'm an investigative journalist from the *Boston Herald*, and I'm doing a piece on the Kathleen Todd murder." Hey, if it ain't broke, don't fix it.

The bartender's eyes widened. "Oh yeah?"

"Yeah. I'm working on profiling her family. It has come to my attention that Kathleen Todd's daughter, Megan Lawrence, was, well, let's just say *close* with Budzinski, the owner of this club."

"Megan Lawrence?" The bartender's furrowed brow looked genuine. Unless he was a drama major, he had never heard of Megan.

"She's in her midthirties," I said, "pretty, blonde, yoga pants—"

"Yoga pants!" The bartender snapped his fingers. "Oh yeah, I've seen her. Always tons of makeup and the yoga pants, drives a black Range Rover?"

"That's her. You've seen her here at the club?"

"Uh-huh. Several times in the last two, three months. I thought she was a vendor—you know, like a liquor saleslady or something."

"So she goes into Budzinski's office?"

"Uh-huh. Early in the evening before the club opens, usually, right about when I come in to get ready for my shift. Not during club hours."

"Office door shut?"

"Yeah."

"When was the last time you saw her?"

"I dunno. Sometime last week? But I mean, she could've been here even today. I don't, like, notice every single thing that happens in the club. Listen, I gotta go."

"Thanks for your help," I said.

"Wow," Otis said to me once the bartender had dashed off. "You're amazing."

"Amazing at lying?"

"Let's just say you're amazing *in general*."

My cheeks were on fire.

Just then, I saw Gothboy straight across the dance floor from where I was sitting.

"*Psst!*" I poked Effie's bony arm. She still hadn't gotten rid of Mr. Jocky. "Stop ignoring me, Aunt Effie!"

Effie turned. "I thought you were ignoring *me*, Agnes, and I wasn't about to interrupt your conversation with Delicious Treat." She smiled and made twiddly fingers at Otis, who could not—*please, Jesus*—hear what she was saying through the hubbub.

"Gothboy at twelve o'clock," I said.

Effie slithered off her barstool. "Let's go."

We plunged into the crowd, Otis right behind us.

"Hey!" Mr. Jocky yelled after Effie. "You never even told me your name!"

We weaved through the pounding, sweaty perimeter of the dance floor and stopped about two yards away from Gothboy. He and two young guys had their heads bent over something. I fumbled my phone from my backpack and tapped on the camera function. "I'll take the pictures," I said to Otis and Effie over the music. "You guys stay here."

They nodded.

I kept my eyes glued to Gothboy and stalked him, shoving through hot bodies, stepping on toes, and getting beer sloshed down my cleavage. I was *so close*. I aimed my camera at Gothboy's hand, which had just pulled something from the pocket of his black trench coat. He was passing it to one of the young guys.

Click.

The guy took it and passed something—folded-up cash, it looked like—to Gothboy.

Click.

"*What do you think you're doing?*" someone snarled, so close that I practically jumped out of my gold pumps. I spun around and found myself face-to-face with . . . Jentry.

Omigod.

Jentry's sneer revealed small teeth with too many gaps.

"Doing? What? Me? Nothing." I dodged sideways, stumbling over feet and elbowing people, and reached Effie and Otis, who had evidently seen everything because Otis wordlessly took my hand and pulled me, at the same time propelling Effie in front of him.

"*Omigod omigod omigod,*" I wheezed. "Is he coming?"

"I think so," Otis said.

"Did you see his face?" I said. "He looked like he wanted to *kill* me."

"No, I didn't see his face," Otis said, "because I was focused on the *gun* it looked like he had stuffed in his jeans pocket."

"Did you get the pictures?" Effie asked.

"Yes. I'm not sure if they came out, though."

Otis said, "Come on, let's go out the back way, past the bathrooms. I'll bet there's an exit out to the alley."

We turned into the hallway. I stole a glance over my shoulder. No Jentry. We navigated through the line of girls outside the bathroom. We turned the corner. The music receded a little. The door to Bud's office stood ajar, and it didn't look like anyone was inside.

"Hey, let's hide in Bud's office," I whispered. "We could lock the door and climb out the window."

"I like it," Effie said, skittering in.

Otis opened his mouth as if to object, but he was still holding my hand, so I pulled him in the office, slammed the door, and clicked the button lock on the doorknob.

The dance music lowered to smudgy wails and thumps. My eardrums buzzed.

Bud's office was just as messy as the last time we'd been there, including the package of Oreo cookies on the desk. Oh, and the desk chair was tipped over.

Effie leaned over the desk. "Oh, dear God," she said. "Another dead body."

My brain turned to oatmeal.

Otis leaned over to look on the other side of the desk too. "Crud," he said. "Bud's dead. Let's get out of here."

Crud? Otis said crud? That was *my* word! "Wait," I said. "Are you sure?"

Otis, Effie, and I squeezed around the desk and bent over Bud. He was dead, all right. No gunshot wounds that I could see.

"I'll bet it was a heart attack," Effie said, straightening. "That bluish-gray skin! And you see, he'd been convulsing for a bit. See the disarray? God, I need a cigarette. My third husband Raoul died of a heart attack in the sauna. Drinking scotch with the pool boy." She shivered. "Let's go."

Otis was already unlatching the window behind the desk. "There's a screen," he said. "I'll try to get it out."

"Hurry," Effie said.

Since we were there, I picked up a file folder from Bud's desk and flipped through.

"What are you doing?" Effie asked me. An unlit cigarette dangled from her lips.

"I don't know, looking for clues?" I said. The file folder held only what appeared to be alcohol delivery receipts.

"Something tells me Megan and Bud weren't the type to handwrite love letters to each other," Effie said. "They'd sext."

"Sext?"

Effie went over to a filing cabinet and yanked it open. "Haven't you heard of sexting?"

Part of me was afraid our escapades were going to land Effie in the hospital. But another part of me felt like she was corrupting my flowerlike innocence.

"Oh my," Effie said. "What have we here?"

"What?" I clumped over to Effie and the filing cabinet as fast as the gold pumps would allow.

"Um, you guys?" Otis said, still fiddling with the window screen. "I don't think touching that stuff is a good idea. There's a dead body in here."

"Natural causes, Otis dear." Effie waved a smallish pad of paper at me. I squinted. The top said *Dr. Jason Lawrence, Lakeshore Family Clinic, Rochester, NY.*

"A prescription pad," Effie said.

"*Megan's husband's* prescription pad," I said. "This is huge! Put it in your purse!"

"Are you crazy?" Effie stuffed the prescription pad back in the filing cabinet and slammed it shut.

"Wait!" I dug out my phone. "I'll take pictures."

A thump shuddered the door. "Hey!" came Jentry's muffled yell. "I know you're in there, you stupid cows!"

Otis rattled the window screen. "It's stuck."

"Open up!" Jentry shouted. The doorknob twisted.

"Hurry!" I whispered to Otis.

"I'm going to have to cut it." Otis dug a pocket knife from his jeans and flipped open a blade. He sawed at the screen. "Unfortunately, this is going to make this office look like a crime scene."

Effie opened the filing cabinet again, and I took pictures of the prescription pad, getting the filing cabinet and other papers jumbled in the drawer for context. Effie slammed the drawer. I stuffed my phone in my backpack.

A huge thump. Jentry was trying to kick the door down. He bellowed, "If you snitch to the cops about anything, I'm gonna kill you!"

Effie's face went stony. Her eyes narrowed, and she marched to the door. "Yoo-hoo, Jentry," she called.

Silence.

"Oh, good," Effie said. "You're listening. Jentry, darling, if you threaten me or my niece again—or follow us about in your pickup truck—we *will* snitch to the police. How do you like *that* for a catch-22?"

We didn't wait for Jentry's reply; Otis had finished cutting a big flap in the window screen. Effie and I climbed through into the wet alleyway. Otis went last.

"Run!" Effie cried.

"I *am*," I said. I mean, I was *trying* to run, but in the gold pumps, it was more like a reindeer prance. We slid and crashed past dumpsters and around the corner of the building onto Main Street.

I slammed right into someone and sent them down onto the sidewalk.

"*Oof*," a familiar voice said. A girl squealed.

I pried my eyes open. I was staring down into Roger's appalled face. Oh—and I was clutching his shoulders and astride him.

"I know it's going to be terribly difficult for you, Agnes," Roger said gently, "but you're going to have to at least *try* to get over me." He writhed out from under me, and I fell back onto my butt on the wet sidewalk, legs splayed. I didn't even feel like crying. I just felt like dissolving and washing away into the streaming gutter. Roger's arm curled around Shelby, and they both studied my shoes.

I knew what they were thinking: *Rebound shoes.*

"What are you two staring at?" Otis said to them, emerging from the alleyway. Then to me, "Come on, Agnes." He held out a big, strong hand, pulled me to my feet, and wrapped his arm around my shoulders. "We'd better get going."

In the meantime, Effie had lit her cigarette despite the rain. "It's only been *two days* since you dumped Agnes," she said to Roger. "How is she supposed to have moved on already? It's a bit much to ask. You should be ashamed of yourself." She pointed her cigarette at Shelby. "You too."

"The heart wants what it wants," Roger said loftily.

Gross. I turned to Otis and Effie. "Let's go."

*   *   *

Otis loped alongside Effie and me to the Cadillac, and we didn't see Jentry. Maybe he was still trying to smash Bud's door down. We all climbed in, Effie in the driver's seat and Otis and me, for some reason, glued to each other in the back seat. His hard, heat-radiating body felt like the only thing keeping me from bursting into tears and/or frantic giggles. This fact annoyed me but not enough to unglue myself. I'd process it later.

"Obviously, we have to call the police," I said, digging for my phone.

"Obviously," Otis said.

"Wait," Effie said. "How are we going to explain to the police what we were doing in Bud's office? And unless Jentry somehow succeeded in breaking the door down, it'll be locked, and they'll find the cut screen . . ."

"I'll ask Lauren to call the police," I said. I dialed Lauren. She was still inside the club with Chester. I explained how Jentry was after us and how we'd found Budzinski dead from what looked like a heart attack in his office. "So could you call nine-one-one?" I asked.

"Sure," Lauren said coolly. "And you know what? I'll steal a phone from one of these college kids—their phones are lying around all over the place—and call from *that* so no one will have to explain a thing."

"You're a genius," I said. "Call me if anything weird happens." I punched *end call*. Then I went to my photos to see how the shots of Gothboy's drug deal and the prescription pad had turned out. "The drug deal shot is blurry, but the prescription pad shots are crystal clear," I said and put my phone away. "In the movies, the police labs can always enhance those blurry shots."

"Yeah, I'm not sure the Naneda Police Department has spy-thriller technology," Otis said.

"I hope Bud really died of natural causes," I said, "so they won't be looking for fingerprints—of which we left about five million."

"Could I make a suggestion?" Otis said.

"Sure," I said.

"Stop this investigating stuff before you get killed? Go to the police and tell them about Jentry's pot operation and the drug deals and the prescription pad? And then, I don't know, go on vacation to Brazil for six months?"

I shook my head. "Number one, Aunt Effie and I can't go on vacation *anywhere*. We're persons of interest and have been forbidden to leave town. Number two, Aunt Effie could be arrested for trespassing at the inn, and both of us could be arrested for trespassing on Jentry's farm even if he *is* growing pot." I didn't add that if I was arrested for *anything*, even if the charges were immediately dropped, it would break Dad's heart.

Effie said, "Detective Albright thinks you're some kind of seductive little criminal too, Agnes."

"Really?" Otis said.

"*And number three*," I said, "we have some really amazing leads! Dr. Lawrence's prescription pad? Hello, that makes Megan look really bad—and it makes Bud and Jentry look bad too. And Roland Pascal is an ex-con, remember? Who knows? He could've been imprisoned for drug charges. Kathleen Todd's murder was about drugs—*prescription* drugs—and I'm going to prove it. So no. Wild horses couldn't make me stop this investigation now. I'm so close to cracking it, I can almost taste it."

I didn't add number four, which was something like, *This investigation is the only thing keeping me from wallowing in a miserable pile of chocolate chip muffins while throwing darts at a target with a photo of Roger's smug, jerky face scotch-taped on the bull's-eye.*

I leaned forward between the seats despite the toxic fume cloud roiling around Effie. "Aunt Effie, I *do* think you should come and stay at Dad's—"

"Hell, no," Effie snapped. "The threats of arrest for trespassing and of ghosts won't keep me out of the inn, and neither will Jentry. I've got pepper spray, and I've lived an exceptionally full life and have no fear of death. I'm not budging."

Otis groaned and slouched back on the seat. "You two are the most stubborn people I have *ever* met."

"Thank you," Effie and I said in unison.

Chapter 19

The rain kept up overnight. In the morning, I dawdled upstairs, lounging in bed, taking a marathon shower, doing laundry in Dad's upstairs stackable, blow-drying my hair—something I never do—and deliberating endlessly between two ill-fitting high school outfits. The thing was, I was trying to avoid Dad. I could hear him in the kitchen talking with Cordelia. But nine o'clock came and went, and I realized that he wasn't going to go to work without talking to me first. I bit the bullet and went downstairs.

"Good morning, honey," Dad said from the breakfast nook. The pouches under his eyes looked puffier than usual. Great. I was killing my Dad.

"Hi." I went to the coffeemaker. Luckily, Cordelia wasn't in the room.

"Fun night?"

"What? Oh. Yeah. I went out with Effie, Chester, Lauren, and Otis Hatch—you remember him?—for a drink. Just a mellow, laid-back night." I poured half-and-half in my coffee to avoid eye contact. I'd downed only one and a half drinks last night at Club Xenon, but the liquor they used was the kind that came in huge plastic jugs. So yeah, I had a headache, and my tongue felt like a pinecone.

"I didn't know you drank," Dad said.

"Oh, now and then."

"I hope Great-Aunt Effie isn't leading you—"

I waved a hand. "Don't be silly."

"The owner of Club Xenon on Main Street died last night."

I gulped coffee. "Oh?"

"Police Chief Gwozdek said it looked like a heart attack, but they sent the body in for an autopsy just to be sure, what with Kathleen Todd's death and all."

"Makes sense." I took a muffin from a plate on the counter. "Say, Dad, why aren't you at work?"

"I wanted to ask you about something—"

Here it comes.

"—something a little, well . . . let's just say I hope there was some kind of misunderstanding."

I furrowed my brow, "innocent and confused" (I hoped), as I bit into the muffin.

Dad cleared his throat. "Megan Lawrence called my office yesterday and said you and Aunt Effie had stopped by her house, saying you wanted to start some kind of neighborhood watch group?"

"Oh. Yeah." I coughed on a muffin crumb, and my eyes watered. "Well, no. I *knew* Megan didn't understand what Aunt Effie said. What happened was, we were there sort of canvassing because Aunt Effie is interested in putting herself up for historical society chairman."

"Really?" Dad's big shoulders sagged in relief.

"Yeah." Mental note: tell Aunt Effie she is considering putting herself up for historical society chairman. "We were just asking Megan Lawrence about the break-in at her house—did she tell you about that? yeah?—and Aunt Effie wanted to ask her how she'd feel about a historical society chairman who took a special interest in, uh, home-security issues."

"Well, Agnes, your hearts are in the right place, but that would really be outside of the bounds of the historical society's role. The police are in charge of—"

"I know, I know. It was Aunt Effie's idea. She gets kind of carried away with these grandiose plans."

"She sure does." Dad looked like he wanted to say more, but he didn't.

He was doing me a favor and, true to his word, keeping out of it. I'd thought that that would allow me to retain some shreds of my adult pride, but, ironically, him indulging me this way only made me feel like a touchy teenager.

Dad stood. "Well, I've got to get to work, but I'm glad we talked, Agnes. I was starting to worry again that you two were meddling in the murder investigation."

"Us, meddle?" I chuckled weakly into my coffee mug. "We're *way* too busy for that."

*   *   *

By the time I rolled up to the Stagecoach Inn on my ten speed, my clothes were as waterlogged as my spirits. Lying to Dad felt awful. It was like lying to Teddy Ruxpin. No way was I backing off on my investigation when I felt so close to the solution, but I needed to wrap it up, and quickly, before I ruined my relationship with Dad forever. Luckily, seeing that prescription pad and those drug deals in Club Xenon last night had been a breakthrough. Kathleen Todd's murder probably had been about prescription drugs, and Megan, Bud, Jodi, and Jentry all looked really sketchy. The problem was figuring out how to pursue this lead without getting into another dangerous situation with Jentry.

I leaned my bike on the kitchen porch railing and went inside.

Effie and Chester were at the kitchen table. The orange-striped cat crouched on the kitchen table on top of some catalogs or magazines, licking what looked like milk from a bowl.

"Gross," I said, shutting the door behind me. "If kitty litter gets in your food, you could get all kinds of disgusting diseases, you know. There's even a parasite that makes you crazy and love cats."

Effie said, "We're not *eating food*, darling. Perish the thought."

I looked at Chester. "What's with you? Going manorexic?"

"He's love-sick," Effie said.

I snorted. "Lauren's out of your league, Chester." I had texted with Lauren that morning, thanking her for calling 9-1-1 and giving her an update. I'd also asked her if there was any chance she'd ever go out with Chester. She'd written back: *Eye roll.*

"Aren't you going to ask *me* why I'm not eating?" Effie blew a stream of cigarette smoke toward the ceiling.

"No." I leaned my butt on the counter. "You never eat."

Effie ignored that. "The ghost came again last night."

"Oh really? Did you leave any cigarettes out for him?"

"I woke up to a shattering sound that penetrated my earplugs," Effie said. "I grabbed my pepper spray and went downstairs, and I found a plate right in the middle of the dining room floor, broken into about ten pieces."

"Oh, okay," I said in a *this is redonk* voice. But goose bumps prickled up and down my back. "And the ghost shattered the plate?"

"I think so, yes," Effie said.

"Where's the plate now?"

"Still on the floor. I couldn't bear to touch it. Chester said he would clean it up, but he seems to be afraid of it too."

"Afraid of poltergeist slime?" I said to Chester.

He made a *nyah-nyah* face at me.

"Speaking of slime," I said, "are we still not going to report Bud and those prescription pads to the police?"

"You don't need to," Chester said. "At the bakery this morning, everyone was gossiping about Bud's death and the prescription pads the police found in his office. Oh, and the cut window screen."

Great.

"The police will be asking Megan's husband about those prescription pads for sure," Chester said, "although I guess Kathleen Todd's funeral is today, so they might have some delays."

"That means that *we'll* have a hard time talking to Megan today too, unless we crash the funeral," I said.

"No crashing." Effie scratched the cat's ears. The cat flicked his tail. "Too high profile."

"Then what?" I said. "I want to *do* something."

"Can't we work here a little, first?" Effie said.

I stifled a sigh. "Sure." Putting off the next step in our sleuthing felt like torture, but I *had* accepted a cash advance from Effie.

"I'm so glad you're in your dumpiest work clothes," Effie said.

I looked down at my outfit: the Rocky sweat pants and a red *Star Trek* T-shirt.

"Of course," Effie went on in a contemplative tone, "you probably weren't expecting to see Otis today."

I spluttered on coffee. "*He's* coming?"

"Well, not that I *know* of," Effie said, "but he does have a way of showing up whenever you're around."

Chester snickered.

I narrowed my eyes.

"Come on, Agnes," Effie said in a sweet voice. "There's no need to pretend with me."

"Pretend what?"

"That Otis isn't a gorgeous, hot-blooded male who's clearly smitten by you and with whom you'd love to dive into the sack. I'm not blind. I had laser surgery on my eyes only two years ago."

"I don't even know how to respond to this," I said. Warmth crept up my neck. "Sure, maybe I gave Otis the wrong idea last night because I'd been drinking—"

"Oh, yes? Enough of a wrong idea that he felt inclined to swoop you into his arms after Roger and that stick of sugarless gum—"

"Swoop? He didn't *swoop*."

"And exactly what sort of wrong idea did you give him, darling? Oh, never mind. I suppose there's really only *one* idea when it all boils down."

"Men and women can be just friends, you know," I said, maybe too loudly.

"No, they can't!" Chester said, his voice cracking. He lurched to his feet and stumped across the kitchen. "Going to work on the dining room wiring."

Effie gazed after him. "Those with English degrees do suffer more *poetically* than the rest of us."

"I assume Lauren told him she only wants to be friends?"

"Mmm."

Smart move. Chester's longest relationship to date was, I believe, two weeks long, and that was an online relationship with someone in Norway.

Effie stood. "I'm going to sort through the hallway coat closet. There are things in there that probably need to be burned."

"I'll be there in a second." I sat down at the kitchen table to finish my coffee. I petted the cat until he got bored of me and hopped down.

The four issues of Kathleen Todd's *Good Housekeeping* and *Better Homes and Gardens* that Effie had stolen from the library stared up at me. I paged through one. Garish ads and articles suggested that a woman could make her husband happy with pot roast, nice living room drapes, and by using the right brand of cold cream. Kinda offensive. Although, what did *I* know? I was a twenty-eight year old dumpy dumpee. Maybe I should've paid more attention to all that happy housewife stuff. Maybe Roger would've liked it.

Thinking about Roger got me thinking about Otis. Which may seem strange, but in a way, my relationship with Roger was, at least at its beginning, deeply influenced by what had gone wrong with Otis in high school. Roger—who even back in college had had pleated jeans and stooped shoulders—had seemed like a safe alternative to guys like Otis. Roger had seemed like someone who would appreciate me for my brains and wit and overlook my butt and other girls' butts too, you know?

I'd sure gotten *that* one wrong.

But oddly, now I was wondering about Otis. It truly seemed like he, well, like he *liked* me. Even that he thought I was . . .

attractive. But how the heck could I ever forget the Hagness Blimp disaster? That had broken my heart.

Shut up, *Agnes*, the rational little bug voice in my head scolded. *Remember that you decided this whole Otis fascination was a reliving of the* sensation *of first love? It'll pass.*

I was swallowing my last sip of coffee when I happened to notice that all four of the mailing labels had been ripped off. Actually, in the way of those really sticky labels, they had only been partially ripped off, and fragments of the printed address remained. It looked like it was the same address on all the labels, because I saw the same letters and numbers repeating. Why would someone rip off the labels? Somehow, this felt important.

I arrayed the magazines in front of me, and in only a couple minutes, I had mentally pieced together the address:

Earlene Roy
19 Scump Pond Road
Scump, NY

This was too weird. I had no clue who Earlene Roy was, but . . . Roy? As in *Gracelyn* Roy? And where in the world was Scump, New York?

I found Effie, smoking in the hallway and staring into the closet, and told her what I had discovered. "Do you think these magazines belong to Gracelyn Roy's family?" I asked.

"But she's new to town, and I don't know any other Roys in Naneda. Do you?"

I shook my head. "Let me check the white pages." I searched on my phone. No Roys.

"Anyway, didn't you say Kathleen Todd donated the magazines to the library?"

"Hey!" Chester shouted from somewhere. "Aunt Effie! Come quick! We've got a serious problem."

* * *

We found Chester standing with his arms folded and scowling at the fireplace in the dining room.

"Is it asbestos?" I asked.

"Is it the ghost?" Effie asked.

Chester pointed to the floor in front of the hearth. A puddle of water glimmered.

Effie gasped.

"Hel-*lo* money pit," I said.

Next, Chester pointed to the elaborately carved wooden mantelpiece. It was blotched with water.

"Is it ruined?" Effie clutched her chest. "That can't be replaced! What happened here? I didn't see any water last night."

Chester shrugged. "It's been raining. There's a leak somewhere."

"Well it's *still* raining!" Effie cried. "We've got to find the leak!"

"Yes, we do," Chester said grimly. "I can't move forward with the wiring if there's an active leak. This is a major setback, and I'm running out of time."

We climbed the grand staircase to the second floor and then up a smaller staircase to the attic. We found the dormer window closest to the chimney, and Chester wrestled it open and leaned out.

"Oh, crap," he said. He ducked back inside.

"What?" I said.

"There's no flashing around the chimney."

"What's flashing?" Effie said, toying with her chunky gold necklace.

"The strips of stuff—usually copper or tin—around the roof where the chimney comes out, to keep the rain off," Chester said. "And the flashing is just . . . gone. Which is really strange."

"Why?" Effie's voice sounded a little shrill.

"Because if there's no flashing, there would be *old* signs of a leak—water damage—in the dining room already. On the floor. On the mantelpiece. Probably on the walls and ceiling. But there isn't."

"Are you saying that the flashing was removed *recently*?" I asked.

"Yeah, I am," Chester said. "As in, since the last time it rained."

"That was like a week ago," I said.

Effie marched over to the open window and thrust her head out. She craned her neck to see the chimney. Then she looked down. "Oh, dear lord," she said. "There are copper strips down there."

The three of us poked our heads out the window. Strips of greenish metal lay curled and bent on the porch roof.

"I guess that's what your ghost has been up to," I said to Effie.

We went downstairs. Effie and I got to work on sopping up the puddle in the sitting room, and Chester went off to the hardware store to buy supplies to fix the flashing.

"I have to admit, I'm pretty creeped out," I said to Effie. I swabbed the floorboards with an old towel. "Someone's been coming into the inn while you've been sleeping. Come and stay at Dad's. Please. At least until you can install some sort of security system or buy a guard dog or something. There's plenty of room."

"No," Effie said. "I'm staying put. Whoever it is, they're obviously just trying to drive me out, not harm me. They climbed on my goddam roof in the middle of the night when I was sleeping, when they could have easily killed me in my bed—"

"But what'll they do when they *can't* drive you out? Is *that* when they come and kill you?"

"Don't be dramatic, Agnes." Effie was poking her phone. "I'm calling Karl Knudsen at City Hall," she said. "I've *got* to make him reconsider the demolition date. Chester will never get the wiring done in time, now that—Hello? Is this the public works department? Wonderful. I'd like to speak with Mr. Knudson." *Waa-waa-waa*ing on the other end. Effie frowned. "Home sick? The poor man. All right, thank you." She hung up. "Knudson is home sick. We'll stop by."

"He's sick!"

"That's right. Sick and *vulnerable*. I've got to make him change the date. Come on. We've cleaned up all the water here, and there's nothing else we can do until Chester gets back."

Chapter 20

I looked up Karl Knudsen's home address on my phone. He lived a few blocks outside of the central historic district on Madison Street. Effie and I set off in the Caddy.

As we drove down Third Street, I noticed Gracelyn Roy's antique pickup parked in front of her house. "Hey," I said, "let's stop by and talk to Gracelyn. We can ask her about the mailing labels on those magazines, okay?"

Effie parked. We climbed out of the car and picked our way up the front walk, steering well clear of the rusty saw blades and tractor parts. Tall sunflowers swayed in the breeze. Goldfish flicked in a pool set inside a monster truck tire.

Effie eyed the pool. "Ingenious," she said dryly.

I knocked on the front door. We waited. No answer. I peered through the window. "I can see right down the hallway to the back of the house," I said, "and the back door is open. Maybe she's in the backyard."

We circled around the house, following a flagstone path, and found ourselves in a small backyard billowing with tomatoes, squash, and pole beans. A fence separated the yard from Dorrie

Tucker's next door. Dorrie's lace curtains were drawn. She'd be at Kathleen Todd's funeral.

Gracelyn squatted beside a raised garden bed, picking tomatoes. She wore a bathrobe, and her back was to us.

"Excuse me," I called. "Ms. Roy?"

Gracelyn swiveled. Her eyes squinched. "Who the hell are you?" The hick accent was dialed up to *strong.*

"I'm Agnes Blythe, and this is Euphemia Winters."

"That's right." Gracelyn stood. "The murderers. I met *you,* granny"—she pointed at Effie—"when you interrogated me at my book signing." She popped a cherry tomato in her mouth. "What do you want?"

"I have a couple questions for you," I said.

"Oh, yeah? And this is what you do? Trespass in folks' yards?"

"First off," I said, "is it true that you were with Roland Pascal at midnight the night Kathleen Todd was killed?"

"He tell you that?"

"Yes."

"Stinker. No privacy in this town."

"Then you *were* together."

"I guess, but what's it to you?"

"Just curious. Another thing: while I was cleaning out the porch at the Stagecoach Inn—we're renovating it, you know—"

"*Renovating* it?" Gracelyn snorted. "I heard it was gettin' razed to kingdom come in a few days."

"Hopefully not," I said. "Anyway, I found these old magazines from the sixties with mailing labels addressed to someone named Earlene Roy in Scump, New York. Any relation to you, Ms. Roy?"

Gracelyn's jaw jutted. "Roy's a pretty common name."

"Not really," I said.

"*Sure it is.*" Gracelyn was moving toward the back porch.

"You haven't lived in Naneda long, have you?" I asked.

"Nope." Gracelyn mounted the porch steps.

"Have you ever been to Scump, New York?" I asked.

Gracelyn swung open the screen door, grabbed something, and twirled around. She braced a shotgun against her arm, and her mouth was squared off in that chimp-at-war way, teeth bared. "Get the hell off my property, or Annie here is gonna take a chunk out of you."

I backed up, stepping on Aunt Effie's toe. "Is that Annie as in Little Orphan or Oakley?"

"Enough with your lip, four-eyes," Gracelyn snarled. "Now *git.*"

"Okeydokey," I said. Effie and I turned, hurried back around the house, and jumped into the car. "Well *that* was a little aggressive." I wrestled with my seat belt, hands shaking.

"I'm amazed how many citizens of this town are packing heat," Effie said, fumbling for a cigarette.

"*Drive,*" I said.

"To Karl Knudsen's?"

I thought about it. "In a minute. First, let's go see Roland Pascal and ask him about prison—and about Gracelyn Roy."

*   *   *

When Effie switched off the engine in front of the McGrundell Mansion, we heard piano music coming from a radio somewhere inside.

"You go speak with Roland," Effie said. "I'll just pop into his trailer and see if the crumpled-up list of references is still in there. If I find it, I'll photograph it."

"Do you know how to work your camera phone?"

"No. Show me."

I showed her.

Effie stole into the trailer, and I went up to the mansion's front porch.

The front door was off its hinges and leaning on a porch pillar, so I took that as an invitation to go in. I found Roland on a ladder in the library, rubbing wood varnish on a high bookshelf.

"Ah, a lady," he said without stopping his work. "Good morning. How lovely you look."

"Don't lie," I said. "Roland, what were you in prison for? Was it drug related?"

Roland's hand slowed in its rubbing only briefly and then resumed its earlier brisk pace. "Prison? Drugs? Dear lilylike Agnes, what can you mean?"

"The tattoo on your hand—it's a convict's tattoo."

"Ah, that? Youthful folly. Not prison. In my adolescence, I and the other village boys desired to look like, how do you call it, *toughs*. To impress the girls." He smiled. "Does it impress you, Agnes?"

"Actually, no. Sorry." I wasn't sure if Roland was bluffing about the tattoo or not, but I *was* sure that I wasn't going to squeeze anything else out of him about it. I switched gears. "I was just speaking with your girlfriend, Gracelyn Roy. Quite the charmer. She pulled a shotgun on me."

Roland smiled as he dipped his rag into a can of varnish. "Ah, yes, she has the feisty temperament, little Gracelyn."

"I think she's hiding something," I said. "Her accent is fake."

213

"Is it? I am a foreigner, so I cannot differentiate American accents. You all sound like you are from *Baywatch* to me."

That was just sad. "You're positive you and Gracelyn were together at midnight the night Kathleen was killed?"

"Did Gracelyn say we were together?"

"Yeah."

"Well then, we were together."

"What the heck is that supposed to mean?"

"Why are you asking such questions, fair Agnes? Perhaps I should telephone the police and tell them you are conducting your own murder investigation?"

"Have a great day!" I said quickly and went outside. Effie was already in the car.

"Any luck?" she asked me.

"Not really. You?"

"I found the references page and photographed it. There are three people listed. Look."

"Awesome." I took out my own phone and dialed the first name, Herbert Thoreau in Cambridge, Massachusetts. No answer. I left a message, wheeling out the line that I was an investigative reporter from the *Boston Herald*. I dialed the second name, Valerie Rose in Caraway, Vermont. Again, no answer. I left the same message. The third number was no longer in service. "I hope someone calls back," I said. "Roland really rubs me the wrong way."

Next stop, Karl Knudsen's house.

* * *

Karl's house was a one-story blue Cape Cod in a neighborhood of modest midcentury homes. The front curtains were drawn. The yard was well kept yet blah—clipped lawn, clipped boxwoods, squeaky-clean garbage and recycling bins. A Toyota pickup and a Porsche SUV stood in the driveway.

"A Porsche?" I said as Effie parked across the street. "On a public works salary?"

"Maybe he has a visitor," Effie said.

We got out. As we turned up the front walk, we heard voices. "He has a visitor, all right," I whispered. "And she sounds *pissed*." A woman's anger-spiked voice bulldozed over a man's placating whine.

"I suppose we should come back later," Effie said, turning.

"Wait." I touched Effie's arm. "What if this is . . . relevant?"

"How could it possibly be relevant?"

"Well, I can't believe I'm saying this, but if we eavesdropped, maybe we'd learn something that we could"—I licked my dry lips—"that you could, ah, *leverage*."

"Agnes Blythe!" Effie whispered. "Are you suggesting that I blackmail Mr. Knudson into stopping the inn's demolition?"

"*Blackmail* isn't exactly—"

"I *love* it." Effie crossed the lawn, her sharp heels sinking into the turf, and disappeared into the shrubs at the side of the house.

What could I do but follow her? After all, eavesdropping had been my idea. Why did I *say* these things? I guess I kept thinking that Effie, as a responsible senior citizen, would object. *Yeah, right.* I jogged after her.

In the shrubs, Effie and I elbowed through branches to position ourselves under a window. Twigs knocked my glasses askew and raked across my arms and scalp. *Ow.* And I had my fingers crossed that no one was watching from across the street, because even if they hadn't seen us disappear into the bushes, they might see the bushes shaking.

"—and I swear to God, Karl, I'm going to call the police if you don't stop this—this *craziness*!" the woman shrieked inside the house.

"Don't call me crazy, Ashley. I *love* you and—"

"Don't you dare talk about love! Love? Hah! Where was the love when we were married? When you'd go bird-watching every goddam weekend instead of spending time with Benny and me?"

Effie and I slowly rose to peek through a window. We had a decent view of Karl's living room. Karl sat cocooned in a blanket in a recliner, feet propped up and a snowfall of used Kleenexes on the carpet. A tall, pretty brunette, maybe fifty years old, paced near the front window. She swung on Karl. "You know what it's called, don't you, Karl? It's called *stalking*. I could get a restraining order! Everyone in town would know about it. You'd have a real fun time walking into work every day with everyone knowing you're a stalking psycho, now wouldn't you?"

"Don't threaten me, Ashley. It's not stalking." Karl blew his nose. "It's just that I haven't gotten over you yet—"

"Our divorce was finalized three years ago! I'm married to Matt! And *yes*, following me around town in your truck and taking pictures of me at the antique store is stalking, and you, Karl, are sick. This is your last warning—and I'm giving you one more chance only for Benny's sake. Cut it out, or I'm getting a restraining order." Ashley stormed out of the living room, and a second later, the front door banged. A few seconds after that, the roar of an engine and the squeal of tires let me know that Ashley had zoomed away in her Porsche.

"Well, there's your leverage," I whispered to Effie.

"And then some."

"Let's ring the doorbell."

"No, no. This is so much better. We can keep our leverage in our pocket and wheel it out if and when we need it. That way, if we *don't* need to blackmail Karl to stop the demolition, why, we can save our leverage for later. I'm sure we'll be seeing a lot of Karl Knudsen in the future as the inn's renovation progresses."

Effie was treacherously organized. And I wasn't sure how comfortable I was with all those *we*s.

"Come on," she whispered. "The front curtains were shut, so Karl won't see us."

We scurried over the front lawn, across the street, and into the Cadillac. Effie revved the engine, and we lurched away.

"That was wrong," I said. "We shouldn't have done that. I feel *dirty*. You can't blackmail Karl, okay?" I needed a muffin or—wasn't it pushing lunchtime?—pizza.

"I won't blackmail him *yet*," Effie said, "but I must admit it feels nice to have something up my sleeve in the event that Chester doesn't finish the wiring in time. Where to next, Agnes? And *don't* say that revolting pizza place on Route 20."

"Pizza? At this hour? *No*. And honestly, I'm not sure what to do next. I'd like to poke around into the drug deals at Club Xenon, but I have no idea where to start. I'm assuming that now that Budzinski is dead, the club will be shut down, and no way am I going back out to Jentry's farm under any circumstance. Maybe we could corner Gothboy and get him to fess up. He seems kind of wimpy. We could find out where he lives and do a stakeout."

"Sounds like a terrible bore," Effie said.

"As far as I know, detectives spend a ton of time sitting in their cars on stakeouts and eating donuts."

"Nancy Drew never ate donuts, and she was forever driving around in her convertible."

"Let's go back to the inn," I said. "You can cheer on Chester, and I can make some calls and try to figure out where I can find Gothboy." I was also sweating it that Effie might really blackmail Karl Knudson about stalking his ex-wife if things got down to the wire, but I didn't want to say that out loud. Maybe she'd forget about it.

Chapter 21

When Effie and I arrived at the inn, Chester's Datsun was parked out front, and so was Otis's motorcycle.

My belly clenched. I was getting hungry, okay?

As I pushed through the kitchen door, my phone rang. I dug into my backpack and answered it. "Hello?"

"Miss Blythe?" a young man said.

"That's me."

"This is Eric Tanaka at the Pressley Program in Syracuse. Remember we spoke about your *Boston Herald* piece on the murder in Naneda?"

Sassy molassy. The winsome little dude who thought I was a big-time journalist and his ticket into the profession. "Yeah, of course."

"Okay, well, I did some more digging into our old files, and I found some stuff that I thought might be interesting to you."

"Go ahead."

The kitchen door opened, and Otis walked in, looking awesome as ever in faded jeans and a T-shirt that showed off his pecs. Otis and Effie started talking. I sank onto a chair.

On the phone, Eric Tanaka said, "Not *all* the old files—paper files, I mean—had been entered into the database by the data entry students, it turns out, so I looked through the boxes of files for the students who entered in fall 1972—they're stored right here in the school—and I found Kathleen Todd's file."

"Are you serious?"

"Yep."

"But you said you couldn't find her name."

"I couldn't—and that's because she had changed her name. But the name change was noted in her file, because I guess she changed it sometime between when she applied for the school and when she actually started the course."

"Okay, and what was her original name?"

"Larlene Black."

"Larlene Black," I repeated. "Any address? Like for an orphanage in Massachusetts?"

"I couldn't find one. The file included her original application for enrollment, but she'd listed a PO box in Syracuse as her address."

"Anything else?"

"Not really."

"Okay, great work, Eric. Keep me posted." I hung up. "I need to e-mail my journalist friend in DC and make her give this kid some kind of internship," I said to Effie and Otis. "Otherwise, I may combust with guilt."

Otis grinned.

Effie was uninterested in guilt. "Am I right in understanding that Kathleen Todd's original name was Larlene Black?"

"Yeah. She completely changed her name. And doesn't Larlene ring a bell?"

"It sounds like a kooky bit character on a 1950s sitcom," Effie said.

"The *magazines*," I said, pointing to the kitchen table. "Think!" I eyed Chester's leftover Cheetos on the table, but since Otis was standing right there, I decided not to scrounge. Cheetos-powder rings around the lips is not a lovely look.

"Still no bells ringing," Effie said.

"Those magazines were addressed to Earlene Roy," I said. "Doesn't Larlene sound like *Earlene*?"

Effie tipped her head. "A bit. But—"

"I think this is our big break in the case. Let's go."

Otis and Effie exchanged a look: *Alert! Cuckoo bird on the loose.*

"Why are you two just standing there?" I asked, pausing on my way to the door.

"I guess the word is . . . *tenuous*," Effie said.

"So? I've got a hunch, and we need to go to Scump. Oh—and I'm doing the driving."

"Your license is at the Goodwill," Effie said.

"So? It's a stolen car, *and* the police told us we can't leave Naneda, so if we get stopped, we're screwed anyway."

"Can I come?" Otis asked.

"Fine," I said.

* * *

Scump, New York, according to the map on my phone, was just over one hundred miles away, near Oneida Lake, north of Syracuse. Kind of a blank spot on the map, honestly. Not quite the Adirondacks but nowhere near Lake Ontario either.

We gassed up. I was behind the wheel, and Effie insisted on chain-smoking in the back seat, so Otis was next to me. This felt weirdly marital, like I was Mom and Otis was Dad and Effie was our chain-smoking toddler. I turned up oldies on the radio—something for everyone, right?—and off we went.

"I'm liking those sunglasses on you, Agnes," Otis said once we were on the Thruway, giving me a sly, sidelong grin. It was so sunny, I'd been forced to borrow Aunt Effie's face furniture.

I gripped the wheel tightly. I couldn't help it: each and every time Otis said something that was, at least ostensibly, a compliment, my blood pressure went up. I was going to have to drag all that Hagness Blimp stuff out into the open before it made me crazy.

"Listen, Otis," I said, "I know you're used to being all ladies' man, and that's cool. Heck, I think you're entitled to it. You're a, um, a handsome guy." I swallowed.

"Gee, thanks, Agnes," Otis said. There was a lilt of humor in his voice.

"I'm not saying that to butter you up. I have no interest in handsome *personally*, although I am fully aware that there are women who do."

"Where are you going with this, Agnes?" Effie called from the back seat. Smoke wafted. "I know it's old-fashioned, but I still believe gentlemen should do the asking."

"I'm not *asking* anything!" I said.

Otis swiveled around to look at Effie. "Anyway, Mrs. Winters, I already asked Agnes out on a date, but she turned me down."

"Don't give up," Effie said to Otis. "She'll come around."

"Do you guys realize I'm sitting approximately ten inches away?" I said.

Effie leaned back in her seat. "Well yes, darling, but you're so obtuse, you might as well be ten *miles* away."

222

My gas pedal foot sank toward the floor. The speedometer crept up. "Okay then, since we're getting into this, Otis, I'll tell you why I didn't accept your invitation for a so-called date. Number one, because I just broke up with my boyfriend—no, fiancé!—of *eight years*. Number two—and this is on a related note—I don't accept pity dates." Actually, I'd never been asked on a pity date before. In fact, before Roger and I got together, I hadn't really done dating of any kind.

"Is there a number three?" Otis asked. His usual bantering tone was gone.

Well, *good*.

"Yes," I said, "there *is* a number three, and thanks for asking. Number three is the way you completely and *utterly* humiliated me before senior prom!"

A long silence. I kept my eyes on the road.

"I didn't," Otis finally said.

"You *did*!" The speedometer flickered toward eighty. I rocketed past a guy in a U-Haul who gave me the finger. "You said you had something important to ask me after fifth period and to meet by my locker. Then, when I got to my locker, a big crowd of your—your—those popular jock assholes and mean girls and your brother Garth were already there waiting for the show, and there was that *sign* on my locker!" Hot, furious tears surged out of my eyes, but I didn't bother to wipe them away. "Hagness Blimp?" My voice cracked. "Ring a bell?"

"Agnes," Otis said gently, "that wasn't me. You thought *I* did that?"

I glanced out of the corner of my blurry eye at Otis. His mouth hung open in amazement.

"Of course it was you! And yeah, okay, I'm willing to admit that people can grow and change out of their highs school selves, although for the most part, people really don't. We're all walking around with the same egos and insecurities we had when we were seventeen years old."

"So true," Effie said.

"Agnes, you've got to listen to me," Otis said. "I didn't set you up. I didn't write those awful signs. I can't believe you thought that was me all these years! Is this why you never returned any of my e-mails during college?"

I snorked my runny nose. Who cared? In a beauty pageant, or heck, even in a Miss Congeniality pageant, I'd be finishing dead last at this point. "Okay, then how do you explain the coincidence that you asked to meet me in *the very spot* where all that happened?"

"How do I explain it? Simple. I was going to ask you to go to prom with me."

"But—"

"My jerk brother Garth knew it. *He* did all that other stuff. The signs. Arranging for his goons to stand around and watch."

"Garth. *Garth?*" I let up a little on the gas. I couldn't believe my ears. All these years, I'd harbored a grudge against the wrong brother?

From the back seat, Effie said, "You still could've asked her to the prom, you know, Otis."

"I would have," Otis said. "But by the time *I* got there, you were gone. I couldn't find you anywhere. You were absent from school for the rest of the year. I tried calling, and you wouldn't take my calls. I went to your front door a bunch of times, and your dad and your housekeeper kept shooing me away. So then I wrote you a letter apologizing for my brother and mailed it to your house. Did you ever get that?"

"Yeah," I said. "But I . . . well, I didn't read it." Lauren had helped me turn it into confetti; we'd assumed it was only more taunting.

"And after that, we graduated, and I went to my mom's for the summer. Back then, Mom lived down in Corning." Otis rubbed the back of his neck.

"The one that got away," Effie said, almost purring.

I wasn't sure if she meant me or Otis. And I didn't know what to think. I mean, I believed Otis. Partly because I wanted to, but also because this story fit so much better with the Otis who had been my goofy pal in AP Chemistry. But heartbreak doesn't just heal instantaneously like a jacket zipping up. All the soreness I'd harbored for so long was still there . . . but now it was sort of dangling out there with no place to land. And the weirdest thing was, now that I couldn't bear a grudge against Otis, there was no reason for me *not* to have a big bad crush on him.

Which meant I was going to have to think of a new reason. Fast.

*   *   *

Scump wasn't one of the darling villages of upstate New York with big old houses, clapboard churches, huge trees, and cute downtowns. No, Scump was a tumbledown gas station/bait shop/used-truck dealership and, farther down the highway, a squat restaurant called The Moose Look, billowing sour smoke. A discount mattress emporium and an all-terrain vehicle dealership rounded out the offerings. They certainly liked their tubby tires in these parts.

"Take the first right after the gas station," Otis said. He was manning the map on my phone. "That should be Scump Pond Road."

"Okay," I said. I was feeling nervous. I'd had two hours to think over what Otis had told me. He suddenly seemed available to me in a way he hadn't before. And he was sitting *right next* to me, sending over faint whiffs of aftershave and waves of masculine self-assurance.

I believe the word *argh* sums it up pretty well.

"This?" I asked, turning onto a dirt road.

"I guess." Otis craned his neck. "I can't see a sign."

"Could be covered in all that growth, though." As we jostled up the rutted dirt road, branches scraped the sides of the car, and rocks clunked against the undercarriage. "Sorry," I said with a glance at Effie through the rearview mirror.

"Don't be. I'm enjoying every second of it. I can only hope that Paul will get to see his precious car when I'm through with it."

"Is Paul your—" Otis began. I shushed him with a dark glance.

We passed trailer homes and small houses sunk back into dank trees, each with an average of four vehicles parked out front and satellite dishes the size of hot tubs. After about half a mile, I spotted a rusted-out mailbox with a peeling American flag sticker and the number nineteen.

"I guess this is it." I turned down the driveway.

Nineteen Scump Pond Road was a long, narrow trailer home balanced on cinder blocks. A sofa rotted sideways into the weedy front yard. A battered station wagon was parked at the bottom of the steps. As I turned the engine off, I noticed one of the curtains twitch. I gulped, and it sounded deafening.

"You okay, Agnes?" Otis said.

"Sure. Except . . . people have guns."

We hadn't even mounted the steps when the door creaked open and a frail woman emerged. A tangle of clear tubes attached her to an oxygen tank on wheels.

"Whaddaya doin' on my property?" she yelled with surprising power.

"Ms. Roy?" I said.

"*Mrs.* Roy. Hate that miz crap. Earlene, everyone calls me."

Bingo.

"Whaddaya want? You city slickers lost?" Earlene wore baggy old jeans and a brand-new-looking sweat shirt that said *Proud to be an American.*

"We aren't exactly city slickers," I said. I mean, come *on.* I looked like a geeky PE teacher in my sweats and *Star Trek* shirt.

"Got yerself a nice Cadillac," Earlene said. "Least it's American-made."

"Yep, she's a real beauty," Otis said.

Earlene looked him over, the oxygen tubes at her nostrils glinting in the sun. "You look like a country boy."

"I am, Mrs. Roy." Otis tossed her his bright white smile.

"What the eff happened to your windshield?" Earlene asked.

"Oh," I said, "um, it was a little accident at the firing range. We were having a picnic . . ." I coughed. "We were wondering if we could talk with you for a minute."

"What about?"

"About Gracelyn Roy."

"Gracelyn?" Earlene's eyes widened.

"And Larlene."

At *Larlene,* Earlene's wasted body quivered. "You ain't cops. What are you?"

"Friends," I said.

A pause. "All right. Come on in, I guess."

Chapter 22

Inside Earlene Roy's trailer home, the odors of microwave burritos and rot mingled. Copies of *Soap Opera Digest* and dusty knickknacks cluttered surfaces. A huge flat-screen TV dominated the living area, switched off. Earlene gestured to a couch caving in with bottom-prints. Effie, Otis, and I sat in a row.

Earlene sat in a newer-looking La-Z-Boy recliner on the other side of the coffee table and tenderly arranged her oxygen tank and tubes. "Okay, shoot," she said.

I took the lead. "Did you know someone named Larlene Black?" I'd already guessed she did, but I wasn't prepared for her reply.

"'Course I knew her. She's my daughter."

My breath caught. "Your daughter?"

"Yep. My only child."

"Did you know she . . . died?"

"'Course. Saw it on the Channel Seven news. But seeing as I ain't laid eyes on that little snot for about thirty-five years, I can't say I feel too sad. You guys want some Crystal Light?"

"No, thanks," Effie, Otis, and I said in unison.

I said, "But Kathleen—that's what she changed her name to—"

"Yeah, I know," Earlene said.

"—well, she told people she grew up in an orphanage in Massachusetts."

"She would've *liked* growing up in an orphanage. Heck, she told me that about every day when she was a kid. A real Miss Priss she always was, acting like she was too good for me and her dad and the whole town of Scump. Called us trailer trash. As soon as she finished up at the high school, she took off. I never did see her again, but I heard about her, through our relations."

"Your last name is Roy," I said, "but Kathleen's—Larlene's—last name was Black?"

"Me and her dad weren't married."

Okay, that added up. "And Gracelyn Roy—she's a relation too?"

Earlene's withered lips curled up at the corners. "My niece."

Oh. My. Gawd. *Magnum, P.I.* had nothing on me. *Nothing.* "So Gracelyn and Kathleen were *cousins*?" This was freaking unbelievable. Somehow, not a single person in Naneda seemed to have caught on to this.

"Uh-huh. Did you know Gracelyn's got real famous?" Earlene pointed to a shelf where Gracelyn's several books were on display.

"Yeah," I said. "We've met her. She lives in Naneda where Kathleen, you must know, had been living for decades. Do you know why Kathleen and Gracelyn would have kept the fact that they were cousins a secret?"

"Nope," Earlene said. "They always did fight a whole lot when they was kids, though. Gracelyn always came out from Buffalo every summer for a couple months. Her dad, Mike—that's my brother—thought it would be good for Gracelyn to see to how

229

real folks live, seeing as she was growing up all spoiled out in Buffalo. Going to a fancy school with them uniforms and never playing outside. Ballet class and French lessons, that's what Mike and his snooty wife raised Grace up on."

"Wait," I said. "*Grace?*"

"That's her name. Gracelyn's the name she just cooked up for them books. To make her seem like real folks, you know? Mike's another one that took off from Scump soon as he could. Became a real fancy lawyer. Makes a ton of money. 'Course, he don't want to share any with his little sister, do he?" Something hard glimmered in Earlene's eyes. "He don't talk to me no more."

"But Gracelyn does?" I asked.

Earlene paused, her eyes drifting past us. Weighing her words. "Yeah," she finally said. "Gracie stops by and sees me every couple months. Makes sure I'm okay, what with all this stuff." Earlene gestured to the oxygen tubes and tank.

"Mrs. Roy," Effie said.

"Yeah?" Earlene looked Effie up and down. It was clear she didn't like the looks of her.

"Do you have any idea why Kathleen would have kept several boxes of your old magazines?"

"No idea what you're talking about."

"Old issues of *Good Housekeeping*, *Better Homes and Gardens*, that kind of thing," I said. "From the sixties."

"Addressed to me, now?"

"Yes."

"Oh, yeah. Those were Larlene's. She saved up her money from babysitting to subscribe to them stupid things. Do I look like I go in for all that Betty Crocker bull?"

"But they were addressed to you."

"Larlene was a kid. They probably wouldn't deliver to a kid's name. Hell if I know. But yeah, Larlene loved them magazines. She'd stare at 'em for hours. Started it up when she was only about ten. She'd ask me why our house didn't look like them pictures, how come we didn't have those meals with a meat and a vegetable and a bread all on one fancy plate, and *I* said, how the heck could I make our house and dinner look like a magazine when we were so poor and her dad was always giving me hell? Me and her dad used to fight like cats and dogs in them days, before he finally took off."

Huh. Sounded like the magazines were a sort of fantasy world for young Kathleen/Larlene, a domestic paradise where everyone was smiling, every appliance was shiny, and every napkin was freshly ironed. In fact, from what I knew of Kathleen/Larlene, she must've carried this fantasy of domestic perfection forward into her adult life. Her position as the historical society chairlady had given her the opportunity to treat the town of Naneda as her personal domestic fantasy land. No wonder nobody liked her. And the boxes of old magazines, well, I figured she must've kept them for nostalgic purposes. Maybe she had decided to donate them to the library when the mildew situation got out of control.

"Where is Larlene's dad now?" I asked.

"Dead. Snowmobile accident up in the Adirondacks. Good riddance, is what I said. Asshole."

"Have you ever met Kathleen's—I mean, Larlene's—daughters, Megan and Jodi?" I asked.

"Not in person, no," Earlene said, "but I did call Megan a couple times asking her for help with my medical expenses 'cause I heard she's got a rich doctor husband. Little snot hung up on me both times."

"Megan knew who you were?" Effie asked.

"Sure, 'cause I told her." Earlene cackled, and then the cackles turned into phlegmy coughs. Once the coughs had subsided, Earlene added, "I don't think Megan's mom filled her in on the truth about her past, so I did it."

"When was this?" I asked.

"Oh, sometime last fall, I guess."

"Did you tell Megan that Gracelyn is her aunt?"

"Yup. That sure was fun. I could tell Little Miss Perfect weren't too happy about *that*." Earlene cackled again. "Aw-right. My show's starting, so you're gonna have to leave."

I couldn't think of anything else to ask Earlene, even though my brain was buzzing with *what-ifs*. Otis, Effie, and I thanked Earlene and showed ourselves out. From behind us came the symphonic strains of a soap opera theme song.

* * *

We drove to The Moose Look since it was the only restaurant in town, and Otis and I were starving. Once I'd had several bites of the "moose special" biscuits and gravy, I was starting to think straight again. I was also trying really hard not to wonder if it was *moose meat* gravy. Admittedly, it was pretty tasty.

"Okay, so even though Gracelyn Roy's *dad* was originally a hick, she isn't really one," I said. "But she's pretending to be for the sake of her book brand. She certainly wouldn't be the first person to put on the folksy act to appeal to the masses."

"But why on earth were she and Kathleen pretending they didn't know each other?" Effie said. "Even after Kathleen was killed, no one made a peep about the two of them being cousins. In Naneda, that means no one knew."

"Gracelyn didn't attend Kathleen's funeral today either," I said. "She was gardening."

Otis said, "Maybe Gracelyn and Kathleen didn't recognize each other after all these years. It sounded like they hadn't seen each other since they were kids." He took a bite of his hamburger.

"That's possible," I said, "although I can't get over how Kathleen ripped down Gracelyn's poster at the library. We're talking Tyrannosaurus rex levels of fury. If Kathleen didn't know she was her cousin, she hated her for *some* reason."

"But the simplest explanation is always the best," Effie said.

"And what's the simplest explanation?" I asked.

"That Kathleen *did* know Gracelyn was her cousin—she had kept her name almost the same, yes? Grace Roy. Grace*lyn* Roy. How could Kathleen *not* have guessed?"

"And how come they hated each other?" Otis said. "Childhood feud?"

"Because Kathleen had spent years pretending that she'd grown up in an orphanage and that she was a pillar of the community, looking down her nose at everyone," Effie said, "but in reality, she was from a trailer home in backwoods Scump."

"Kathleen would've been afraid of losing her social power if people found out about her background," Otis said. "She was a snob, and she probably assumed everyone else in town held the same views." He wiped his lips and pushed his plate away. He'd polished off the burger, but several perfectly good fries still languished on his plate. I simply do not understand people who can leave fries on their plate.

"Want some fries?" Otis nudged his plate in my direction.

"What? *No*," I said. "So here's a theory: Kathleen knew that Gracelyn was a fraud, hick-wise, which would have threatened her blooming empire. She's got all those books out, and she's in talks with a television network for her own show. I'd guess that a *ton* of money is at stake for Gracelyn, and if her fans found out she was really from a well-to-do family and had gone to private school and had taken ballet and French lessons, well, they might turn their backs on her."

"So Kathleen threatened to expose Gracelyn?" Effie said. "Prompting Gracelyn to turn around and *murder* her?"

"Why not?" I said.

"But if Gracelyn has so much at stake," Effie said, "why didn't she simply stay away from Naneda? Why would she move to a town where someone knew about her past? It doesn't make sense."

"The only thing I can think of is blackmail," I said. I took a deep breath. "Okay, Gracelyn Roy, prime suspect. I want to talk to Megan and find out more about her mom and aunt's relationship. I'll call Megan from the car on our way back."

"What about the drugs and Club Xenon?" Otis asked.

"Still not sure," I said.

* * *

Otis drove, and Effie smoked in the back seat. I dialed Megan's cell phone. Luckily, I'd gotten her number when we'd visited her.

"Hello?" Megan said in a snippy voice. Gentle hubbub in the background.

"Hi, Megan, this is Agnes Blythe—we met yesterday when my aunt and I stopped by to ask about the break-in at your—"

"How *dare* you call me!" Megan whispered hotly. "I'm at my mother's goddam *wake*, and you call me to do more of your snooping? I reported your lies to the mayor, by the way."

"Yeah," I said. "He told me."

"Did he ground you? Because I heard you're living at home. You know, Agnes, when *I* was twenty-eight—you're twenty-eight, aren't you?—I was happily married, and I think that's when I bought my house. It must be tough to be such a loser."

Okaaaay. Megan was *ultra*–ticked off. I was pretty sure I knew why too. "I guess you found out today from the lawyer that your mom was planning on disinheriting you, huh, Megan? Lucky break that she kicked it before she signed that will."

"You *little*—"

"Or are you upset about Bud and his heart attack?" If I could provoke Megan into blowing a gasket, maybe she'd spew a clue in the process. "Because I know that he was your lover, Megan, and that you gave him your husband's prescription pads. What about the Rolodex? Did you give that to Bud too?"

Dead silence on the other end. Then Megan whispered scratchily, "You know about the Rolodex? Never mind—let's talk about this in person. Just you and me. Now isn't a good time. Half the town showed up for Mom's wake. Bunch of nosey parkers."

"Name your time," I said.

"Ten o'clock tonight. My house."

I glanced at the dashboard clock. Pushing six. I could make it. "Ten o'clock," I said and punched *end call.*

"Whoa," Otis said admiringly.

"Good work, Agnes," Effie said, lighting up another ciggie in the back seat.

"Didn't the sight of Earlene Roy and her oxygen tank spook you even a little?" I asked her.

Effie spouted smoke. "I'm supposedly seventy-two, darling. Do you really think I'm going to stop now? God, I think *stopping* would kill me."

235

"Quite the spokesperson for the American Lung Association, aren't you?" I said.

Otis had to check up on things at work, and after that, he had an unbreakable date to play gin rummy with his grandma, so he wouldn't be tagging along on the rendezvous with Megan. We dropped him off at Hatch Automotive.

I was relieved to see him go, because I needed some time away from him and his smiling brown eyes and his arm muscles—how could they look that *solid*, by the way? Did he lift weights, or was all that toned tanned goodness from hefting around engine parts and . . .

Focus. Okay, essentially, it was too soon after my breakup to think about tearing off another guy's clothes. Not that I'd ever actually *torn off* Roger's clothes. He was the sock-folding type.

Chapter 23

In lieu of returning to Dad's, I helped Chester at the inn for a few hours and ate Thai takeout by LED lantern light in the inn's kitchen. When Effie and I pulled up in front of Megan's house a few minutes before ten, her black Range Rover was in the driveway. No lights shone onto the dark lawn. No one answered the doorbell.

A dog yapped behind the house.

"That must be Megan's Maltipoo," I said.

The dog kept yapping.

"Maybe Megan is in the backyard and didn't hear the door-bell," Effie said. "We *are* a little early."

"Okay, let's check."

We took the flagstone path that led alongside the house to the backyard.

More yapping.

"The dog is inside," Effie said.

Low lights shone inside. The Maltipoo boinged back and forth behind the French doors.

"Um . . . he's not wagging his tail," I said. My mouth went sticky.

"Why would he? He wanted to tear our throats out when we saw him before, darling."

"Yeah, but . . ." I'd had a lab mix as a child, so I recognized the shrill alarm in the dog's bark. We crossed the patio. "My feet feel like cement."

"It's only those sneakers you're wearing."

"That dog is upset about something."

"Perhaps about the two intruders in the backyard?"

I cupped my hands and peered through one of the French doors. Inside, the oven hood light was on, and all those white cabinets and slabs of Carrera marble seemed to glow.

"*Omigod*," I whispered. "Megan's on the floor!" Megan made a sad little heap of bathrobe and blonde hair over by the sink. I rattled the door handle. Locked.

Effie tried another handle. The alarm system beeped once as the door opened. Disarmed, thank goodness. We dashed inside.

I threw myself on the floor beside Megan. As soon as I saw her face, I knew we were too late. One cheek squashed against the floor, mouth open. Her skin was ashen, and her eyes stared.

"Looks like another heart attack," Effie said, "but surely Megan couldn't have had a *heart attack*. All that yoga—"

"Call the police!" I tried to shout. It came out like an Alpine yodel.

Effie rummaged in her handbag. "Oh God. Oh God. Oh God. Where the hell is my Xanax?"

"Get your *phone*!" I shouted. I managed to scoot away from Megan.

Effie found her phone and called 9-1-1. While she was explaining herself in faltering tones to the dispatcher, my eyes fell on the marble island. Plastic-wrapped plates of cookies and brownies and foil-covered casseroles cluttered the island. I guessed that people had given all that food to Megan, the way people often give food to mourners. Only one dish had been opened, a gooey, cheesy macaroni casserole with a few servings sloppily carved from one side. I went over to the dishwasher and peeked in. The only thing in there was a cheese-globbed fork. Megan had eaten the macaroni straight out of the casserole dish.

Effie hung up. "The police and ambulance are on their way."

"I think that casserole is poisoned." I chewed the hangnail on my thumb. At least if Megan had been murdered with a casserole, the murderer wasn't, say, in the house *this very second*.

"It's called *carbs*, but the effects aren't that instantaneous. *Kidding*." Effie started digging in her purse again. I was about to yell at her for being too nonchalant about the whole thing, but she suddenly looked as frail as a wet sparrow. She found a prescription pill bottle, uncapped it, and popped a pill. She held up the bottle. "Want one?"

"No, thanks." I glanced around the kitchen. "Do you see the Rolodex anywhere?"

"No, I don't, but let's have a quick look." Effie started yanking open drawers. Sirens keened in the distance.

I went over to the built-in home office. It was organized with color-coordinated sticky pads, folders, and pushpins. No Rolodex on the desk. I checked all the drawers and shelves. No Rolodex. I checked inside the kitchen cupboards. Perfectly organized pantry items and white dishes. No Rolodex.

"I'm kind of creeped out about searching the rest of the house," I said, hesitating in the doorway that led to the dining room.

Sirens wailed closer and closer.

"It's too late, anyway," Effie said. "You don't want the police to catch you searching the house."

"Oh, crud," I said.

"What?"

"We've left fingerprints all over this kitchen!"

"Calm down. The police already know we've been here."

"Yeah, but not opening *every single drawer and cupboard.* They'll know we were searching for something." My upper lip broke out into a sweat.

"Oh. I see your point. I'm going out for a cigarette."

I followed Effie outside. We stood on the patio, Effie smoking and me chewing my hangnail, and that's how we were when the police and paramedics arrived.

A burly policewoman told us that we were going to have to go to the station to make statements. She corralled us into the back of a squad car and locked us in.

"Is this really happening?" I said. I massaged my temples. Dead bodies were piling up. I was locked in the back of a police car with my great-aunt. And I could *not* make my brain stop trying to solve this puzzle. Maybe popping Xanax *was* a good idea; Aunt Effie was at that point as cool as a cucumber.

"I loathe the smell of those little dangly tree things," Effie said. "Air fresheners, they call them. They're little polluters!" She fished a lipstick and a compact out of her handbag.

There was no way that, when Effie and I went to prison, we would have to share a cell, right?

"Wait a second." I sat up straight. "When I called Megan, she was at the wake, and she mentioned the Rolodex. She literally said *Rolodex.*"

"Your point?" Effie smeared on lipstick.

"My *point* is that someone at the wake overheard her making plans to meet us and discuss the Rolodex, and this someone got Megan to eat the poisoned casserole before we could talk to her. This is all about the Rolodex!"

"Fewer than twenty-four hours ago, you swore that this was all about drugs, Agnes."

"I know, but maybe the Rolodex has, I don't know, the names and phone numbers of drug customers."

"Bud is dead. Megan is dead. We don't know of anyone else involved in drugs except Jentry and Gothboy." Effie popped the cap back on her lipstick. "Honestly, it's a bit bizarre, because Megan didn't look like she *ever* ate carbs, let alone macaroni casseroles."

"Her mom and her lover were murdered," I said. "If it was me, I'd be eating entire pans of sticky buns."

"Well, you are a Blythe."

"You know, it makes me think that whoever gave Megan the casserole *knew* that she couldn't resist—*specifically*—a cheesy macaroni casserole."

"Which would suggest it was given to her by someone who knew her well."

"*Really* well."

"Like her sister, Jodi."

"Yeah."

And around and around we went. *Crud.*

*   *   *

"I'm not going to lie," Detective Albright said to me in the police station interrogation room hours later. "It's not looking good for you and Mrs. Winters. This is the second body you've just happened to stumble upon."

241

"Uh-huh," I said. "The second one." I guess the cops still had no clue that we'd *also* stumbled upon Bud's corpse.

"Why were you at Megan's house this evening?"

Effie and I had agreed to stick to the same fib I told Dad. And speaking of Dad, he was going to be really upset that I didn't have a lawyer present at this interview. Yes, Albright was grilling me, but if I had a lawyer present, *I* couldn't grill *Albright.* "Well," I said, "my great-aunt wants to be the next historical society chairman, and we had arranged to meet with Megan to talk about the society and the kinds of improvements she'd like to see in the organization."

"On the evening of her mother's funeral? At ten PM?"

"It was her idea."

"I think you were snooping," Albright said. "People have been telling me how you and your great-aunt are driving around in a car with a duct-taped windshield, asking questions. What happened to that windshield, Agnes?"

"I think it was hit by a rock. What people?"

"Can't say."

Not good. I was losing control of the situation. I cleared my throat. "So how's the bowling?"

Albright's face lit up. Then it closed, suspicious. "Don't try your Mata Hari stuff on me, Ms. Blythe." His eyes drifted down to the *Star Trek* logo plastered across my bosom.

Well, okay. If Albright thought I was a Mata Hari, then I should work it, right? I leaned forward and tried to bat my eyelashes. I was so tired, I felt like a blinking iguana. "Was Megan Lawrence, um . . . murdered?"

Albright gazed into my eyes. "You know I can't tell you that."

"It *was* murder, wasn't it? Poison. I saw that macaroni casserole."

"Okay, okay. It's going to be in the newspaper tomorrow, anyway. Yes, Megan was most likely poisoned, and forensics say it looks like the same poison that was used on Bud Budzinski. They're running tests on the casserole."

My breath caught. "Budzinski was *poisoned*? I thought—I mean I *heard*—that he had a heart attack." Those Oreos on Bud's desk. Had they been poisoned?

"Everyone thought it was a heart attack at first. But considering that the screen in the office where he was found had been slashed and that Kathleen Todd was murdered, Budzinski's body went straight to autopsy. He was poisoned with aconite."

"What's that?"

"A garden plant. Has a few different names. Monkshood?"

"I've heard of it."

"It grows wild, too, but not around here."

"So someone fed a flower to Budzinski?"

"All parts of the plants are toxic, especially the roots. Budzinski had chocolate sandwich cookies in his stomach, and fresh monkshood root was found in there too. But look at what you've done to me." Albright straightened his thick glasses. "Using your feminine wiles to get me to spill the beans."

"If you really think Aunt Effie and I are the murderers, I'd already know all this."

"You know I don't want you to be arrested, Agnes—I mean, Ms. Blythe." Albright's voice was husky.

"Isn't this sort of . . . inappropriate?"

"Come on, Agnes. I think we both know what you've been doing, showing up here in your cute little outfits. You ought to lie low. Stay home. Catch up on your television—there's a *Doctor Who* marathon tomorrow. The bowling alley's another wholesome place to spend time."

243

"Right," I said. "The bowling alley. Well, is there anything else?"

"No."

I stood.

"Oh. Wait. Yeah. Police chief wants you and your aunt fingerprinted."

"Fingerprinted?" *Uh-oh.* Once they had our fingerprints, they would match them to the *one million* fingerprints Effie and I had left in Bud's office and Megan's kitchen. As in, they'd know we'd (1) been in Bud's office and (2) been searching for something at Megan's. "Sure," I said in a tight voice. "I'm happy to give you my fingerprints."

* * *

After getting fingerprinted, I looked around the police station for Effie. Even though it was after midnight, a lot of people were milling around. I could practically smell the tension mixed in with stale coffee. But no Aunt Effie. She wasn't in the parking lot either, although I hadn't expected that since we'd arrived at the station by squad car.

I set off down the sidewalk. Dad's house was only six blocks away. A deep, rustling hush held the town close, and houses were dark and snug. Never had Naneda felt so creepy. Three people had been murdered—*three*. Somewhere out there, the murderer might be plotting even more deaths.

I dialed Effie.

"Did you offer up your fingerprints?" she asked.

"Yup. You?"

"I had no choice, and the ink absolutely *ruined* my mani."

"You realize that once they match our prints to all the ones we left in Bud's office and Megan's kitchen, they're going to arrest us?"

"Oh, yes. I expect it'll be sometime tomorrow."

"Where are you?"

"In bed at the inn, actually, and I've already taken my sleeping pill, and the sound machine is on."

"I thought I heard whales. Pepper spray handy?"

"Naturally. And my handbag with the metal studs."

"Well, good night, then. I'll come over first thing in the morning. We're running out of time to figure this thing out."

When I reached Dad's house, lights burned in the kitchen. *Great.*

Dad and Cordelia were waiting in the breakfast nook, both in bathrobes.

"I've been worried sick about you, Agnes," Dad said. "I just got a call that you were taken to the police station again? You discovered Megan Lawrence's body? You let the police question you again without counsel present? You could be getting yourself into some serious hot water."

"Uh-huh," I said. I got down a glass and filled it at the sink. I gulped down the entire glass and refilled it. "This town's going to the dogs."

"I *told* you she's not taking it seriously," Cordelia stage-whispered to Dad.

"Yes, I am," I said. I polished off the second glass of water. "I'm taking it *very* seriously."

Cordelia pursed her lips. "If you *were*, Agnes, you'd sit tight at home until it all blows over instead of running around with your crazy aunt and getting into trouble. What is it with you two? You're like a couple of teenagers—"

"*Cordy.*" Dad shushed her with a hand and turned to me. "Agnes, I'm just . . . worried."

"*Tell* her, Gary," Cordelia said.

"Tell me what?" I asked.

Dad looked green. "The house was broken into today."

"*What?*"

"I came home from the supermarket this afternoon to find the place just *ransacked*," Cordelia said. She blotted tears with a Kleenex. "Drawers had been pulled out in the kitchen and your father's study, and all the closets had been searched. Your room in particular, Agnes, had been *thoroughly* gone over." This was said in an accusing voice.

My thoughts flew to yesterday, when the security system had been tripped during my nap. That hadn't been the wind after all. The murderer thought *I* had something.

"Was anything stolen?" I asked.

"Nothing that we noticed," Dad said.

"How did they get past the security system?"

"You didn't set it!" Cordelia shrilled.

Oops. "Did you file a police report?"

"Of course. And it took me *hours* to set the place to rights again," Cordelia said. "This is all because of you and Euphemia, Agnes! You two are meddling, and it's just stirring up trouble. Do you know what the FedEx man told me today? He told me that he thinks Euphemia is *living* at the inn! Is that true?"

I cleared my throat. "Oh. *What?* Um, no, of course not. She's staying at a bed and breakfast somewhere over by Skaneateles, I think she said."

"She's *lying*, Gary," Cordelia said to Dad in an undertone. "She's always been a terrible liar."

Dad's eye bags drooped lower than ever.

Yes. I am a sucky daughter. And I was about to be even suckier. "Dad," I said, "were you at Kathleen Todd's funeral today?"

Cordelia threw her hands up. "Here she goes with the snooping again!"

"Why do you ask, Agnes?" Dad said.

"Was Kathleen's daughter Jodi there?"

"Yes, of course."

"What about Jodi's boyfriend, Jentry?"

"I'm not sure I'd recognize him."

I racked my brains. "What about Susie Pak?"

"Susie Pak was there, yes—"

"Dorrie Tucker?"

"Yes."

"Roland Pascal, the French carpenter guy?"

"Yes—but Agnes, I know what you're doing. You're playing detective with Aunt Effie."

"The *whole town* knows it," Cordelia said in an acid voice.

"This town is like the primitive villages I read about in my anthropology courses," I said. "Gossip, witch-hunts, feuds, and clans. It's just human nature."

"Agnes," Dad said, "I'm going to call Mr. Grimaldi the criminal defense lawyer in the mor—"

"Dad, no," I cried. I squeezed my eyes shut, took a deep breath, and opened them again. "I am so, so sorry I am upsetting you, Dad, and making you worried, and, let's face it, humiliating you and ruining the family name. But I have nothing to hide." That was seventy-five percent true. "Hiring a lawyer would cause an uproar in town. It will make me look *guilty*."

"That's better than going to prison, Agnes."

"Listen, Dad, there is *no way* I am going to prison." I wished I was as sure as I sounded.

"Well, I can't do anything without your consent, that's for sure," Dad said. "You're an adult. But I do think you're making a grave mistake."

"Stop worrying so much. This is all going to be cleared up before we know it. Good night."

I went upstairs. My room was as tidy as ever. No sign that it had been ransacked by a homicidal intruder.

And by the way, I was growing increasingly suspicious that this homicidal intruder was Jentry. We hadn't seen or heard from him since our run-in at Club Xenon. No way would he just call it quits—Aunt Effie's threats notwithstanding. Jentry was out there somewhere, and he was up to something. I felt it in my gut. And *no*, it wasn't the moose special I'd eaten for lunch, but thanks for asking.

Just as I was plugging my phone into its charger, I got a text from Otis: *I heard Megan L was killed? Are you OK? Please let me know. Worried.* I texted him back: *I'm OK. Yes, Megan L is dead. Poisoned.* Otis wrote, *Holy cow. Need help?* Me: *I'm fine.* Otis: *OK, well let me know if you need anything. Promise?* I stared at that last text for a while. What was happening here? How had things gotten so . . . intimate with Otis all of a sudden? And was it really a problem? Before I could stop myself, I texted *Promise.*

I showered, got into my pajamas, and crawled into bed. And let me tell you, I slept *so well.* Was there something wrong with me? I mean, there I was tripping over dead bodies left and right, about to be fingerprint-matched to three crime scenes, in a house that had been broken into and trashed only hours earlier, and lying to my poor Dad—yet I slept like a freaking baby.

Maybe Roger was right. Maybe there was something to be said for being adventurous.

Chapter 24

In the morning, I texted Chester in time to get a ride with him to the inn. He had stopped at Flour Girl for a white paper bag bursting with baked goods and three giant to-go coffees. The coffee was a very good thing because Cordelia hadn't left any muffins out for me in Dad's kitchen, and she'd washed the coffee carafe. I'd had no choice but to eat one of the carrot cupcakes I had found in the fridge.

I sat down across the inn's kitchen table from Effie. Chester left for whichever room he was currently rewiring. With the demolition scheduled for tomorrow, I had pretty much given up on the inn being saved. I didn't say this to Effie, though. I saw the slightly bonkers gleam of hope in her eyes.

"Okay, we've got to figure out who the murderer is ASAP," I said. "I'm expecting the police to show up any minute to arrest us."

Effie sipped coffee placidly. "I took especial care with contouring my makeup. There will be the mug shots, you know, and I refuse to look haggard like the last time."

I choked on coffee. "You've had your mug shot taken before? No. Never mind. I don't want to know." I took out a pen and our original list of suspects. I crossed off Bud since he had kicked it:

~~Bud Budzinski~~
Gracelyn Roy
Dorrie Tucker
Jodi Todd
Roland Pascal
Susie Pak

"We can't eliminate anyone but Bud, can we?" I said. "This sucks. We need to write down everything we know *for sure* is true about the murderer."

Twenty minutes later, Effie had smoked two cigarettes, and I had downed an apple Danish, a cruller, and enough coffee to fuel Air Force One. We had exactly four items on our list, and nothing was for sure.

1. Murderer was prob. at the wake and overheard Megan talking to me.
2. Murderer wants Rolodex, since that was only concrete thing mentioned by Megan in conversation.
3. The murder isn't about Megan and Jodi's inheritance, b/c Bud also murdered.
4. Murderer knows about monkshood/had access to monkshood.

"Okay," I said, chewing the pen. "First of all, Dad was at Kathleen's wake yesterday, and he told me Jodi was there, and so were Susie Pak, Dorrie Tucker, and Roland Pascal. Dad wasn't sure about Jentry. Also, if the Rolodex is at issue, who do we know was interested in the Rolodex? Dorrie Tucker, for one—remember, she asked Detective Albright about it."

Effie tapped ash. "Susie Pak seemed to be looking for something when she came around here."

"Then there are all the break-ins. I keep thinking those were Jentry—" My phone buzzed.

Cordelia had sent me a text: *Police are here looking for you. Are you at the inn?*

I stood, stuffing my phone, the paper and pen, an almond croissant, and an apple Danish into my backpack. "We've got to go," I said. "The police may be heading over here as we speak."

"You want to go on the lam?"

"No. But I do want to buy a little more time to crack this case before we get tossed in the clink."

Effie was on her feet too.

*   *   *

We didn't see the cops as we pulled out of the inn driveway and onto Main Street. "Where to?" Effie asked.

"The only thing I can think of—not that I'm thinking too clearly—is to take a look in every suspect's yard and see if we can find monkshood growing anywhere."

"Jodi was growing flowers out at Shakti Organic Farm, I seem to recall—but let's go to the McGrundell Mansion first, since it's the closest."

"Roland Pascal, a green thumb?"

"I am simply being *efficient*."

"Okay," I said. I knew Aunt Effie was scared to go to the farm, but I couldn't exactly complain since *I* was scared too. I pulled up a picture of monkshood on my phone. Tall stalks supported clusters of helmet-shaped purple flowers. The leaves reminded me of carrot greens. "These should be easy to spot."

Effie parked across the street from the McGrundell Mansion, and we got out. Roland was nowhere to be seen, but his Airstream trailer and pickup were out front.

"Look," Effie said. "The trailer is hitched to the pickup. Maybe he's planning on leaving."

"Well, the outside of the mansion looks amazing," I said.

We circled around the side of the mansion. Tinny radio music emanated from somewhere inside. "He's here," I whispered.

"Oh, good," Effie whispered back. "I'd adore a glass of wine."

"*Focus!*"

We reached the back garden. Geometrical shrubs framed luxuriant late-blooming flower beds. I inspected every purple flower, but none of them looked like monkshood.

"Let's go," I said.

We'd made it into the Cadillac when Roland burst out the mansion's front door in paint-spattered coveralls. "Pardon me!" he called. "Ladies! For what do you snoop?"

"*Go,*" I whispered to Effie.

She hit the gas so hard that I almost banged my forehead on the dash.

Next we headed over to Third Street to check out Gracelyn Roy and Dorrie Tucker's gardens.

"Uh-oh," I said. "Don't stop—there's a police car." A squad car idled in front of Gracelyn's house, and two cops talked to each other on the sidewalk. I slumped low in my seat as we cruised past.

"Do you think they're going to arrest Gracelyn?" Effie asked.

"I think they want to arrest *us*." I looked in the side-view mirror. One of the cops was squinting after the Cadillac as we retreated down the block. He jotted something in his notebook before we rounded the corner.

Uh-oh.

"Now what?" Effie asked. "Jodi's farm?"

"I guess." The thought of returning to that farm made me pull out the squashed apple Danish from my backpack and take a huge bite. "No, Susie Pak first. Here—I looked up her address. Six-oh-two Maple Crescent."

We drove across town to a small subdivision of new homes. They were all beige, with baby trees and weed-free lawns. Susie's house was somehow the blandest house in her cul-de-sac. I could almost picture her vacuuming her front lawn. No white Mercedes SUV out front, but the two-car garage was closed.

"Is it possible Susie has a flower garden out back?" Effie said doubtfully, looking at Susie's empty front lawn. "I'd peg her as the artificial flower type."

"Anything is possible at this point."

We got out of the car and circled around the back. No flowers. No, nothing except Miracle-Gro-doused turf.

We returned to the Caddy and drove off. Just as we were turning onto the road leading to Jodi and Jentry's farm, my phone buzzed. I read the new text message. "Aunt Effie," I said, "remember we called Roland Pascal's references, and I left a message with a lady named Valerie Rose in Vermont? Well, she just texted me and said to call her back and that it's important."

"Well, what are you waiting for?" Effie said.

A siren screamed behind us. Effie started, veered, and straightened out. I swiveled in my seat. "They're right behind us," I said. "Pull over! *Please* pull over. I can't deal with a car chase with the cops."

That was it, then. It was all over. So frustrating!

Effie pulled over next to a field and switched off the engine. The police car parked behind us, and two chubby cops emerged. They were the same two we'd seen in front of Dorrie and Gracelyn's earlier. Effie buzzed her window down.

"Euphemia Winters?" one of the officers said, stooping to look in Effie's window. He definitely needed to go up a size or two in his uniform. Not that I should talk.

"Yes?" Effie said.

"Would you get out of the vehicle, ma'am?"

Effie unbuckled and got out. The cop pulled handcuffs from his back pocket.

"Boys," Effie said, taking a step back, "what ever happened to foreplay?"

"Hardy-har-har," the other cop said. "Mrs. Winters, you're under arrest for auto theft, grand larceny in the fourth degree." He recited the Miranda warning, which was surreal since I'd only ever heard it at the movies and on TV.

Effie obediently stuck out her bony wrists, and the cop slapped the cuffs on.

"Take care of the car," Effie said to me.

"Oh, no," Moustache Cop said. "Car's getting towed to the station. Stolen property." He bent to look at me. "You're gonna have to get out, ma'am." He plucked the keys from the ignition.

I grabbed my backpack, got out, and watched as the cops led Effie to the squad car. She looked like a toothpick propped up by a couple of russet potatoes.

"Aunt Effie, I'm going to call Dad," I yelled. "You're not going to spend a single day in jail." My voice died away. Because I had no clue what Effie had actually done down in Florida. Had she murdered that guy Paul? Did she smuggle knockoff handbags? Had she embezzled millions of dollars from a retirement community? Anything seemed possible.

"Thank you, darling," she called. The cops helped her into the back of the squad car, and they rolled away.

I stood there for a minute with my mind wiped blank like a dry-erase board. Then I remembered the almond croissant in my backpack. I stood there eating it while cars and trucks whizzed by on the road. I didn't know what to do. Going to Jodi and Jentry's farm to look for monkshood was the obvious next step, although that was sounding like a too-stupid-to-live move at this point. But wait—I *did* have one other lead, one last fragile thread . . .

Valerie Rose in Caraway, Vermont. I'd totally forgotten that she'd texted.

I took out my phone and redialed the number from the text.

"Hello?" a woman said.

"Is this Valerie Rose?"

"Yes."

"I'm Agnes Blythe—the investigative reporter working on the piece about the Kathleen Todd murder?"

"Oh, yes. I was hoping you'd call." Valerie's voice grew urgent and husky. "Listen to me, I'm truly afraid that Roland Pascal had something to do with that murder."

"Really? Why?"

"Because he's a criminal."

The five-dots prison tattoo. I *knew* it. "Did you, um, want to speak to the police about this?"

"*No*. I can't—if my husband found out—well, the thing is, Roland and I had a bit of a fling—you won't publicize that, will you?"

"Of course not."

"Good. I'm worried, but I can't go to the police, or my husband will learn about my little . . . lapse. Roland did some work in my house, you see—my husband and I own a gorgeous old 1860s second empire that was sorely in need of some restoration on the interior moldings. They were already in bad shape, but just before I finally decided to hire Roland, they suffered some terrible water damage."

"Water damage?" My belly trout-flopped.

"Yes. From rainwater coming in around the chimney. Well, it turned out that Roland had ripped the flashing off while performing a so-called inspection on my roof."

"Why?"

"To *cause* the water damage! Because he was so determined to work on my house. Obsessed. It sounds odd, but he sort of *fell in love with* my house."

"Did you report this to the police?"

"Well, no, because Roland . . . Roland had—*has*, actually—a bit of leverage. You see, I didn't *realize* he had ripped off the flashing until I called in an exterminator about some squirrels in the attic, and by then, well . . . I've been working from home, and my husband was working in Asia, and Roland is so charming and talented. One thing led to another, and before I knew it, we were . . ."

"Got it."

"Don't tell a soul!"

"I won't. Promise."

"There's something else. Roland loves wine, and so sometimes, if his work was done for the day, he'd start drinking—and once he'd had too much, and he hinted that he'd served prison time in France."

"Did he say what for?"

"No, and when I tried to search for some kind of evidence on the Internet, I turned up nothing. Not, of course, that that means a damn thing. He could've changed his name. I terminated our fling right after he'd mentioned prison, of course. I can't have a drunken ex-convict in my bed—it cost a *fortune*, and two antiques dealers had to search for it for thirteen months."

"Thanks so much, Ms. Rose. I really appreciate the tip, and I'll be tight-lipped about your, um—"

"Lapse," Valerie said firmly.

"Your lapse." I hung up.

Hot pot of coffee. This was major. I was going to need help. I thumbed to my old text messages.

Otis: OK, well let me know if you need anything. Promise?

Me: Promise.

I took a deep breath and tapped out a message to Otis:

I need help.

I pushed *send*. Thirty seconds later, my phone rang.

"Agnes?" Otis said. "Are you okay? What's wrong?"

"I'm fine. Aunt Effie was just arrested, though."

"What happened?"

I told Otis how Aunt Effie's Cadillac was hot, and how I worried there were other things—criminal things—that she hadn't mentioned to me, and how Effie and I had both been fingerprinted last night so it was only a matter of time before I was arrested too. "But that's not what I need help with," I said.

"I'm listening."

"You know the carpenter, Roland Pascal?"

"Uh-huh."

"Well, it turns out he's probably an ex-con, he's a confirmed scam artist, and"—I swallowed hard—"and I want to confront him."

"Agnes—"

"Just listen, okay?" I hurriedly explained how Valerie Rose had gotten back to me and tipped me off about Roland's water damage racket. And you know, even though Roland was a scam artist and possibly a murderer, that somehow got back-burnered to my total and absolute *fury* that he had sneaked into the Stagecoach Inn and ripped off the flashing. It was *violating*. It was like he'd sneaked up behind me and given me an atomic wedgie.

"Water damage?" Otis said.

"Yeah. Water damage like the Stagecoach Inn suffered two nights ago. I've been thinking it was Jentry who broke into the inn and all those other houses—including my dad's house. But now I'm thinking it was Roland."

"Why?"

"To try to force Aunt Effie into hiring him to fix it. I don't know if this means he's a murderer, but he isn't looking like Mr. Law-Abiding at this point."

"Was there water damage at your dad's?"

"Not that I know of." On the other hand, I was thinking as straight as a plate of cooked spaghetti.

An engine's rumbling made me turn. A police tow truck pulled up in front of Effie's Cadillac and started doing that annoying backup beeping.

"What's that?" Otis asked.

"Tow truck."

"Wait—are you just standing on the side of the road? I'll come and get you. And you need to take what you've learned about Roland to the police. Confronting him would be, well, sort of impulsive."

"I am *going* to do it." Wow. I sounded just like Aunt Effie when I said that. "I need your help, Otis. I need a witness. And *then* I'll go to the police. Are you in, or are you out?"

"Tell me where you are. I'll be there as soon as I can."

Chapter 25

Fifteen minutes later, I was zipping along the highway on the back of Otis's motorcycle, clinging to him for dear life. He'd brought an extra helmet for me, and through the visor, I saw Naneda in a Claude Monet blur. We rumbled to a stop across the street from the McGrundell Mansion. I dismounted.

"You okay, Agnes?" Otis asked. "Dizzy?"

"A little." I passed him my helmet and hitched up my backpack. "Look. Roland's Airstream is . . . bouncing."

Otis removed his own helmet and looked. "Wow. Well, I'm pretty sure a bouncing trailer can only mean one thing. Maybe we should come back later."

"*No.* I don't have much time." I crossed the street and marched up to the Airstream's long rear window. I figured I'd peek inside and make sure Roland wasn't, say, dismembering a corpse with a power saw before I knocked on his door.

Otis joined me. Slowly, we lifted our eyes to the bottom edge of the window.

The ratty curtains were drawn, but a two-inch crack offered an ample view.

"Uuuuuh," Otis whispered, crouching. "I am *not* old enough to see that, and I never will be."

"Is that Roland's *back* that looks like a giant toupee?"

"Aw shucks, Agnes, you aren't into furry backs?"

I gave Otis a light kick.

"I couldn't see who the lady was," he whispered.

I peered through the window. "It's Gracelyn Roy . . . isn't it?" I couldn't tell, actually. Someone with a bra that looked like it had been designed by the Army Corps of Engineers. I didn't want to look any closer than that. I crouched down beside Otis. "Whoever Roland is with, this is a great opportunity. He's vulnerable, so I'm just going to knock on the door and point-blank demand some answers about the connection between his water damage scam, his prison time, and the murders."

"Agnes, I'm new to this detective stuff, but I'm pretty sure it's always a bad idea to confront murderers."

I scrambled to my feet. "I don't care." I circled around to the trailer door. A vehicle was cruising to a sloppy park a little way up the street, but I ignored it.

I pounded on the trailer door. The rustling noises inside intensified and then stopped. A pause. Stomping footsteps. The door cracked open. Unfortunately, I wasn't standing on a step stool, so I was eye-level with Roland's bushy belly. Luckily, he'd pulled on some boxer shorts.

All the same, *blech.*

"Hi," I said. "I've come to ask you about a couple things."

"Oh, yes? I have things to ask *you* as well, fair Agnes."

"You do?"

"For what were you snooping earlier today in the mansion's rear garden?"

"Oh. Um, monkshood."

"What is monkshood?"

"Don't pretend you don't know."

"But I do not."

"It's the poisonous flower that was used to murder Bud Budzinski and Megan Lawrence."

"They were poisoned?"

Roland truly seemed surprised. Never mind; I still had beef with him. "Listen, I know it was you who broke into the Stagecoach Inn and ripped off the flashing around the chimney, and let me tell you, I am *royally* ticked off about it! Did you know—" I didn't finish because Roland's eyes widened, looking at something behind me.

He muttered, "*Mon Dieu.*"

I turned.

Gracelyn Roy stood a few yards behind me, Annie the shotgun leveled at Roland.

Who the heck was the lady in the trailer, then?

"Agnes," Otis said slowly. "She's got a gun."

"*Duh.*"

"Move it," Gracelyn barked at me. "You're gonna mess up my aim."

Roland slammed the trailer door.

"Come out, you lying, cheating bastard!" Gracelyn screamed.

I couldn't move. I *wanted* to, and my pulse whirred like an egg beater. But I couldn't.

"Git on!" Gracelyn roared at me, making shooing motions with her shotgun. "I'm going to blast straight through that door."

"*Git on?*" I said. "Come on, *Grace*, we all know the hick routine is fake."

Her eyes slitted. "*What* did you say, missy?"

"You heard me. I know you grew up rich in Buffalo."

"Oh, who gives a damn?" Gracelyn said, ditching the hick accent. "I'm here to shoot Roland, so move out of my way."

"Can't," I said. "Frozen."

"All dressed up like a PE teacher and you can't move your butt an inch?" Gracelyn said. "*Typical* of this town."

Since I couldn't move, I decided to ask a few questions. "Why on earth did you move to Naneda, Gracelyn? The town where your own cousin lived—someone who could expose your secret?"

"Um, Agnes?" Otis said. "This probably isn't the best—"

"How do you know Kathleen was my cousin?" Gracelyn said. Now the shotgun was leveled at *me*.

"Just answer the question." Out of the corner of my eye, I saw Otis take out his phone. He'd be dialing 9-1-1.

"You want to know why I came to Naneda?" Gracelyn said. "I'll tell you why. To force Kathleen into paying for her mom's goddam medical expenses! Earlene didn't have any health insurance when she got emphysema, and she guilted *me* into paying the bills. What was I going to say? 'No, go ahead and die?' I've been paying for everything—treatments, home visits—I even paid off that depressing trailer she lives in because she somehow managed to take out a second mortgage on it."

Otis was speaking softly into his phone, but Gracelyn didn't notice. She was too wrapped up in her rant.

"Earlene's sucking me dry with no end in sight," she said. "So when I bumped into Megan at a charity event in Buffalo and realized she was Kathleen's daughter, I had a great idea. I'd move here, settle right in, and get Kathleen to take financial responsibility for Earlene."

"Did you threaten to blow up her Brooks Brothers image if she refused?" I said.

"Yep."

"That's blackmail."

"That's life. Now move it." Gracelyn yanked me aside by my backpack loop and flung open the trailer door.

Dorrie Tucker burst out, wide-eyed and clutching clothes to her chest.

Dorrie and Roland? Just . . . *wow.*

Dorrie squeezed past Gracelyn and me, whispering as she went, *"I heard what you're looking for, and Jodi Todd grows monkshood at her farm."* Then she ran off down the street. Her bottom bounced in high-waist granny undies.

Jodi *was* growing monkshood. Can you say *booyah*?

"Go on and run!" Gracelyn shouted after Dorrie. "I'm not going to shoot you! You're just another victim of his lies!"

"Agnes, come on." Otis took my hand and pulled me away from the trailer.

Roland burst from the trailer with keys in hand and jogged to the front of the pickup to which his trailer was hitched. He looked like an ape running across hot coals.

Gracelyn swung around and fired the shotgun.

Otis half carried, half dragged me through the trailer door. He landed heavily on top of me, just inside.

Another gunshot. The roar of the pickup's engine. We were moving.

"Get back here, you cheating dog!" Gracelyn screamed. Bullets clanged.

The trailer swayed like a whale's tail. Otis thumped off of me, and I rolled around on the filthy orange-and-dirt carpet until I got wedged under a built-in table. Dishes and books and all of Roland's assorted junk went flying everywhere. It was a junk blizzard.

Sirens whooped close by. Roland gassed the pickup.

Otis pulled himself up to see out the rear window. "The police aren't far behind," he said. "It looks like three squad cars. Oh, crud, it's going to be a chase."

"Maybe we should try to jump out," I said, still clinging to the table legs. "Who knows where Roland is going. He could go for miles!"

"Not if the cops have anything to say about it."

The trailer made a sweeping arc as we turned a corner. Otis went splatting on the floor.

Then we were gaining elevation, Roland devouring the dips and turns of the road like a NASCAR driver. On and on we went. Sirens wailed. I'd just decided that we were on the road that led out to Naneda Lake State Park when we did a sickening, wide swing. The trailer lifted onto two wheels, there was molar-shattering impact and screeching metal, and then . . . we stopped.

For a couple seconds, I couldn't move. My lungs made a sound like air leaking out of a tire.

Otis got up and staggered over to the trailer door. Outside, megaphones and sirens squawked. I struggled to my feet too and peered out the curtains. Cop cars were wedged all over the road. Was this the end?

Otis reached for the door handle.

"Wait," I said. "Don't."

"What?"

"Because . . ." I darted over to the windows on the other side of the trailer and looked out. The forest was *right there*, sloping up, and—I peered left and right—we *were* on the road leading to Naneda Lake State Park. We were no more than three miles from Jodi and Jentry's farm. I turned to Otis. "The police don't know we're in here, right? So why don't we just . . . sneak out the window? It looks like it'll crank wide open."

"Agnes, that's—"

"*Listen*, Otis. Please." In a mad scramble that probably made me sound like an escaped mental patient, I told Otis how Dorrie Tucker had whispered to me that Jodi grew monkshood on her farm. "If I walk out that trailer door, I have no doubt in my mind that I'll be leaving here in the back of a squad car. There is no way my fingerprints haven't been matched up to all three murder scenes by now, and who knows what Aunt Effie has confessed to in jail. I've *got* to go to that farm and see for myself if there really is monkshood growing there. I don't want to give up now—I'm *so close*. Can't you understand that? And if not, well"—I swallowed—"go, but don't tell the police I was in here."

Otis gave me a long look, like he was trying to decide whether I needed a straitjacket or a Wonder Woman headband. Outside, men's voices grew louder. "Okay," he said. "We'd better get going."

Otis pushed open the window, looked both ways, and hopped out feet first. I went next, and Otis took me by the waist to help me down. We were practically in the ditch. Right on the other side, thick forest undergrowth clustered. We leapt across the ditch and burrowed in. Branches scratched, leaves fwapped, and we came up for air in a little clearing. We looked back. Blue-and-red lights flashed through the branches, but no one was shouting.

We'd made it.

* * *

"Okay, which way to the farm?" Otis asked softly.

I looked around. "I'm pretty sure that's north," I said, pointing, "and Jodi's farm is to the northwest of the state park, which is back that way, so we need to follow along the side of this hill for a little while and then drop down into the valley."

"Wow. Were you a Girl Scout?"

"Maybe."

At first we crept through the dense hardwood forest with a lot of over-the-shoulder glances. Once we'd rounded a curve in the hillside, we started hiking in earnest, striding and swinging our arms. Dried leaves crunched underfoot, and yellow-and-orange foliage splotched the tree canopy.

"I feel like I'm getting away with something," I said.

Otis laughed. "You are. You're on the run from the police."

"Not *really*. With any luck, they'll never know we were in that trailer."

"What are you going to do if you see monkshood in Jodi's flower patch?"

"Photograph it and get the heck out. Then . . . start walking back to town, I guess." Naneda was miles and miles from Jodi's farm, and we both knew it. I glanced over at Otis. There he was, this frankly *beautiful* guy, trooping along through the forest with me. Evading the police. Heading for a pot farm where a possible murderer—or two—lived. And why? I had no idea. "Thanks, Otis," I said shyly.

"For what?"

"Come *on*. For what? I'm pretty sure you're risking arrest by sneaking away from that trailer with me, and we're headed for who knows what at the farm."

"We're friends, Agnes."

"Being friends back in high school doesn't oblige you to do crazy things for a person once you've reached the age of reason."

"We were friends," Otis said, climbing over a boulder ahead of me. He turned and reached out a hand. "Good friends. And we're still friends now."

I took his hand, big and warm, and he helped me over the boulder. As soon as I hopped to the ground, I slid my hand away. I didn't like the ideas that popped into my mind at his touch. Let's just say they probably wouldn't make the PG-13 cut.

We continued through the trees, side by side.

"You know, it's funny," Otis said. "All these years, with all the girlfriends I've had—"

"I suppose there have been a lot?" I blurted. *Argh.*

Otis scratched his ear. "I guess. I get along with women."

Yeah. With pecs like that, you get along with women all right.

"But with all the girlfriends I've had, I was always looking for that friendship." A pause. "You know, the friendship *we* had."

It took work to pry my tongue from the roof of my mouth. "Oh. Interesting. And did you find it?"

"Nope."

More tongue prying. "Oh." I concentrated on my orange sneakers going one in front of the other. I did *not* like the sound of what Otis was saying. Yes, hearing him talk about *us* made my heart squeeze, but . . . friendship? I mean, there I was fantasizing about pushing his T-shirt up to his armpits and nuzzling his belly button, and *he* was saying he missed being *friends* with me? Uh-uh. No. No more "friendship first" relationships for me. That's exactly what had gone so horribly wrong with Roger. No, I was going to hold out for a passionate relationship with a guy who was deliriously *in love with* me.

"Back in high school," Otis said, "I really, really liked you, Agnes."

Liked? *Liked?* "I liked you too," I said primly.

Otis looked confused, and the conversation petered out.

After about fifteen more minutes of walking, the forest opened out onto a vista of green-and-gold sloping fields and vineyards framed by stands of trees. In the distance, the long swathe of Naneda Lake glowed blue-bright.

I shaded my eyes from the afternoon sun and scanned the landscape to the northwest. "There," I said. "Down there—see that red barn? That's Jodi and Jentry's farm. We can cut straight across this field below us here, go through that cluster of trees, and then the next field after that is on their farm. But first, I kind of have to, um, use the restroom."

Otis grinned for the first time since our little "friendship" talk. "Me too. Meet you back here in three minutes."

We split up, did our business in the trees, convened, and set off down the steep field of tall grasses and flowers. "I hope I don't get a tick," I said. "This is tick grass."

"Too late in the season," Otis said. "You could lie down in this grass and roll around and be totally fine."

I walked a little faster. Rolling around in fields of grass was *not* something I needed to be discussing with Otis right then—with all due respect to Sting.

Chapter 26

Otis and I reached the bottom of the field, where a broken-down barbed wire fence gave way to trees. We picked through the barbed wire, through the trees, and stopped when we reached the other side. A cow-dotted pasture stretched before us and, beyond that, Jodi and Jentry's farm. Sunlight shimmered on the fruit orchard. Solar panels on the barn roof glinted.

"No vehicles parked in front of the farmhouse," I said. "That's a good sign. Maybe nobody's home. Okay. See the flower patch between the orchard and the rows of vegetables? That's where we're headed. I don't remember seeing flowers anywhere else on the property when Aunt Effie and I were here before, and I don't see any now."

"There are flowers growing in this field right here," Otis said.

True. I peered around. "Monkshood is purple—I don't see any purple. Do you?"

"Nope."

I pulled my phone from my backpack and checked the battery. Fourteen percent. That ought to do it. "Ready?"

"Ready."

We hunched down and hurried across the field. In the orchard, we picked around rotten fallen fruit. We reached the flower bed, where orange, pink, red, yellow, and white flowers tangled their leaves and stems together into one big buggy mass.

"Purple!" I whispered. "I see purple!" I waded through clinging stems to a tall stalk. My heart leapt to my throat. "Omigod. This is monkshood. It's *monkshood*!"

"I think someone's coming, Agnes," Otis whispered, crouching low. "Get down!"

"But I found monkshood!"

"*Get down.* Maybe he hasn't seen us."

I fell to my knees. "He?"

"Gothboy, over by the barn."

Gothboy? I could deal with him. Jentry was the one to avoid like a rat with hantavirus—Jentry and his Dobermans—which, come to think of it, I didn't hear barking. My fingers shook as I fumbled for my phone in my backpack. I dropped the phone, and it disappeared into the mesh of vegetation at my feet. Frantically, I patted around for it.

"Stop moving!" Otis whispered.

Somewhere off in the distance, I heard the gargle of an engine. Maybe—*please-oh-please*—it was out on the main road.

My fingers closed around my phone. I swiped it on, fumbled around to the camera app, and aimed it at the monkshood stalk. The sunlight was bright, and I got several good shots, including one with the red barn in the background. I stuffed the phone into my backpack, zipped it, slung it on my back, and started crawling toward Otis.

The engine noise crescendoed, then abruptly stopped. A door slammed, a man's voice said, "Sic 'em," and then two dogs were barking like they'd spotted giant T-bone steaks on legs.

I reached Otis. "The pasture," he whispered, eyes wide. "Hurry."

We crawled to the edge of the flower bed where it met the orchard.

Gothboy stood looking down at us, his black trench coat flowing back like a cape and his powdery-white face expressionless. He held a shovel aloft. He went for Otis first, whacking his beautiful head with the back of the shovel as I croaked, "*No!*"

Otis slumped face-first on dirt and rotten plums. The dogs were somewhere nearby, but I didn't see them; I only heard their shrill, snarling barks.

Gothboy came at me next, shovel high. I dove sideways and felt the breeze from the shovel first, opened my mouth to cry out, but blinding force at the back of my skull knocked everything dark and silent.

* * *

The first thing I was aware of was that my head felt like a giant, aching block of cement. The next thing I noticed was that my back was cold—so, so cold—and it was dark, and I couldn't really move, and my arms and legs were sort of bent and tangled like a baby horse's. Why was it so freaking cold? Where was I? Was this hell? Omigod—was this a *coffin*?

I tried to jerk my legs.

"Ow!" someone said really, really close by. "Careful."

"Otis?" I whispered. Our voices sounded smothered. "Where are we?"

"Inside a chest freezer."

Panic sizzled through me.

"Stay still!" Otis whispered. "Your knees are right on top of . . . me."

My knee wasn't the only thing on top of Otis; we were smushed together like gummy worms. He was on his back with his knees bent, his head forced forward by the side of the freezer. I'd been dumped sideways on top of him. My knees were—*oh Gawd*—nestled between his, er, *legs*, and my face was pressed into the crook of his neck, my glasses by some miracle still on. My right backpack strap was cutting off the circulation in my arm. Otis's warm breath on the side of my head would've been totally awkward under other circumstances, but in this case, it was reassuring. Especially with that deep, black, persistent cold enfolding us on all sides.

"Sorry," I mumbled against Otis's neck. "Let's get out of here."

"I think we're locked in."

"*What?*"

"I came to when Jentry and Gothboy dumped you on top of me, and right after that, they shut the lid, and it sounded like they locked it."

"How long ago was that?"

"Only a couple minutes."

I pushed at the lid just a few inches above me. Frost burned my fingertips; the lid didn't budge. "We're going to die in here!" I said. "We're going to freeze!"

"Suffocation is possibly more of an issue."

Okay. Okay. All I had to do was stop breathing. And stop thinking.

"Maybe there's a way to break the lock," Otis said. "Let me feel—could you move your back a little—yeah—and then—oof! That's my stomach!"

"Sorry," I whispered. "Is that better?"

"Yeah." Otis bumped and fumbled with something next to my head. Frost fell onto my scalp. "Crud," he said. "The latch is completely inside the wall of the freezer. There's nothing to work with."

"*What?*"

"Someone will come along, Agnes—"

"We might die!" Icy tears squeezed out of my eyes. I burrowed my face closer into Otis's neck. His skin was chilly, but he smelled good.

He wrapped his arms around me tight. "It's okay," he said into my hair.

"I want to tell you something, Otis," I mumbled in his ear. "I wasn't completely honest earlier. Yes, I liked you back in high school, but also . . . I was also in love with you." Our hearts thumped together for a few beats. My voice sank to a whisper. "I still am. I never stopped. I dreamed about you all the time. I wondered about you, even though I thought you'd—you know. With the sign on the locker."

Otis's arms tightened still more around me. "I would never do anything like that to you, Agnes. Never. Okay? And I—" Muffled noises outside the freezer made him fall silent. Voices. A door slamming.

Otis and I both started shouting and screaming and thumping with feet and fists on the freezer walls with all our strength. After about twenty seconds, the lid lifted, and someone stared down at us. I blinked painfully in the light.

"Oh, for frick's sake," a woman said. "Jentry's been at it again with his ridiculous commando games? When he gets back with the beer, I'm gonna tear him a new one."

"Jodi?" I said, pulling myself upright.

"Ow," Otis said underneath me.

Jodi narrowed. "The mayor's daughter. Somehow I'm not surprised. What were you doing here? Taking pictures of Jentry's pot? You're such a little snoop! You're sick! Where's your old battle-axe of an aunt?"

"Um. In jail," I said.

Jodi made a nasty smile.

I climbed out of the freezer. We were on the back porch of the farmhouse. Warm afternoon sunlight slanted through the trees, but my joints felt like chunks of ice.

"Wait," Jodi said, looking around me. "*Otis*?"

Otis climbed out of the freezer, teeth chattering. "Yeah?"

Jodi tossed her blonde dreads over her shoulder. "Don't you remember me? Jodi Todd? From Camp Ti-Ki-Rah? We were both counselors back in high school one summer."

"Um . . ." Otis brushed frost from his hair.

"My sister and I went to boarding school, but we were here in Naneda most summers—"

"Oh, yeah," Otis said. "Jodi. Now I remember. You were the craft counselor."

"And you were the lifeguard." Jodi raked her eyes down and up Otis. "God, I had *such* a crush on you."

Otis wrapped an arm around me. I felt him shivering. "I'd love to hang out and reminisce, Jodi," he said. "but your boyfriend almost killed us in this freezer, and we really need to get out of here."

"Say, Jodi," I said, "I happened to see that you're growing monkshood in your garden. Care to explain?"

"I grow all kinds of medicinal plants out there."

"Monkshood is medicinal?"

"Yes. I harvest it and sell the roots to a homeopathic drug manufacturer in Ohio."

"Okay, well how did Dorrie Tucker know you were growing it out here? She told me I'd find it, and I did."

"Dorrie Tucker? No idea. Maybe just a good guess—we've discussed growing medicinal plants before at the farmer's market. She's an avid gardener—"

"You don't put monkshood in the bouquets you sell at the farmer's market?"

"No way. That would be dangerous."

"What do you know about your mom's Rolodex?"

Jodi's eyes squinched. "How do you know about that?"

"Your sister Megan mentioned it to me, for starters, not long before she died. People are looking for that Rolodex, Jodi. The *murderer* is . . . and I can tell by the expression on your face that you know all about it."

Jodi bit her lower lip. "Yeah, okay, I know what's in that Rolodex—sort of. But why should I tell you?"

"You don't have to. You could tell the police—"

"No cops!" Jodi threw her hands up. "I don't want them coming around here or poking any more than they already have into my business. With all the crap Jentry gets mixed up in—I want my kid to have a dad, even if he's a bad dad, okay?" Jodi licked her lips. "And . . . if I tell the cops what's in the Rolodex, they might cook up some reason to arrest . . . *me*."

"Because you've been withholding evidence," I said.

"I guess."

"Mommy!" A little blond kid burst out of the kitchen door and pointed at me. "Mommy, that lady is on TV!"

Jodi, Otis, and I rushed inside.

An old television set droned on the kitchen counter. Bold letters on the bottom of the screen said *Manhunt*. A news lady from Rochester Shore 7 News was saying, "Police are uncertain whether or not Agnes Blythe is armed, but she is considered extremely dangerous. She is wanted for questioning regarding the three murders that have rocked sleepy Naneda in the past week. Here's one more look at the police composite sketch of Agnes Blythe." A black-and-white sketch flashed on the screen. Supposedly me, although honestly it looked like a cross between a hard-boiled egg and a Neanderthal with glasses. Great.

"Should we call the police, Mommy?" the little kid asked.

"Go play with your Legos, Aspen," Jodi said. Aspen scampered off.

Otis had my hand and was tugging me toward the back door. "We'd better go," he whispered in my ear.

"*Wait*," I whispered back. I swung to face Jodi. "Come on, tell me about the Rolodex," I said. "Give me a chance to solve this thing before it's too late."

"Why?" Jodi said. "You're nothing but an amateur snoop. You *should* be arrested—for being a pain in the ass."

"That's probably true. But I'm trying to figure out who killed *your* mom."

"Hated her."

"Okay, well"—I swept a hand around Jodi's kitchen with its stacks of canning jars, food dehydrator, and light fixture made out of deer antlers—"then help me out in the spirit of doing-it-yourself." I held my breath.

"Okay," Jodi said, shaking her head. "Fine. I'll tell you about the Rolodex. I never saw it in person, but my sister Megan did, and even though Megan and I didn't exactly get along, she told me about it last Christmas after she got totally plastered on eggnog martinis."

"Okay," I said. "And?" This was like trying to squeeze the last bit of ketchup from the bottle.

"Apparently Mom was collecting dirt on everyone in town—their secrets, you know—and keeping track of it in the Rolodex."

My mouth fell open. "Seriously? That's . . . awful."

"Mom *was* awful."

"What kind of secrets?" Otis asked.

"The usual stuff. Affairs, cheating on taxes . . . oh—here's some stuff I remember: Dr. Baxter, the electrical engineering professor, wrote all of his son's college application essays. That owner of the jewelry store downtown? He has a thing for boy bands. Oh—and you know Penny Jean Spence?"

"Scariest church lady in town?" Otis said.

"Yeah—*she* has a secret stash of naughty nighties."

"How did your mom know all this stuff?" I asked. "It's so . . . *private.*"

"Mom had ways of twisting people's arms," Jodi said. "She was so manipulative. When I was, like, sixteen, she read some love notes I'd gotten from this cute guy who raked the leaves at my boarding school in New Hampshire, and she used them to force me to get Dad to buy her a diamond tennis bracelet. She was screwed up."

"That sounds like . . . blackmail," I said. Lots of people had commented on how Kathleen had had a way of getting people to do what she wanted, even though she was not well liked. Then I made the most glorious deduction *ever*: The reason Karl Knudsen the code-compliance officer had done Kathleen's bidding and set the demolition date for the Stagecoach Inn was because Kathleen must've known he was stalking his ex-wife. Kathleen must have *blackmailed* Karl into bumping up the demolition date.

"By the way," Jodi said, "how do you know *I'm* not the murderer?"

"Because if you were, you would've left us in the freezer until we were blocks of ice."

"Fair enough."

"Honestly, though, I have my suspicions about Jentry," I said.

Jodi laughed. "Jentry? He doesn't have it in him to kill anybody."

"He *did* lock us in your freezer," Otis said. "You know, to be fair and all."

"He's just messing around," Jodi said. "Come on. Jentry's going to be back any minute with the beer. I'll tell him you guys escaped all by yourselves." She picked up car keys from the counter and yelled, "Aspen! Come on!"

* * *

Once we were bumping down the farm's driveway in Jodi's battered Volvo, Jodi said, "If I say get down, *get down*. Cops are going to be out looking for you. Now where to?"

Otis and I were in the back on either side of Aspen in his booster seat. A plan was taking shape in my mind, but I needed time. Time, and a place to hide for a few hours. "I'm not sure," I said. "Your place, Otis?" I didn't even know where he lived. Weird, considering—*gulp*—I'd told him I was in love with him. To which he *hadn't responded*.

"No, the cops might look for you there," Otis said. "Let's go to my grandma's. She'll be at the county fair for the next couple hours, and I have a key."

Chapter 27

Otis gave Jodi directions to his grandma's house, which was on the edge of the historical district. We got there without any police sightings, thanked Jodi, and waved bye-bye to Aspen. We went in through the kitchen door.

Inside, Otis's grandma's house was like a museum of doilies and hard candies in crystal dishes. It felt snug and safe.

"Hungry?" Otis asked, going to the fridge.

"Yeah. Starving, actually."

Otis took out Wonder Bread, peanut butter, and a jar of marshmallow fluff and made us sandwiches.

"I'm pretty sure the murderer has been killing to get their hands on that Rolodex," I said, "so . . . I have a plan. If I pretend to have the Rolodex, I can sort of lure the murderer out."

"How?"

"We can spread the word around town that I have the Rolodex—"

"A rumor?"

"Exactly. This town is a total rumor mill, so why not make that work for us? Once the murderer hears I have the Rolodex, they might get in touch with me, or try to find me or, well, or *something*. They might show their face."

"That sounds very dangerous."

"I don't care. I'm seeing this through to the end. I'm about to be arrested, and once that happens, I have no idea what the police will or will not believe out of all this stuff I've figured out. Detective Albright suspects I'm guilty, and Police Chief Gwozdek hates Aunt Effie. They might let the murderer get away with it! Anyway, my plan might not even work. If Gracelyn was arrested for shooting at Roland's trailer and she's the murderer, this isn't going to work. If Roland is the murderer, it's not going to work either, since he will have been arrested for evading the police by now."

Otis, leaning on the counter, rubbed the back of his neck. "Okay. Tell me what I can do to help."

* * *

A few minutes later, I dispatched Otis in his grandma's Buick—she'd gotten a ride to the county fair with a friend—to go find Chester and Lauren. The plan was that the three of them would go to gossip hot spots around town—the Cup n' Clatter, the fair, the Black Drop, the Green Apple—and spread the rumor that I, Agnes Blythe, had Kathleen Todd's Rolodex. They would say they had no idea where I was, they'd act all concerned for my safety and/or sanity, and we'd all keep our fingers crossed that the murderer would call me. I was pretty sure all the suspects had my phone number.

After Otis left, I broke into a box of Nilla Wafers in his grandma's kitchen. Would this work? Or would the police track me down and arrest me?

Otis had been gone about half an hour when my phone buzzed. It was a text from Cordelia: *You are wanted by the police. Your father is very disappointed in you. Also, did you steal a carrot cake cupcake from the fridge?*

Seriously?

I ate more cookies, even though they were stale. I had only seven percent charge left on my phone. Not good. The clock ticked. The flour canister shaped like a sad kitty stared at me.

Another buzz. This time it was a text from Chester: *Demo tractors and trucks are parked at inn. Prepare for the worst tomorrow. BTW the rumor is really taking root here at the fair. You are going to have to pay me back for all the fried dough I'm having to buy.*

The Stagecoach Inn was going down. How awful, especially for Aunt Effie. Time for more cookies.

Another twenty minutes passed. My phone buzzed for the third time. It was a call, not a text, and . . . I recognized the number on the screen.

"Agnes Blythe," I said, trying to sound calm.

"Susie Pak," a no-nonsense voice barked.

"Oh. Hi. What's up?"

"Shut up and listen. I've got your lover-boy here."

"Huh?" Who was my lover-boy? I frowned. "You're with Otis?"

"Otis? No. I got your lover-boy Roger here, Agnes, the genius professor, but he doesn't look too genius right now with all that sweat under his arms. Looks like a map of the Great Lakes on his nice button-down."

"Yeah, Roger has a sweating issue."

"You know they can give you Botox injections for that, right?"

"Why are you telling *me*? Tell *him*."

"You know they can give you Botox under your arms for that, lover-boy?" Susie said.

In the background, Roger's feeble voice: "Agnes! Agnes you've got to *do* something! This lunatic has kidnapped me!"

Susie was back on the line. "You heard it yourself, Agnes. Lover-boy has been kidnapped."

"What's going on here, Susie? Are you planning on murdering Roger too?"

"I will do whatever it takes to get that Rolodex."

I made a little fist pump. My plan had worked!

"Now listen," Susie said. "I give you lover-boy, you give me the Rolodex. Straightforward trade."

"What if I don't have the Rolodex?" I said since, well, I *didn't* have the Rolodex.

"Then lover-boy goes boom."

Chester had said Susie frequented Skeeter's Shooting Range. She had a gun. I was going to have to play this *just right*.

"She's serious about this, Agnes!" Roger squawked in the background.

"We'll do the trade-off at the Tunnel of Love," Susie told me. "At the county fair."

"The fair? That's not exactly a private spot," I said.

"We're already here."

"She just nabbed me by the cotton candy booth while Shelby was using the restroom!" Roger cried. "She's an animal!"

Susie said to me, "Plus, I don't want lover-boy sweating all over my SUV upholstery. I just had an interior detail that cost a fortune."

"And the Tunnel of Love because . . . he's my lover-boy?" I asked.

"That's right. And I don't want to be in a wide-open space where people can see what's going on. Tunnel of Love, six o'clock sharp. Got it?"

"Uh, yeah, got it."

"If you're late, or try to bring the cops or anyone else, lover-boy gets iced. It'll be real crowded at the fair, and I'm quick. Anyway, who would believe cute little Susie Pak would shoot some sweaty genius professor for no reason?"

"Probably no one," I said.

"You got it."

The line went silent.

It was five thirty-one.

I pictured Roger, quivering and helpless. He'd never been good at sticking up for himself when it came to assertive older women. It was a mommy thing. Still, we had a long shared history, and I cared about him even though he was a jerk, so I had to rescue him, right?

There were a *lot* of problems heaped on my cafeteria tray. But the foremost one was that the fairgrounds were five miles away. No way would I make it there on foot by six o'clock. The plan had been for me to call Otis as soon as the murderer contacted me, but we hadn't counted on anything like Roger being kidnapped. Susie said she'd kill Roger if I brought backup, so I was going to have to go it alone.

I peeked into the garage, hoping to see a second Buick or a bicycle or, heck, a Rascal scooter. But there was nothing on wheels.

I went into the backyard. Lots of flowers and a porch glider. No vehicles. However—I peered over the fence—there was a bicycle leaning on a shed in the next-door neighbor's yard. *Perfect.*

But first, since I was wanted by the police, I needed a disguise.

* * *

Ten minutes later, I climbed over the fence and skulked through the neighbor's gate with the bicycle. It was a dirt bike small enough for a nine-year-old, with undersized wheels. I was wearing Otis's grandma's pink wrinkle-free slacks and matching jacket, orthopedic shoes, and a floral scarf to cover my hair. The slacks fit *perfectly*, but I didn't care because in the guest room I had found—get ready for it—*a Rolodex!* It was filled with about fifty years' worth of Grandma's addresses. With a little finesse, I might be able to rescue Roger before Susie realized it was the wrong Rolodex.

I hopped on the bike and set off. By the time I saw the glow of county fair lights, my legs were jellified, and I was panting. I ditched the bike in the crowded parking lot and headed on foot to the main entrance. Inside the revolving gate, four barns stood between me and the carnival where the Tunnel of Love would be. I checked the time on my phone. *Shizap.* Five minutes till six.

I decided to take a shortcut through the barns. I zipped my phone into my backpack's outer pocket and started jogging. I passed through a livestock barn and into the crowded arts and crafts barn colorful with quilts, oil paintings, half-eaten pies, and flower arrangements. Pushing through the crowd, I accidentally stepped on a small blue Keds sneaker.

"Ooo!" a woman squealed.

"Sorry," I said. I tried to squeeze past.

"Wait. Agnes Blythe?"

"Oh, hi, Mrs. Tucker." It only seemed proper to call Dorrie *Mrs. Tucker* after I'd seen her galumphing away in her high-waist underpants only hours before. "Having your flower arrangements judged?"

"I *am* the judge," Dorrie snapped.

"Sorry about earlier," I said. "I didn't know you were in the trailer with, um—"

"*You shut your mouth!* Wait a minute. Aren't the police looking for you?"

"Gotta go," I said. I shoved through people in T-shirts, plaid, and denim, denim everywhere, and I was sure, in a sixth-sense way, that someone was following me even though I didn't recognize anyone when I glanced over my shoulder.

I burst out of the arts and crafts barn, pressed on through a barn filled with rustling cages—Bunnies? Chickens?—and then I was in the carnival.

Blinking lights, clattering machinery, nightmarish hurdy-gurdy music, and seething rivers of people. Adults clutched plastic cups, and kids munched cotton candy. Stalls peddled burgers, hot dogs, beer-battered bacon, fried butter, fried *anything*, really. I couldn't see the Tunnel of Love; I couldn't see much, honestly. I'd have to canvass the carnival to find Roger and Susie.

"Yo, Agnes. Nice disguise. It's like a preview of what you're going to look like when you're eighty."

I swung around. "Oh. Hey, Chester."

Chester was munching French fries from a huge, grease-splotched paper cone. "What's up?"

"You have mustard on your soul patch, and I'm in a hurry." I elbowed into the crowd.

Chester caught up to me. "Did the murderer contact you?"

"Yep."

"Wow. Who is it? Want a fry?"

"Sure." I grabbed one and stuffed it into my mouth by folding it into thirds. Salty, greasy nirvana. "It's Susie Pak."

"Not surprised."

"Why are these fries so long? They're like a foot long."

"Foot-long fries, baby. The miracle of genetic engineering."

"Gross." I gulped it down. "Can I have another?"

Chester tipped his fries cone toward me.

We kept moving, and I searched for the Tunnel of Love.

"So what are you up to?"

"Susie Pak called to tell me she kidnapped Roger."

"Are you joshing me?"

"Nope. And she said—and I quote—'*lover-boy is going to go boom*' if I don't hand over the Rolodex in, like, one minute from now."

"Did you call the police?"

"Too dicey. They want to arrest me, remember?"

"This sounds dangerous."

"It is. And you can't come with me. I'm supposed to go alone." I grabbed another fry and smushed it in. We zigzagged through a tot crowd waiting to board the Tiltin' Teacups and rounded a corner.

I stopped hard. Chester bumped into me, and some of his fries launched into the air.

"Hey!" Chester said. "Each one of those is precious and unique, Agnes!"

Up ahead, the Tunnel of Love throbbed with blinking red lightbulbs. A heart-shaped exit was disgorging a train filled with couples from its dark bowels. Signs in juvenile handwriting said *Romance! True Love! Thrills!* None of the couples getting off the ride looked like they were in the throes of true love, although one couple looked like they'd just broken up.

"So where's the Rolodex?" Chester asked. "In your backpack?"

"Didn't Otis tell you? I don't actually have the Rolodex. But I have *a* Rolodex."

"So you plan to *bluff* your way through a high-stakes trade-off with a triple murderer?"

"Well, yeah."

Chester shrugged, stuffing in more French fries. "I'm going to call nine-one-one. In the meantime, worst-case scenario, Roger explodes. That wouldn't be *so* bad."

"You're not taking this seriously, are you? Susie is psycho."

"Hey!" a woman said behind me. "Agnes Blythe!"

Susie. Here goes. I turned.

Multicolored carnival lights spun and bounced on the lenses of Susie's big black sunglasses. Roger was right next to Susie, squashed up close. In fact, he had an arm around her waist like a lover. Susie's arm was under his tweed jacket.

"She's got a gun," Roger peeped. "Agnes, for God's sake, give her whatever she wants! She's a lunatic! She's—*oof.*"

Susie shut him up by grinding something—a gun, I assumed—into his back.

Roger's eyes teared up. And yeah, he was sweating like a pig at a Hawaiian luau.

Susie seemed to be looking Chester up and down. Hard to tell with the tsetse fly sunglasses. She turned to me. "I told you not to bring anyone with you."

"Him?" I said. "He's not with me. Anyway, does he look like a hero to you?"

Chester had already disappeared into the crowd.

He'd call the police, of course, but it was too late for them to help *or* hinder me.

"Where's the Rolodex, Agnes?" Susie asked.

"In my backpack."

"Hand it over."

I swallowed. "Okay. But I want to do it at exactly the same time you hand Roger over."

"No."

"Then no deal."

"You want lover-boy to bite the dust?"

"He's *not* my lover-boy. Why do you want the Rolodex, anyway? As far as I can tell, it's just full of people's unsavory secrets."

"You *do* have it. Give it to me!"

"It was you who broke into all those houses this week, wasn't it? You were looking for the Rolodex."

"Wrong. Jentry did that."

"Jentry!" I *knew* it. Roland must have broken into the Stagecoach Inn to rip the flashing off the chimney. The other break-ins had been Jentry. "Is that why he followed my aunt and me around when we were, uh, investigating stuff?"

"Sure. I told him to see what you snoops were up to and report back."

"He *works* for you?"

"He does now, ever since I told him I knew about his ganja farm and he'd better snap to or I'm calling the cops."

"Surely Susie's Speedy Maids never cleaned at Jentry's—"

"Kathleen Todd mentioned the ganja to me once. Bad move. She knew all about it because Jentry is her daughter Jodi's boyfriend. Kathleen never called the cops on him because of her daughter and grandson."

"Ok*ay*." My brain was spinning like an off-balance Maytag. "And you use the information in the Rolodex to blackmail people?"

"Wrong again," Susie said. "*Kathleen Todd* was using the Rolodex to blackmail people."

Well I'll be a monkey's uncle.

"Wait," I said. "You were using Susie's Speedy Maids as an excuse to go into people's houses for months, weren't you? Or was it *years?* Poking around and finding out everyone's dirty secrets. Then what? You gave the secrets to Kathleen Todd?"

"Gee, you're almost as smart as lover-boy here, Agnes Blythe. Except I didn't give Kathleen Todd the secrets. I sold them to her. I'm a businesswoman."

"If you aren't a blackmailer, why do you want the Rolodex?"

"None of your business!"

Susie had completely violated her clients' trust, and furthermore, it probably wouldn't be hard for anyone to deduce that the private information in the Rolodex had been gathered by Susie's maids. Her business and her reputation were at stake, and there would surely be serious criminal charges brought too.

"Enough chit-chat," she said. "Hand it over."

"Please, Agnes, just do what she says!" Roger said.

I gave him a look.

"I'm *sorry*, Agnes," he said. "I miss you! Shelby's so—"

"I don't care," I said, putting up a hand.

"So you're just going to let this psycho lady shoot me? She's got a gun that looks like something from *Die Hard*!"

"Hand over the Rolodex," Susie said to me. "What's the matter with you, anyway? You've got the attention span of a gerbil." She glanced out into the crowd, and her lips went pale. "*Cheese and crackers.* Get moving, lover-boy." She jammed her gun into Roger's back. He whimpered.

"What about our trade?" I said.

Susie didn't answer. She pushed Roger to the front of the Tunnel of Love line.

What was going on? Had Susie seen cops in the crowd? *I didn't see any.*

The Tunnel of Love jerked into motion, the train creaking and rattling into the darkness. The carny was just closing the gate, but Susie, herding Roger in front of her, shoved through.

"Hey," the carny said in a mild, stoner-ish voice, "it's two tickets per person."

Susie kneed him in the Jackson Pollocks; he doubled over. Susie and Roger clambered up the steps and jumped onto the love train's last car. They disappeared into the blackness.

Chapter 28

I tasted bile and Franken-fries. Not a stellar combo. But Roger's date with boomery was about to commence, so I slipped past the carny, stampeded up the steps, and plunged into the Tunnel of Love.

The dark tunnel reeked of stale beer and gear oil. The train up ahead clacked insistently on its track. I lumbered forward.

The point of the Tunnel of Love was to give teenagers a dark place to make out, so there wasn't much to see except, encased in the walls behind Plexiglas, crummy lit-up dioramas of supposedly romantic places. I stumbled past the Eiffel Tower and a castle made of spray-painted Styrofoam. Around the first bend, I spotted the caboose of the ride and caught a flash of Susie's white jacket. I picked up my pace, nearly crashing when I stumbled on a beer can.

Pretty soon I was just yards behind the caboose. Susie and Roger didn't seem to notice me; I guess the ride's clacking was too loud.

I didn't have a plan. That was sinking in. I scrambled along, trying to keep pace with the love train. A plan. A plan . . .

Then I realized: I could hit Susie. With Otis's grandma's Rolodex.

I dug it out, still trotting along, and huffed and puffed closer and closer to the caboose. I held the Rolodex aloft, its index cards fluttering. I was about to bring it down on Susie's head when she suddenly swung around.

"You following us?" she said. "Sorry, then, about lover-boy. He was okay-looking before he started sweating."

"Help," Roger said in a choked voice.

I swung the Rolodex, trying to whack Susie, but I only whapped the air above her head and then Roger's shoulder.

Susie muttered something that I guessed were Korean curses, and then *bang*! Something on the ceiling shattered.

Roger screamed. So did the rest of the people on the ride.

I dropped the Rolodex and with all the strength I had left in my body, I grabbed the back of the moving caboose and heaved myself forward. I'd envisioned myself doing a track-star hurdle, but in reality I dumped myself headfirst onto the seat between Susie and Roger.

More screams. Roger sobbing, Susie cursing, and a long metallic moan as the train was brought to a stop. Everyone else on the ride stampeded forward through the tunnel. I managed to get myself sideways so my feet were on Roger and my head was smashed between the seat and Susie's leg.

"Get off me, you maniac!" Susie screamed. She slapped my head.

"Ow!" I yelled. More squirming—I think I kicked Roger in the throat—and then I'd somehow gotten my mitts on Susie's gun. It was absurdly large, and the handle was warm. I wrenched it away from her.

She cursed, but whaddaya know, I was stronger! That was *one* person in the adults-under-ninety world I was stronger than. Gold star!

I mostly righted myself and pointed the gun at Susie.

Her face, lit up by the pink-and-blue light of the diorama behind me, registered fear. Her hands fluttered up in surrender. I guess that meant the gun was loaded.

"You okay, Roger?" I said over my shoulder.

"I will be when you get your behind off my shoulder."

"Okay, Susie," I said, "start talking about the murders—Roger, pay attention. You'll be the witness to her confession."

"Wait," Roger said. "Agnes, I want to say something."

"Can it wait?" I said, not taking my eyes off Susie.

"No." Roger's tone was half-pompous, half-wounded.

"Okay, what?"

"Agnes, I've made a mistake. About breaking things off with you."

"*What?*"

"I was also wrong about what I said, about you being not adventurous."

Susie snickered.

"You're the most exciting woman I've ever met," Roger went on, "and I—I miss you."

I glanced at Roger behind me. He looked flabby and crumpled. Okay, technically *I* was crumpling him with the weight of my body, but you know what I mean. "What about Shelby?" I asked.

"Forget her! She's so immature! I don't even care about abs—she's been on my case about toning my abs even though I told her I'm writing a paper for an *extremely* prestigious conference. Jesus. Take me back, Agnes. Please."

This was it. The magical moment that every dumpee dreams of. Yet it only felt stale and laughable.

"You can work things out with Shelby," I said. "Let her help you tone your abs, and then you can help her read books or something—hey!" Susie was taking the opportunity to climb stealthily out of the caboose. "Hold it, or I'll shoot."

Susie thumped back to a seat, hands once more up in surrender.

"All I want to know, Susie, is why you murdered Kathleen Todd, Bud Budzinski, and Megan Lawrence. Was it just to get the Rolodex back?"

"I didn't murder anyone."

The gun in my hand shook a little. "Then who did?"

Something flickered across Susie's face. "I don't know."

"You're lying. You're . . . *afraid* of someone."

Susie licked her lips. "Okay, fine. It was—"

"No," someone said from the darkness.

Susie, Roger, and I swiveled to look over the back of the caboose.

A stumpy form slowly unpeeled from the shadows. Blue diorama light bounced off a gun and a pair of Keds sneakers.

"*Dorrie Tucker?*" I breathed.

Dorrie came closer. Closer.

"I've got a gun, Dorrie," I called. Darn that tremor in my voice.

"I don't believe for a second that you know how to shoot that thing, Agnes Blythe," Dorrie said. "I've never seen you at the shooting range." She stopped a yard away. Pink light bathed her soft cheeks and puffy hair. Her lips pursed with distaste. A shiny purse dangled from her shoulder. "You three are to do as I say, or there *will* be bloodshed. Am I clear?"

"Um, yes," I said.

Roger whimpered softly. Susie nodded.

"Susie Pak, and whoever this smelly little man is, walk—slowly—away through the rear of the tunnel," Dorrie said. "Do not look back."

Roger and Susie clambered out of the caboose and scurried away.

"Gee, thanks for the help, Roger," I shouted after him.

"Now, Agnes," Dorrie said, "hand over the gun."

I looked down at the gun in my hand.

"Now!"

I handed it over. What was I going to do? Dorrie obviously knew her way around a Glock or whatever that was she was pointing at my heart.

"Thank you." Dorrie slid Susie's gun into her purse. "Now you are going to take a nice walk with me. If you try to run or cry for help, Little Snuggums here"—she waggled her gun—"is coming out to play. Okeydokey?"

"Okay," I croaked.

Dorrie pushed open a side door I hadn't noticed, and twilight seeped in. I went first, Dorrie right behind me. A noisy crowd congregated over by the Tunnel of Love's entrance, with security personnel mixed in. No one noticed Dorrie and me as we tromped down side steps and through a gate in the temporary fencing.

"Where are we going?" I asked over my shoulder.

"Don't speak unless you are spoken to."

Dorrie concealed her gun under her cardigan, keeping it pressed against my middle. We wove through the crowd, and then we were cutting in line for the Ferris wheel, and somehow Dorrie shoved me onto a seat and sat down beside me. We swooped back and up into the air. The metal safety bar hadn't been lowered, and I couldn't reach it.

Adrenaline jetted through me. What was worse? Being shot point-blank or falling off a Ferris wheel? Take your pick.

I hitched an arm over the back of the rocking seat. The glittering fair sprawled out below. Dorrie was busy doing something with her gun—checking the bullets?—and a feeble little idea fluttered into my brain. I sneaked my free hand around to the outer pocket of my backpack—this was the side away from Dorrie—unzipped it slowly, very slowly—

The Ferris wheel stopped. We were almost at the top, and it had *stopped*.

Creak-creaaakk, creak-creaaak went the hinges of our seat.

"Could we put the safety bar down, maybe?" I said. My stomach boiled with nausea.

"No," Dorrie said primly. "I am going to push you off just as soon as the Ferris wheel starts up again and we're at the top."

Less chance of a witness if she pushed me off the top, I guessed. Sight lines and all that.

"Wow," I said, "what's that down there by the Tiltin' Teacups? A giant pink bunny?"

"Where?" Dorrie craned her neck.

I took the opportunity to view my phone at an awkward angle under my elbow and sneakily turn it on.

Three percent battery. That meant it could power off at any moment. I tapped open my voice memo app, cleared my throat, and spoke loudly in the hopes of getting Dorrie to follow suit so we'd be caught clearly on the recorder. "So, Dorrie, how was it killing Kathleen Todd?"

Dorrie sniffed. "Not as satisfying as I'd imagined all those thousands of times."

"You're confessing?"

"Why not? You'll be dead in a few minutes. And my mama always told me it helps to get things out in the open. Better than chamomile tea for sleeping, she said."

"Okay, so why did you kill Kathleen?"

"I'd had it up to here with her bullying! And then I found that horrible Rolodex. She'd left it at my house by mistake. Of course, I'd had suspicions that she was doing that sort of thing. I mean, she knew everyone's secrets. *Everyone's*. But *I* was in there. Her most loyal friend!"

"Oh yeah? Was it about how you murdered your husband? I didn't have him for social studies, but a friend of mine did. I heard he was a bully."

"*How did you learn about Bruce?*" Dorrie hunched toward me, her voice going horror-movie raspy. Our seat swung violently.

"Lucky guess." I clung to the cold metal seat. Water filled my eyes. "Okay, so you saw Kathleen's Rolodex, and she had stuff in there about how you had—what, poisoned?—your husband. Then what? You confronted her?"

"She was so surprised. Thought I'd never stand up for myself. For a long time, I *didn't* stand up for myself with her. But she'd started calling me Dorrie the Doormat, just like Bruce used to. Then she'd laugh and say 'you don't *mind*, do you?' and I'd simply smile and nod, smile and nod."

"Your choices were for you to do whatever Kathleen wanted, or she'd turn you in to the police for killing your husband."

"That was the position she wanted *everyone* in town in. She'd didn't blackmail people for money, oh no. She wanted obedience. She wanted a whole town full of her slaves."

"What did she make you do?"

"Ran me ragged as her assistant. Gave me tongue-lashings whenever she needed to vent. Nothing Bruce hadn't gotten me used to. But she was overlooking the fact that I had killed Bruce and I could kill again."

"Did you plan it?"

"Not really. I had daydreamed about it often before I ever saw the Rolodex because, well, she was such a domineering . . . *you* know." Dorrie touched her hair. "When I saw the Rolodex—she'd accidentally left it in my house the day she died, in a box of historical society files—I went to her house that evening to tell her how angry I was with her about it. She wasn't home. I went to where I knew she would be."

"The Stagecoach Inn?"

"Yes."

"How did you know she'd be there?"

"Because she was obsessed with that filthy old place! She'd always wanted it for herself—she wanted to restore it into something out of a glossy magazine, just like your crazy auntie wanted to—but old Herman Colby refused to sell it to her. That didn't stop Kathleen from coveting the inn. I'd followed her there once before and seen her wandering the rooms, touching the woodwork with a dreamy look on her face. Kathleen Todd was crazy. She wanted everything around her to be perfect, and when it wasn't, it made her cruel."

All those haunting stories about the inn, about lights going on and off in the middle of the night . . . that hadn't been a ghost. It had been Kathleen Todd.

"That night, she was visiting the inn one last time, I suppose," Dorrie said. "Saying good-bye since she had gotten Karl Knudsen to set the demolition date."

"If she loved the inn so much, why would she want it demolished?"

"Don't you watch *Dr. Phil*? If she couldn't have the inn, no one could. I only meant to confront Kathleen about the Rolodex. But she somehow got her scarf caught in that wringer contraption. It felt so good, having *her* trapped for a change, hearing her beg me for help. But, stupid woman, she couldn't leave well enough alone and called me Dorrie the Doormat one too many times. So I cranked that wringer until it shut her up."

I swallowed. "Then what?"

"Then I left."

"You must've been wearing gloves," I said. "If you'd left fingerprints, the police would have arrested you right away."

"Yes. My gardening gloves."

"So maybe you *were* thinking of murdering Kathleen when you headed to her house that night."

"Maybe."

Dorrie was the type who wasn't going to take full responsibility for anything. "You started the rumor about my great-aunt and me at the Black Drop the next morning."

"I thought *that* was quite tidy. I was there when you threatened to strangle Kathleen, and I was also shopping at the Green Apple when your auntie and Kathleen had words."

"It wasn't tidy at all," I said. "You slipped up, Dorrie. You mentioned my great-aunt's sound machine in your rumor, but only the murderer could have heard the sound machine."

Dorrie pursed her lips. "Nobody's perfect."

"Do you still have the Rolodex?"

"Yes. I plan to use it, just like Kathleen did. I'm just waiting for things to die down."

"What about Megan?" I asked. "What about Bud?"

"Bud told me he knew about the Rolodex and Bruce's death when I visited him the day before yesterday about that appalling neon sign. He had to go, and good riddance. We don't want *that* sort in Naneda."

"And you overheard Megan talking to me on the phone about the Rolodex at her mom's wake, right?"

"Oh, yes. Megan was sleeping with Bud, you know. *No* morals. That's probably why Kathleen wrote Megan out of her will."

Yeah. That was probably why Kathleen had been powerless to get Budzinski to remove his neon sign, too; he had the leverage of knowing about Kathleen's blackmail scheme.

"It's so easy to poison people when you know what their favorite foods are," Dorrie said. "Bud was stuffing his face with Oreos when I visited him about the neon sign. And skinny-minnie Megan, well, she would break her strict diet for a macaroni-cheese casserole. I'd seen her do it at her mother's house. She just couldn't help herself."

"How did you know that Jodi was growing monkshood?"

"She told me all about it once, at a gardening show. She sells it to some hippie medicine company."

"You told me about Jodi's monkshood earlier to put me off the scent. Did you also send Jentry after me today?"

"Oh, yes. I knew he'd be furious about you snooping at his farm again, so I called him—his telephone number is in the Rolodex, actually—and told him you were headed there. I hoped he'd get rid of you. But you're like a garden mole, Agnes. You keep popping up. *So* annoying. People poison moles, you know, although it's much more effective to drown them or stomp their little skulls in. After I get rid of you, Susie Pak is next on the list."

"You're sick."

Dorrie gasped, affronted. "No, I'm not! You're a bully, Agnes Blythe, just like the rest of them!"

"I hate to break it to you, Dorrie, but *you're* the bully—and a serial killer, and probably a sociopath too."

"Stop *picking* on me!" Dorrie hurled herself sidelong across the seat, lunging at my throat with both hands. The seat teetered. Holding my phone tight, I threw my arms around the vertical side bar. Dorrie fell sideways. She clawed at the seat for one sickening second before the rocking seat dumped her out. She screamed, and there were some heart-stopping vibrating clunks, other peoples' screams, and . . . dead silence.

I hugged the side bar and leaned over to look. Dorrie was clinging to one of the spokes radiating from the wheel's central axis, whimpering.

"Lower the wheel!" someone screamed at the carny. "She's gonna fall!"

The Ferris wheel juddered into motion again. As my seat sank to the ground, I watched Dorrie slowly turn on the spoke she clung to until she and her pleather purse were upside-down. Then she was helped off by the carny and crumpled into a dead faint.

Chapter 29

The next morning at ten o'clock, I idled at the wheel of Dad's Subaru in front of the Naneda Police Station. I was driving without a license, but I hadn't told Dad, who had been so grateful that (a) I wasn't a murderer and (b) I hadn't been murdered, that I didn't want to ruin the good vibe when he passed over the keys.

The police station doors swung open, and Aunt Effie emerged. To be honest, I'd expected to see her bent and haggard after a night in jail, but she looked . . . *great*. Perfect makeup, smooth hair, and the outfit she'd been wearing when she was arrested yesterday still looked crisp. She trotted down the steps and got into the passenger seat.

"You collared the killer, Agnes," Effie said, buckling herself in. "Good job, darling. I just *knew* you would, by the way."

"Dorrie Tucker!" I said, driving out of the parking lot. "Can you believe it?"

"I can." Effie lit up a Benson & Hedges. "I never liked her. Sniveling, prim-and-proper little victim. Those are so often the worst bullies—although I really shouldn't speak ill of her. I saw you on the late news, by the way. Where on earth did you get that pink pantsuit?"

"Do we really need to talk about my clothes?" I turned north, toward the Stagecoach Inn.

"No." Effie slid a look at my jeans and T-shirt. "Unless you *want* to."

I actually thought I looked pretty good. My contacts had arrived at the pharmacy, and Cordelia had picked them up for me, and she'd also laundered my non–high school clothes. Just between you and me, I had *very* lightly lined my eyes with a brown eyeliner pencil I'd found in my dresser and slicked on a layer of cotton candy Lip Smacker. Oh, and I had slept like a log since, after I'd given my statement and handed over Dorrie Tucker's recorded confession to the police (my phone battery had held out *just* long enough), I had been given a checkup from a doctor who gave me a bottle of Xanax.

"Paul dropped the auto theft charges, Dad told me?" I said.

"Mm. Silly old fool didn't even realize *I* took his car. He noticed it was missing when he arrived back from Prague and didn't even pause to think that *I* might've taken it. For God's sake, we'd been living together for months. Enough of that. Paul can rot in hell. Now. I heard *all* about your amazing detective work on the news in jail—except for what you and Otis were up to when you were locked in the freezer at that horror-movie farm."

"We weren't up to *anything!*" The truth was, I hadn't seen Otis since we'd parted at his grandma's house yesterday. He had called a few times last night after I had gone to bed, and then I'd slept late into the morning. The fact that I'd confessed to being in love with him and the fact that he hadn't replied in any way, verbal *or* nonverbal, was starting to give me ants in my pants.

"Oh, I'll *bet* it was nothing," Effie said, "judging by the way your cheeks are hot pink all of a sudden."

I turned onto the Stagecoach Inn's overgrown driveway. When we emerged in front of the inn, demolition vehicles were there—dump truck, yellow tractors, dumpster—but like a beacon of hope, so was a sedan with *Town of Naneda* printed on the door. This, I knew, belonged to the city electrical inspector.

I parked. "Ready?" I asked Effie.

"Ready. Oh God, I hope Chester wasn't bluffing about his abilities all this time."

"Fingers crossed," I said, feeling sick. I had no idea if Chester even knew how to plug in a power strip, let alone rewire an entire building in record time. But he claimed to have done it.

"Come along, Agnes, and stop chewing your thumbnail," Effie said. "Oh, look, a motorcycle. Isn't that Otis's?"

My heart sank. It *was* Otis's motorcycle. *Donkey dust.* I couldn't deal with him *and* the electrical inspection at the same time.

Inside, a burly, sunburned guy in a hard hat cornered Aunt Effie. "You the owner?" he said. "I'm pretty hacked that this inspector told us to hold off. My guys are union. They got a strict break schedule."

Aunt Effie laid a hand on his arm. "I'm *so* sorry, darling. Won't you and your boys wait in the kitchen? I'll call for coffee and donuts, mm-kay?"

The burly guy's face softened. "Well, okay."

Effie sailed past him, and I followed her back to the kitchen. "Agnes," she whispered, "call Doctor Donut *immediately* and see about having them deliver two dozen donuts and one of those boxes of coffee." She passed me a credit card.

I took care of that on my phone in the kitchen. Meanwhile, Effie went off to find the electrical inspector. The donut delivery set up and paid for, I ushered the five demolition guys into the kitchen and told them their coffee and donuts would be there shortly. Then I went to find Effie and the inspector.

I found them, along with Chester and—*eep*—Otis, in the grand dining room. The inspector was a fastidious-looking man with a clipboard. He worked in silence as the others hovered and fidgeted.

Otis's face lit up when he saw me in the doorway, and he came over. "Hey," he said.

"Hey."

"I'm so glad to see you're okay. You look great."

I reached up to give my glasses a nudge and then remembered I wasn't wearing them. I scratched my nose instead. "Oh. Thanks. How is the inspection going?"

"Really well, actually, and I think he's almost done."

"*Really well?*"

"Yeah, Chester seems to know wiring."

I looked over at Chester, who was obviously sucking in his paunch as he talked to the inspector. "Well, he *is* really smart," I said.

Chester had told me on the phone all about the crazy aftermath of the drama at the fair. Dorrie had been taken away to the hospital, where she was treated for low blood pressure, contusions, and sprains (apparently a sprained ankle had prevented her from ever making a break for it). Roger had been taken to the hospital in an ambulance (to be treated for shock, I guess), and Susie had been arrested for firing her gun in the Tunnel of

Love. It turned out that after Chester had seemingly ditched me to my fate with Susie outside the Tunnel of Love, he had indeed called the police. Once I had given my statement to the police and they had listened to Dorrie's confession on my phone, they had gone to the hospital and arrested her. I would have to testify in court, but with the recorded confession, it would be a cut-and-dry case.

"Sorry about your grandma's Rolodex," I said. The police had found it in the Tunnel of Love, but it was in rough shape. "I'll get her a new one."

"I already did."

Heavy pause.

My throat tightened. Otis wasn't ever going to respond to what I'd confessed to him in the freezer, was he? I was going to be permanently trapped in the weaker position of Person Who Loves Unrequitedly. And we were going to be pals, just like in high school. *Yay.*

The sound of a car engine out front saved me. "Who's that?" I said. "Better check."

When I reached the porch, a white-haired man was just climbing out of a Lexus two-door sports coupe. He wore slacks, pointy loafers, a yellow sweater, and sunglasses.

Otis was next to me. "Florida license plate," he whispered.

"This the Stagecoach Inn?" the man said, mounting the steps on stiff knees.

"Yes," I said. "You must be Paul."

"That's right. Paul Duncan." He had that snappy, old-fashioned way of talking, kind of like an elderly Jimmy Stewart. "Where's Effie? Is this the place she inherited? Whew. Needs a little TLC, I'd say—and about half a million clams. Is this the way in?" Paul went past Otis and me and through the front door.

"I don't have a good feeling about this," I whispered to Otis. "Effie hates his guts."

"Why? He seems nice."

"Why? Actually, I have no idea."

Another ponderous pause.

"Well," I said, "I guess I'll go inside and see how—"

"Wait." Otis touched my arm. "Just a minute."

I swallowed. "Why?"

"You know why."

"No, I don't!"

Otis's brown eyes glowed. "You do."

Why was he so *close*? Pals didn't get in each other's grills like that. I backed up a few inches. "Okay, fine. The freezer incident. Yeah, well, the thing is, Otis, when people think they're about to die, they'll say all kinds of crazy things."

"Oh, yeah?" Otis closed the distance between us. "What kind of things?"

"I'm *not* going to say it again. At the time, I wasn't thinking rationally. Has it occurred to you that . . . that *thing* I said wasn't even, strictly speaking, an accurate representation of the truth?"

"Nope." Otis took my head in his hands. "I know you meant it."

He kissed me, for the first time ever, standing on the front porch of that ramshackle inn with the birds twittering and the lake softly lapping. The rational part of my brain fluttered away like a moth, leaving nothing but blissed-out mush. Did I care that he hadn't said anything about loving me too? Not at that moment, no. Later, though. There was plenty of time to fret and fidget and get a sweaty upper lip about that *later*. At that moment, everything was . . . perfect.

Voices bubbled louder inside, and then the front door burst open, and people crowded out. Otis and I pulled apart, reaching for each other's hands.

"We passed inspection, Agnes!" Aunt Effie cried. Through the doorway she shouted, "Paul, hurry up with the champagne!"

"Congratulations," the city electrical inspector mumbled, trotting down the steps to his car.

"Good job, Chester," I said.

Chester looked self-important. "I told you I could do it."

"I shouldn't have doubted you for a second," I said.

The burly demolition guy came out, followed by four equally burly workers. "Hey, what's going on?" he asked Effie.

"The demolition is off!" Effie crowed. "Champagne?"

The guy shrugged. "Sure."

Someone switched on extraloud country music on the dump truck's stereo. Paul appeared with a tray of champagne bottles and paper coffee cups. Corks popped, champagne frothed, and we drank toast after toast out on the porch until everyone was buzzing with goodwill. I finally let go of Otis's warm hand—he was talking engine parts with one of the demolition workers—and cornered Effie.

"Well?" I said to her softly. "What's up with Paul?"

"*Such* a darling!"

"What? Last thing I knew, he was a pustule."

Effie sipped her champagne. "I changed my mind. Everything that happened in Prague was a mix-up."

"You never told me what happened in Prague."

"Didn't I? Oh. Well, we were at a simply adorable restaurant in the Old Town, and he got down on bended knee with a little velvet box, and I fully expected a large diamond ring, naturally, but when he popped it open, there were little pills inside."

I frowned. "Little pills?"

"*You* know." Effie raised her eyebrows suggestively. "Little *blue* pills?"

Oh. Oh! For . . . masculine complaints. "Seriously?"

"Yes! Of course I was *utterly* insulted, and I packed my bags, got on the first flight back to the States, and when I reached Naples, Florida—that's where Paul's condo is—I took his Cadillac and drove straight up here, determined to make a fresh start with the inn. But—don't mention any of this to anyone—Paul's mix-up was *really* due to memory loss from his incontinence drug, and he really *did* mean to propose."

"Oh. That's great! Yeah, about the inn . . . Now that you and Paul have made up, I guess you're going to get married—after he gives you the ring—and then what? You'll go back to Florida?" Why in the *heck* was my throat so tight?

"I'm staying put. I've fallen in love with the inn, you see, and do you know, Paul is going to invest in the entire endeavor, whatever it takes. He's got buckets of money. He'll be the majority shareholder, but I don't mind. I have ways of making him do whatever I like, if you know what I mean."

"Ew. No, I *don't* know what you mean—and don't tell me."

"What about you, Agnes? Now that you're no longer a person of interest in a murder investigation, you're free to leave Naneda—and I wouldn't blame you a *bit* if you did." Effie studied me with her sharp blue eyes.

"Oh. Well, actually, I was thinking . . ." I took a deep breath. "I was thinking of staying in town for a while. Maybe I'll start my grad program next year, if they'll still have me." I had sort of missed the first week of classes. "If, that is, you still need help with the inn?" I fell silent. Then I realized I was holding my breath. Home, in its weird, secret ways, had sneaked up on me and hugged me tight. Maybe I was crazy to stay. Maybe I *would* be smothered. But maybe—my gaze floated over Otis laughing and Chester stuffing Doritos in his mouth, along the peeling paint of the inn's railing, past the orange-striped cat hunting in the grass, and out to the glistening blue of the lake—maybe this was where I was supposed to be.

"Agnes, darling," Effie said. "You've got the job."